PRAISE FOR J.D. TRAFFORD

"*Little Boy Lost* isn't just an engrossing novel; it's one that enlightens as well."

—William Kent Krueger, *New York Times* bestselling author and Edgar winner

LITTLE
BOY
LOST

ALSO BY J.D. TRAFFORD

No Time To Run

No Time To Die

No Time To Hide

LITTLE BOY LOST

J.D. TRAFFORD

THOMAS & MERCER

Published by Thomas & Mercer, Seattle

www.apub.com

Amazon, the Amazon logo, and Thomas & Mercer are trademarks of Amazon.com, Inc., or its affiliates.

ISBN-13: 9781503943940
ISBN-10: 1503943941

Cover design by David Drummond

Printed in the United States of America

To my wife and my family for all your love, patience, and support

—J.D.

CHAPTER ONE

It started with a pickle jar, half-filled with pocket change and a few dollar bills. The girl came into my office. She set the jar on my desk and sat down in the chair across from me. Her feet barely touched the ground.

Her name was Tanisha Walker.

"How old are you?" I asked.

She sat up a little straighter. "Eight and a half."

"Got a daughter about that age, little older." I leaned over and picked up the jar, examining it. On one side somebody had written in big block letters with black marker: Cuss Jar.

"Your mama know you took this jar?"

Tanisha shrugged. The beads in her hair clicked. "Ain't my mama's jar." She thought about it for a moment, biting a nail, and then elaborated. "It's my granny's, an' she won't mind . . . least don't think she would. Why should she? Ain't doing nothin' 'cept sitting there, and so she—"

I held up my hand, cutting off the nervous ramble. "Maybe." I put the jar back down on my desk. "Guess that depends on what you plan on doing with the money."

"Gonna hire you with it." She was serious. "Like they do on TV."

I took a moment to consider her intentions.

It'd been a long time since I'd lived the life of a typical lawyer. I certainly wasn't like the ones on television. I didn't have any staff. I answered my own phone and made my own copies. I drove a rusted-out Honda Civic, not a BMW. My suits didn't fit quite right, and my office was located in a half-empty strip of old storefronts on the north side. The storefronts stuck out among the burned houses and vacant lots like the remaining teeth in a broken mouth.

But I wasn't a charity, either.

I had bills due, and after looking at that pickle jar, I figured that this girl was only going to be able to pay me about ten dollars for my services. At the moment, I wasn't feeling that desperate. Maybe tomorrow.

"Why a lawyer?" I asked. "Right now you should be in school, not hiring lawyers."

"My brother's gone missing."

"Well that's an issue for the police." Passing the kid off on somebody else seemed like a fair resolution.

"I called the police, done nothing." The girl crossed her arms in front of her chest. "They don't care. They're glad he's gone."

"Who'd you talk to?"

The girl shook her head. "A white dude."

"Did you file a report? What about your mama or your granny? What are they doing?"

The girl looked away. She didn't want to talk bad about her mother or grandmother, and I didn't intend to ask her about her father. A little black girl in this part of Saint Louis living with her mama and granny— I knew she ain't got no daddy.

Then my lawyer brain kicked in. Assumptions made during an initial interview are where most mistakes are made. If she were white, I'd have asked about her daddy straight away. So I forced the question.

"Where's your father?"

The little girl shook her head. "Don't know."

And that, my friends, was a kick in the gut. Even though it was exactly the answer I had expected, I hated when the stereotype rang true.

I leaned toward her, trying to let the girl go gently. "I'm not sure you need a lawyer. Sounds more like you need a detective."

That answer did not sit well with the girl. She had come to hire an attorney, and it was doubtful that she was going to leave without some sort of a commitment. Saint Louis girls are stubborn like that, especially on this side of Forty.

The phone rang.

I answered on the second ring, hoping it might be somebody with a real legal problem and more than a pickle jar.

"Law office." I turned away from Tanisha and looked out the window. "This is Justin Glass."

"Good," said the voice on the other end of the line. "I'm needing a money-hungry ambulance chaser, like real bad, man."

"I happen to be with a potential client at the moment." I looked back at the girl in time to see her eyes widen as she inched up to the edge of her seat, clearly pleased to hear herself referred to as a client of any kind. I turned away from Tanisha as my younger brother, Lincoln, called my bluff.

"Client?" He laughed. "You do know that the word *client* is defined as an individual who actually pays your poor ass some money? And we both know—"

"What do you want?"

"Hoping to buy you lunch today, catch up a little."

I rolled my eyes and sighed. The Glass family business was politics. Our father was a local hero of the 1960s civil rights movement, a founding member of the Congressional Black Caucus, and the most senior United States congressman in Missouri. My brother, a state senator with ambitions, was always conspiring with our father's chief of staff to expand our empire. When I was younger, I may have cared, but that feeling was lost. I had no interest in any of his ideas. "Don't have time today," I said. "Maybe next week." I hung up the phone and then turned back to Tanisha.

She looked at me with big brown eyes, holding her breath.

"I really appreciate you coming in here, but"—I pushed the jar of coins slowly closer to her—"I've got some real important matters going on right now."

I rolled back my chair a little farther from my desk. I was seeking some distance, knowing that I was about to disappoint her. It wasn't the first time I'd drawn back from somebody needing my help. "Just not sure that I can—"

Tanisha knew what was coming. A tear rolled down her cheek.

I, nonetheless, marched forward. "Like I said, I'm just not sure that you need a lawyer. I don't think I can help you."

Tanisha nodded and wiped her eyes dry. She then took a breath and came back at me, hard. "Ain't nobody want to help us." She stood. "Ain't nobody else. Just you." She looked at me with such intensity, such honest longing. It was as if this girl knew all my secrets and all my problems, but those didn't matter. A flawed man was better than nothing.

The silence grew.

Tanisha didn't back down.

I can't tell you why I took the case. I had thought that any remotely noble part of me had died years earlier, along with my wife. I wish that I could say that this was the moment when I woke up from a long, dark sleep, but that's not true.

Regret and doubt filled me the moment I told Tanisha that I'd make some calls.

CHAPTER TWO

My old air conditioner had stopped working. From the time I left to get a sandwich to the time I returned with it, the temperature inside my office had risen about fifteen degrees. This was late August in Saint Louis, a final boil before the summer turned to fall.

I picked up a ragged old copy of the Yellow Pages and used it to prop open the door. Then I tinkered with the air conditioner for about thirty minutes before giving up.

By the time I sat down at my desk, the back of my shirt was soaked through with sweat. Breathing hard, I stared at the open front door and hoped for a cool breeze.

Relief never came.

I had a small contract with the Saint Louis Public Defender's Office. I handled a few general arraignment calendars every week when other lawyers were on vacation or otherwise unavailable, and I tracked the cases through that didn't resolve at that first appearance. It wasn't much, but the steady check helped keep the lights on. I figured that there might be enough money left over this month to get a new air conditioner; at least that was my hope.

Theoretically I could ask my mother or her father—who we called the Judge—for some extra money, but I wasn't going to do that. It was bad enough that my daughter and I lived with them rent-free because I couldn't afford a place of my own.

I loosened my tie, picked up the phone, and looked at the information that Tanisha Walker had written on my yellow notepad. I called a contact at the Saint Louis Police Department and got lucky. He was at his desk and answered his phone.

"Schmitty." I tapped my pen on the desktop. "This is Justin Glass."

He told me to hang on, and I listened to Sergeant Schmidt get up and close his office door. Then he got back on the line and asked me what I wanted. He wasn't happy about the call, because cops never like talking to criminal defense attorneys, but he couldn't hang up on me, either. One of the perks of having my last name.

"Wondering if you could find out what's going on with a kid named Devon Walker. About sixteen; missing for a month. His little sister filed a report."

"Thug?"

"Don't know," I said. "Why?"

"If he was a thug, I'd check with the gang unit. See if they got background on him."

"You should check, but I really don't know." I thought for a second and then decided to level with Schmitty. "Isn't really a criminal case. Neighborhood girl asked me to check into it. So it's more of a favor."

"And our rewards will be in heaven?"

"That's what I'm banking on."

I told Schmitty that I'd call back or stop by his office the next day after court. Then I spent the next hour attempting to finish a motion to suppress a stolen gun, arguing that the cops didn't have a legal basis to search my client's apartment. I was asking for the court to keep the prosecutor from using the seized gun as evidence at trial. Lawyers called such evidence "fruit of a poisonous tree."

Nothing came easy.

I pecked away at the memo. The heat in the office made it difficult to concentrate. The thick air discouraged any sudden movement or elaborate thought.

Realizing I'd forgotten to eat my sandwich, I worked my way through it, sweating the whole time. Then I pecked a little more at the memo before eventually giving up.

I turned off the computer and decided that I would leave early. Since the law practice was far from flourishing, I didn't have any large files to bring home or papers to review. I gathered up my personal things, putting them in my battered briefcase, and then picked up the yellow notepad.

Tanisha Walker's careful handwriting filled the page. Little curls and loops decorated the ends of certain letters. She had written down her name, her phone number, the names of her family members, and her address. I checked my watch, looked at the information on the notepad again, and decided that I had time to make a stop on my way to pick up my daughter from school.

◆ ◆ ◆

Tanisha Walker and her family lived in one of a dozen brick houses clustered tightly together on the corner of Montgomery and Parnell. There wasn't much more than three feet separating one house from another, and the close spacing looked even more odd considering that they were surrounded by acres and acres of vacant land.

Once there was a city neighborhood. Now there were only survivors, hanging on for a few more years before a wrecking ball took them down, too. The absentee owners probably bought each house for a few hundred dollars at a foreclosure auction, and it was only a matter of time before they got tired of waiting for the big payout. Properties hadn't increased in value for years, and easy city development money was never going to come, partly because Saint Louis was broke and partly because the Northside was viewed by most as a lost cause. Why rebuild housing that nobody wants when you can subsidize an Ikea or a professional sports stadium?

I sat in my car and studied Tanisha Walker's house. It was the biggest one of the group, two stories instead of one. The lawn was mostly dirt with a few clumps of shrub.

A little boy played alone out front in nothing but a diaper. He was maybe three. A faded toy car sat nearby—the kind that was large enough to sit inside, with pedals and a steering wheel. The boy ignored it, content to play in the dirt.

I looked down at the information on the notepad. There were six kids living in the house—not counting Devon, the missing brother. Tanisha's otherwise tidy handwriting had broken down a little near the end of the list. My guess was that the little boy's name was either Deon or Dice. For the sake of him finding gainful employment in the future, I hoped that his name was Deon.

I debated whether or not to get out of the car and talk to the adults who were hopefully inside, but I decided to wait. I wanted to get the file from Schmitty first, and I also just wanted to get away.

CHAPTER THREE

My daughter's given name is Samantha Charlotte Glass, but she never acted much like a Samantha. She acted more like a Sammy, so that's what I called her. Sammy was tall for her age, funny, and whip-smart. She was also the fastest kid in the fifth grade.

I continued to watch for Sammy as the crowds thinned. The steady stream of kids leaving the school diminished to a trickle and then to nothing. I waited a little longer, but nobody came. The buses pulled away, and the schoolyard emptied.

Missed her.

I turned the key, and my car rattled to life. Then I pulled away from the curb and headed home.

My mother and her father, retired federal district court judge Michael M. Calhoun, lived in a Compton Heights mansion that had been in the Calhoun family for over a hundred years. Sammy and I lived in the carriage house behind the main structure. It was small but big enough for the two of us.

My great-great-grandfather had purchased the lot and then moved the family into the house when it was completed. At the time, Compton Heights was a showcase for the 1904 World's Fair. It offered large lots, beautiful winding streets, and strict deed restrictions. Promises were made to the purchasers that the neighborhood would be forever protected from the influx of blacks migrating north and from boardinghouses filled with poor Germans. The deed restrictions—although later found illegal—largely worked, and the neighborhood has remained one of the most affluent in Saint Louis.

Although the Judge had now become a typical great-grandfather toward Sammy—something that I was still not used to seeing—he had always treated me with indifference and my father with disdain.

It was a feeling that had festered over the past forty years.

A staunch supporter of President Richard Nixon and the Vietnam War, the Judge was convinced that my father had brainwashed my mother during their first year at Washington University. He believed that my father, a young man he assumed was a member of the Black Panthers, had taken his perfect little white girl and transformed her into a leftist campus radical.

The truth was exactly the opposite. It had been my mother who had lured my father to protest meetings and marches. She was the radical. My dad just wanted to go on a date.

The Judge's dislike grew even more when my dad was elected to the United States Congress at age twenty-six and took his daughter away to Washington, DC—a place the Judge, like so many others, referred to as "Hollywood for ugly people" and "an incestuous breeding ground for idiots."

When the Judge's wife passed away, my mom moved back into her childhood home in Compton Heights to help him navigate. She had become tired of life as a congressman's spouse in Washington, DC, and it was a good excuse to leave.

I'm glad she did, because I'm not certain where Sammy and I would be if she hadn't convinced the Judge to allow us to move in when our lives had fallen to pieces. We could've moved into the main house, she insisted, but I needed some separation. After being fired from my job and going deeply into debt, I couldn't handle the further indignity of being a middle-aged widower living down the hallway from my mom.

◆ ◆ ◆

"Time for dinner, sweetie." I poked my head into the ornate library. It was such a warm space. Sammy and the Judge sat on a large leather sofa in the corner. They were surrounded by shelves, floor to ceiling, filled with books.

They were reading *The Iliad*.

I took another step into the library. "Come on, Sammy. You've got school tomorrow."

Sammy looked up at the Judge, pleading with him to convince me to allow her to stay. The Judge, however, did not interfere.

"We'll read again tomorrow." He placed a bookmark on the page where they had stopped and then gave Sammy a gentle pat on the back. "I promise."

Sammy's face curled up into a pout. "We were just getting to the duel."

"Duel?" I didn't remember that part.

"The duel to end the war," Sammy explained.

The Judge smiled, proud that she understood the sometimes-convoluted story, then elaborated on her behalf. "In the fourth part there was an offer to end the war by duel. Both sides agreed to a truce and to allow the winner of the duel between Paris and Menelaus to dictate the terms."

"See." Sammy nodded. "We can't stop now."

I shook my head. "Yes, we can, and yes, we are—no matter how riveting Paris and Menelaus might be. Give the Judge a hug and we'll go." I pulled Sammy off the couch and to her feet.

She turned and gave the Judge a hug, and then I put my arm around her and guided her out of the library.

Just as we were about to leave, Sammy turned. "See you tomorrow, Judge."

"Good night, sweetie." The old man blew Sammy a kiss, and she blew the Judge a kiss right back.

We walked down the hallway, through the dining room, and into the kitchen. My mother was at the stove.

"Thanks for watching Sammy."

My mother turned. "Never a problem." She looked at Sammy and smiled, and then she looked back at me. "You can stay if you want."

I shook my head. "Not tonight; maybe tomorrow."

"Just let me know." She paused. "Did Lincoln happen to call you today?"

The question caught me by surprise. "He called," I said, "wanting to go to lunch."

My mother nodded, although it seemed like she'd already known the answer to her question. "Get a chance to talk?"

"We didn't," I said. Then I changed the subject. "There was a young girl in my office, neighborhood kid, wanting to hire me to find her lost brother."

Her eyebrows raised. "New case?"

"Gonna compensate me in quarters and dimes." I smiled wide. "Unusual method of payment, but I can't turn down any type of client at the moment."

"No, you can't." My mother's eyes sparkled, playing. "Good for you to help."

I shrugged. "We'll see how good it is." I turned and opened the back door. "See you tomorrow." Then I shut the door behind us as we walked into the backyard.

It was a perfect August night. The temperature had dropped down to seventy-five, which felt cool compared to the heat and humidity of the day. A few stars managed to shine through the dense city sky, and fireflies bounced around the sweet gum trees.

We walked down the stone path and through the garden.

"Any homework tonight?"

"I did it already," she said. "Got it done right when I got home."

I nodded as we walked. "Did you take the bus?"

Sammy started to answer and then paused. "Why?"

"Came to your school today, thought I'd give you a ride."

"Oh." Sammy stuffed her hands into her pockets. "Yeah. I took the bus. I didn't see you waiting."

"Figured that," I said as we approached the door, "but I was watching pretty close."

Sammy didn't respond.

CHAPTER FOUR

In the morning, Sammy did not want to go to school. She delayed at every opportunity. First, she claimed that she didn't have any clean clothes, even though there was a basket of clean clothes by her dresser. Second, Sammy claimed that we were out of her favorite cereal, even though there was an unopened box of Frosted Mini-Wheats on the top shelf. Third, Sammy claimed that she couldn't find her homework, even though it was in a folder next to her backpack. Finally, she claimed that her stomach hurt, and that might have been true.

"Listen, Sammy." I put a comforting hand on her shoulder. "I'm gonna drive you to school this morning so you don't have to worry about the girls on the bus."

Sammy shook her head. "It doesn't matter whether I'm on the bus or not. They hate me."

"They don't hate you," I said, even though I didn't know what I was talking about.

"The girls say I'm stuck up. That I think I'm better than everybody else because I'm rich."

I took Sammy's hand and led her over to the wooden bench in our entryway. We sat down. I knew that I couldn't explain our economic situation to an eleven-year-old. Sammy was smart, but she wasn't going to understand how she could be a part of a famous family and live in the fanciest part of town, but I couldn't afford an air conditioner for my office.

"You've got to ignore those girls."

"How? You should hear what they say about us, about the Judge and Grandpa and Uncle Lincoln and you." Sammy started to cry. "Nobody likes me." She looked away. "Or maybe some do, but they're afraid to be my friend."

"I'll talk to your principal."

Sammy looked up at me, panicked. "No, Daddy, don't do that. It'll make it worse."

"I have to do something. You have to go to school."

"It's awful." Sammy looked away again, eyes bloodshot with tears. "Girls say I'm *acting white*. They leave Oreos in my locker, Daddy." Her head dropped, defeated. "Black on the outside, white on the . . . Oreos."

Now tears welled up in my own eyes. I put my arm back around her and squeezed her. "They're ignorant." Weight pressed down on my chest with a mix of sadness and anger. The idea of sending Sammy back into that school building another day made my own stomach hurt.

If Monica were still alive, she would've known the right thing to say. Sammy was just like her mother. That mother-daughter conversation, however, was impossible.

Then I caved.

"Why don't you come to work with me today?"

Sammy wiped the tears away. Her body visibly relaxed. "Seriously?"

I nodded. "Just for today, and we'll try and figure something else out."

The decision to bring my daughter to work with me at the courthouse was arguably not my finest moment as a single parent, but you know what they say about desperate times. It was a general arraignment calendar, which is inherently chaotic. Keeping track of a tween girl amid the crowd of low-level street criminals made it even more of a scrum.

In the hierarchy of legal proceedings, misdemeanor and petty misdemeanor arraignment court is near the bottom. It's a sea of people who are usually homeless, mentally ill, addicted to drugs, or all the above. They haven't been charged with major crimes like murder or robbing a bank, but *quality of life* offenses—loitering, open bottle in a park, urinating in public, possession of a small amount of drugs, shoplifting.

I deputized Sammy as my assistant. I gave her the stack of files we'd picked up from the public defender's office that morning and told her to sit in a chair in the hallway with them while we worked through them together.

"Who's on top?" I asked.

Sammy handed me the first file, reading the name. "Schultz."

"Thank you." I took the file from her, and then I shouted, "Schultz." Nobody responded, but the mass of people in the hallway quieted down. I looked at the label. "DeAnne Schultz. Is there a DeAnne Schultz here?"

Still no response. I handed the file back to Sammy. She put it on the bottom of the stack, then handed me the next file. "Bates," she said.

I took the file and shouted, "Bates."

An older man, about twenty feet away, raised his hand.

"Cecil Bates?" I asked him.

"That's me."

"Good." I nodded and walked over to him. "Mr. Bates, I'm your attorney, and we've got about forty seconds to figure out whether you're going to plead guilty today or we're going to set this matter on for trial."

I turned and shot Sammy a wink, and she winked back. At least she was having a good time.

◆ ◆ ◆

The law factory started in earnest around ten in the morning. By the time the judge took the bench, I had spoken with about 70 percent of the people who were identified in my stack of files. There were a few people who came late that I didn't get a chance to consult. The remainder did not show up, and when their cases were later called, the judge would issue a warrant for their arrest.

Sometimes I didn't see the logic in spending the money to arrest, transport, book, and jail a guy who didn't show up for court to receive a seventy-five-dollar fine for pissing in an alley, but that was how it worked. That was justice in America.

I kept my frustration with the system contained. I did my job, made my arguments, and collected my check. It was dangerous to think too much while on the clock. Railing against the Man was restricted to off-duty hours. In the evenings or at happy hour with the other public defenders and low-rent street lawyers, I was allowed to complain as much as I wanted about the system's failures and inefficiency. But when I was at court, I had to get the job done.

It was a sentiment shared by most of the veteran attorneys at the public defender's office. One public defender even had a sign taped to her door that said:

District Court Mission Statement:
Shut Up and Put the Chocolates in Boxes

It was an acknowledgment that we were often the practitioners of assembly-line justice, and a not-so-subtle recognition that most of our clients were black.

"Next case, *State versus Hernandez*, file number 65-MD-14-293849." The clerk picked up a copy of the criminal complaint and police reports and handed the stack of paper to the judge.

In the meantime, Sammy located the *Hernandez* case in our stack of files as the defendant walked from the back of the courtroom to the front. She handed me the file, and I noted my appearance for the record and stated that the defendant qualified for the services of the public defender's office.

The judge looked at Sammy and then at me. He was about to say something, but didn't. Sammy wasn't causing any problems, and if she wasn't slowing down the assembly line, he didn't care. "Mr. Glass, what's the status?"

I looked at my client and he nodded. "My client would like to plead guilty to the shoplifting charge, if the charge of trespass would be dismissed."

"Is that true, Mr. Hernandez?" The judge peered down at my client from the bench.

"Yes." He nodded. He'd been through the routine before.

The judge turned to the prosecutor. "And that's the deal?"

"Yes, Your Honor."

"Very well, proceed with the waiver of his trial rights and the factual basis for the plea." The formalities of the plea agreement were placed on the record, and the judge accepted the deal. He adjudicated my client guilty after the four-minute hearing, then picked up his pen and crossed *Hernandez* off the list of cases on his docket.

The system lurched forward.

"Next case, *State versus Cecil Bates*, file number 65-MD-14-358217." The clerk picked up a copy of Cecil Bates's criminal complaint and police reports, then handed the stack of paper to the judge.

I got the file from Sammy, and once everybody was in their places, the judge officially appointed me to represent Mr. Bates. The same script as the others was followed. "Mr. Glass, what is the status?"

I looked at my client, and he vigorously shook his head. "Mr. Bates would like to plead not guilty, and we'd like to set this matter on for pretrial and trial."

The judge sighed and rolled his eyes. It was an expression and gesture that would never appear in the court reporter's transcript, but the judge's body language made it clear that he did not approve of Mr. Bates wasting the court's valuable time and clogging up the system. They were all guilty, after all.

"Very well." The judge looked at his clerk, and she barked out a date for a pretrial hearing and trial. The judge repeated it, and I wrote the date down on the file. "Hearing is set," the judge said. "Next case."

I patted Mr. Bates on the back, gave him my card, and pointed him toward the judge's law clerk, who was waiting with a written notice of the date and time of his next hearing. Then I turned to Sammy to retrieve the next file, continuing to work through the remainder of the cases.

We finished the morning arraignment calendar at eleven thirty. In just an hour and a half, the court had processed sixty-three cases. Ten were set for pretrial and trial. Twenty warrants were issued, and the remainder of the defendants pled guilty.

"That was fun." Sammy pressed the elevator button in the hallway, smiling. "Where are we going now?"

I put my arm around her. I was glad that she was happy, and for a second I allowed myself to believe I was actually a competent parent. "We're gonna take those files back to where we got them this morning and then go over to the police station for a few minutes."

"Then get a milk shake?"

"How about we get lunch first, something super healthy like a chili dog. Then we can get a milk shake."

Sammy nodded. "Deal."

CHAPTER FIVE

The main government buildings for the City of Saint Louis were all clustered together on the southern edge of the Gateway Mall. The mall was a long park that stretched from one end of downtown to the iconic Gateway Arch on the Mississippi River. As we walked past city hall toward the public defender's office and police headquarters, Sammy asked whether we could stop and visit Annie.

Annie was Angela Montgomery. She and I had grown up together, the two oldest children in two famous political families. Annie was also the first female mayor of Saint Louis and one of the only African American female mayors in the country.

I played it cool as we continued down the street, glancing over my shoulder to ensure that nobody was around to overhear the conversation. "I don't think that would be a good idea."

"But I love the castle." Sammy referred to city hall as "the castle" because of its ornamental towers and columns. The four-story structure even had a grand imperial staircase like in the movie *Cinderella*. Sammy liked to spin around on the marble floor and then pretend to lose her shoe going up the steps.

"I'll call Annie and see if she wants to have dinner sometime. How about that?"

Sammy nodded, agreeing, although she was disappointed and a little confused. She wasn't sure why we couldn't just surprise the mayor of Saint Louis—with whom I was currently having an on-again, off-again extramarital affair—and hang out in the middle of the day.

I let it go. It was complicated.

◆ ◆ ◆

After chatting with some colleagues at the public defender's office and handing off the majority of the files, we walked farther down Tucker to a large structure at the corner of Tucker and Clark. It was the city's main police headquarters and connected to the police academy. Built a few decades after city hall, the building was quite plain in comparison.

Inside headquarters, there was calm. Most of the excitement was now dispersed among the various neighborhood precincts and the new jail down the street.

This building was where the police chief had his office, as well as his more senior officers, human resources personnel, and the geeks. The geeks were computer nerds who analyzed the city's crime data and generated a myriad of reports that advised commanders where the city's beat cops should patrol. Twenty years ago patrols were doled out by instinct. Now there was an algorithm.

Sammy and I walked into the empty lobby. At the far end, there was a reception desk. We went up to the desk and were ignored.

Every time I tried to speak, the heavyset blonde with the painted face raised a finger and quieted me. It didn't matter that I was wearing a suit and carrying a briefcase. To her, I was just another boy who needed to be taught that his hurry wasn't hers. She would not be interrupted. She was in the middle of reading an important article about Hollywood's best and worst beach bodies.

Two minutes passed. The woman still had not looked up from her magazine. Then she nodded, laughed, and stood. Her point had been made, and I, hopefully, understood who was really in charge. "Who are you coming to see?"

"Sergeant David Schmidt."

She nodded. The woman looked down at Sammy and then back up at me. "And you are?"

"Justin Glass." I looked her in the eye and I held it.

The last name clicked somewhere in the deep recesses of her bureaucratic brain, and her attitude softened. "Just a second." If she wasn't careful, she was going to seem almost friendly.

The woman looked at an office directory, then picked up her phone and punched in a number. "Sergeant," she said. "This is your angel at the front desk." The woman looked me over again. "I got a Justin Glass and a little girl up front wanting to see you."

She listened, then nodded and hung up the phone. She pointed at the sign-in sheet. "Gotta sign in here." She handed me a pen and then reached into her desk drawer. "And wear one of these at all times." She removed two visitor badges and handed them to me. "Sergeant Schmidt is on the sixth floor." She gestured toward the elevator. "Welcome to paradise."

◆　◆　◆

Schmitty's office was small, but the fact that he had an office at all was a testament to his seniority and savvy. Despite a steady rotation of new police chiefs every three to four years, Schmitty remained. He was promoted off the streets and got that office because he had the unique ability to keep a low profile but always be present when big decisions were made. Schmitty was valued for his advice, but rarely blamed if things went badly.

"Sit." Schmitty closed the door and pointed to a chair across from his desk. "Is this your girl?"

I nodded, looking at Sammy. "She's helping me out today."

Schmitty sat back down behind his desk. "No school?"

"Something like that." I put my hand on Sammy's shoulder and gave it a squeeze.

Schmitty knew that I was being deliberately vague, but he didn't press for details. It was none of his business.

"Your missing boy is something else," he said.

"Doesn't surprise me."

Schmitty looked at Sammy and then back at me. "Let's just say that Devon Walker is very well known to the police working that area. Young as he is, he's already been in and out of juvie about a dozen times."

"Any idea where he went?"

Schmitty shrugged. "He's got a warrant out for his arrest. Serious case. He's also a person of interest in a couple of other ones, aggravated robberies. I think the prosecutors were about ready to bring additional charges, maybe even a certification to adult court, but then he disappeared."

Schmitty paused, waiting to see whether I had a question, which I didn't.

"Nothing exactly shocking about him vanishing," he continued. "Not at all uncommon for kids like him to cross over to East Saint Louis or take the bus over to Kansas City or Gary or up to Chicago. There are usually relatives or gangbanger friends who are willing to let a kid like this crash for a while. Eventually they get kicked out, come back here, and we pick 'em up."

"So you think he'll come back?"

"Maybe." Schmitty glanced at Sammy and then turned back to me. "Or maybe he's just gone."

"Like, forever?"

"Also not uncommon," Schmitty said. "And, frankly, not too many people around here are going to be shedding a lot of tears for Devon Walker if that's the case."

"Understood." I nodded, hoping that would be enough information to satisfy his sister. "Thanks for looking into it."

"Well"—Schmitty bowed his head—"when the royal family requests a favor, I comply." He then reached into his desk drawer and removed a file. He set it on top of his desk. "This is an extra copy of Devon Walker's juvenile record and incident reports. Because he's a minor and there are ongoing investigations, it's all confidential. Theoretically his family might be able to get it with a court order, but I'm not so sure about that." He stood. "I have to go to the bathroom. You can see yourself out."

"I will." I stood up and shook Schmitty's hand. "Thanks again."

"Not a problem." Schmitty walked around his desk. He left, leaving me and Sammy alone in his office.

"OK." I opened my briefcase, then leaned over and picked up Devon Walker's file. I slid the file into my briefcase and turned to Sammy. "You ready to go get that milk shake?"

Sammy didn't respond. She didn't move.

"Come on now." I motioned to the doors. "Time to go."

She stood up slowly. "Does that man know you're taking his file?"

I smiled. "Yes and no."

CHAPTER SIX

We sat in Daddy's Booth in the back of Crown Candy. Sammy referred to it as "Daddy's Booth" because my name was listed on a plaque hanging on the wall above the table. The honor was given to any person who had consumed five large malts in thirty minutes, which was actually the equivalent of drinking about eight regular malts.

The rules required a challenger to drink both the malt in each glass and the remaining mixture in the stainless steel cup that accompanied it. I had accomplished this goal as a teenager. My brother, Lincoln, had bet me his prize Ozzie Smith rookie card that I couldn't do it, and, well, that was all the incentive I needed.

Sammy and I ordered our chili dogs and milk shakes. Then Sammy removed a thick book from her backpack. I had lost track of all the books that she was reading. She usually had three or four going at once, most having to do with a dragon, a supernatural cat, or a kid wizard.

As she started to read, I pulled Devon Walker's file out of my brief-case. Part of me didn't want to know. I would have rather sat back and just enjoyed the hustle and bustle of one of the country's longest-operating soda fountains. Reading about Devon Walker's doomed life was only going to make me depressed. Tanisha, however, was coming back to my office that afternoon. I wanted to show her that I had made an effort. Then maybe she'd see that there was nothing more that could be done and leave me alone.

I flipped through the file. It was in reverse chronological order. The most recent contacts with the police were on top, and his earliest contacts with the police and the court system were near the bottom of the file. Interspersed throughout were about a dozen photos.

I skipped the reports initially and just looked at the pictures. Near the top, there was a series of photographs taken by the police's gang unit. The first two were mug shots. Devon Walker stood in front of a blank wall like it was a driver's license photo. His expression was blank. His eyes were dead. He didn't appear afraid, nervous, or angry. He was only sixteen, but getting arrested had become a way of life.

Then there were photographs of Devon's tattoos. There were a few that appeared to be the names of girlfriends, which I'd mention to Tanisha and see whether she knew who or where they were. Most were gang references and symbols of the lifestyle. On his neck was a tattoo of a pair of dice. On his arm there was a gun, above it the words *Blood Money*.

The gang references were to three small cliques that had been terrorizing the north side of Saint Louis for the past seven years. These were not organized street gangs established to sell crack cocaine or other drugs, like the Bloods and Crips of the 1980s. They were just groups of three to ten kids who robbed, beat, raped, and got high because that's what gangsters did. It was their destiny. A cop in Northern Ireland once coined the phrase *recreational violence*. That pretty much summed it up. The cliques filled a void.

Devon was one of the growing number of kids who were bored, uneducated, and disconnected. Violence was something they just did, because there was nothing else to do.

I turned to the next set of photographs, a little deeper in the stack, and the tattoos were gone. Then I found the next set, and then another. Devon was getting younger.

The pictures transported me back in time.

Eventually I got to the end. It was a picture of a six-year-old boy. He still had some of his baby fat. His eyes weren't dead. They were wide and alive. He smiled for the camera, because that's what a first grader does when his photograph is being taken. Didn't matter that this picture was being taken by a cop.

The shock of seeing a picture of a little boy in a police file gave way to curiosity.

I flipped the page in order to figure out why he was arrested. The report was from a school resource officer. A classmate had told the officer that Devon threatened to "cut his lips off" on the playground, and the officer found a hunting knife in Devon's backpack. Criminal charges were dropped because it was ridiculous to prosecute a child that young with the possession of a dangerous weapon on school property. But, under the school district's zero tolerance policy, Devon was expelled for a time.

I flipped back to the photograph.

Devon Walker didn't look much different than I did at his age—or much different than any other six-year-old black boy. I tried to imagine how somebody that young would know that stabbing or cutting another person with a knife was even an option. What had he seen others do? What had he heard?

Then I thought of Devon's little brother, sitting alone in the front yard of their house.

"You OK, Daddy?" Sammy asked.

I looked up from the file. "I'm fine, tiger. Don't you worry about your pops."

CHAPTER SEVEN

We walked down two blocks from Crown Candy to my office on the corner of Fourteenth and Warren. I opened the door. The temperature in my office hadn't changed since the day before. The air conditioner had not magically repaired itself during the night.

Sammy coughed. Her face curled back. "Kinda stuffy." She waved her hand in front of her face. "Can't we open a window or something?"

"Wish it was that simple." I turned on the lights. I looked around the sparsely decorated space and sighed. "Just stay here for a second." I picked up the stack of mail that had been shoved through the door's mail slot, then walked through the reception area to my office in the back. "I'll check my messages, then we can go next door."

I picked up the office phone and punched in the code to retrieve my voicemail, then set about sorting through the mail. Solicitations and credit card offers went into the garbage. The remainder went into my briefcase for later.

It took a few minutes to listen to all my messages.

There were six. Four were potential clients seeking legal representation. I wrote down their contact information and the crimes that they were accused of committing. I'd call them back once I got Sammy settled down, but I didn't have much hope. Most people who called my office were only working their way down a long list of criminal defense attorneys that they had found on the Internet or in a phone book. By the time I got back to them, they had usually hired somebody else. If they hadn't hired somebody else, that meant that they didn't have any money.

The fifth message was from Cecil Bates, one of the public defender cases that I had handled this morning. He wanted me to call him back immediately to discuss his defense strategy. He had been doing research at the public library, and he wanted to share with me several United States Supreme Court cases that he had found.

Warning flags went up all around me.

I wrote down Cecil's information and considered how quickly I should return his call. If I called him back too soon, he might come to expect that response every time he contacted me. If I waited too long, he'd sour on me. He'd make my life hell until his case was resolved. These were the kind of real-world problems that never get discussed in law school.

I pressed a button and moved on to the last message. It was my little brother, Lincoln.

"Listen, Justin, you gotta give me a call," he said. "It's important that we talk as soon as possible. Things are happening with Dad and you need to be a part of it."

I shook my head. More political schemes. Then I deleted the message.

◆　◆　◆

Most of the storefronts along Fourteenth where my office was located were empty, but there was some life. Ameren, the local electric utility, and a couple of nonprofit foundations had provided a combination of loans and grants to paint the facades, restore the interiors, and add new streetlights and benches.

The street looked nice for the first time in a quarter century. The beautification effort was intended to be a spark for renewal, but the spark had definitely not turned into a fire.

The lack of economic activity was likely caused by the lack of people. The city had lost 63 percent of its 1950 population. Hundreds of thousands of people gone. It's hard to make money selling things when there aren't people around to buy them.

I prayed nearly every day that it would happen. I wanted to believe that people would rediscover the Northside and move back, but my head told me that was near impossible. Saint Louis was a city built for a million, but it now had a population of just over 300,000. People had moved to the suburbs over sixty years ago, and it was crazy to think that they were going to come back now. They'd settled into pleasant lives far removed from the grit of city life, and every time the city got closer to them, they moved even farther away.

Sammy and I walked a half block down the street to the Northside Roastery. I opened the door, and a little bell rang. Hermes came out from behind a curtain separating the front and back of the shop. "Mr. Glass, I sensed you were coming." Hermes spoke in a thick Bosnian accent, and he claimed to have some psychic abilities inherited from his mother's side of the family.

He and his brother, Nikolas, were two of the thousands of refugees who had been relocated to Saint Louis from Bosnia-Herzegovina during the war in the 1990s. "Come over here. What I get for you?" Hermes walked to the counter. "I've got some wonderful pastries, very fresh, and my Tower Grove French Roast is near perfection."

"I'll have the French Roast, iced." I looked over at Sammy. "Still full?"

Sammy nodded. "Maybe a juice for later?" She didn't want to disappoint Hermes by failing to order anything.

Hermes looked from her to me, seeking confirmation.

I nodded. "And a juice."

30

Hermes clapped his hands. "Yes. Perfect." He turned with a flourish, bent down to a small refrigerator under a stainless steel table, and opened the door. "Orange, apple, strawberry-lemonade?"

"Apple." Sammy looked at me and smiled. Hermes's enthusiasm was contagious.

I liked it, too, but it was unclear to me how he stayed open. It was rare to see more than one or two other people in his coffee shop. My guess was that most of the money was earned by his brother, Nikolas. He stayed in the back whenever possible, and he wasn't nearly as friendly.

Hermes had told me once that Nikolas was a computer genius. He purportedly bought, repaired, and resold computers on eBay and Craigslist. That was probably true, but I got the sense that Nikolas also did other things with computers that were far less legitimate.

Sammy and I got a table by the window that looked out at the street. Unlike the one in my office, the coffee shop's air conditioner was working just fine. A luxury. We sat in the cool, surrounded by the smell of freshly roasted coffee beans.

The smell came from an antique roaster in the corner of the shop. It was a huge cast iron contraption. The body was painted dark blue. A metal arm swept underneath the roasting batch of green coffee beans like the second hand of an old pocket watch. It hummed and cranked. Every few minutes, Hermes wandered over to check the beans. He poked at them with a wooden spoon, ensuring that they were not being burned.

Sammy got out her thick book, and I got out the Devon Walker file.

It took me an hour and a half to carefully work through the entire file. From age ten until the time that he disappeared, Devon was in nearly constant contact with the police and juvenile probation. The older reports described a young kid on the periphery, surrounded by others who were dealing drugs and getting in fights. As the police reports became more current, Devon had moved from the periphery to the center.

He was in the passenger seat of a car when the driver pulled a gun and started firing shots in the air near a bus stop by Saint Louis Avenue and Twenty-Second. He was involved in a fight at an Arby's on Lindell. And then there was, according to the incident summary, a blurry black-and-white security video of him and three friends stomping on and robbing a man at the MetroLink light rail station on Grand.

Once the man was down, Devon had pulled off the victim's pants and run. They had left the bloodied victim half-naked on the train platform. The pants were found a few blocks away, but the cell phone and wallet that had been in the pants were gone.

A warrant had been issued for Devon's arrest, but it was still outstanding. Devon disappeared about the time that the warrant and a probation violation had been issued.

I pushed the file aside, took a sip of coffee, and then, through the window, I saw Tanisha walking toward my office.

I told Sammy that I'd be right back, then headed out the door after Tanisha.

She was looking in my office window and knocking on the door by the time I caught up to her. "Tanisha," I said, then pointed at the locked office door when she turned to me. "Sorry about that. It's too hot in there to get any work done. Want to come down to the coffee shop?"

She was skeptical. "Did you find my brother?"

"No." I shook my head. "But we can talk about it."

CHAPTER EIGHT

Later, I dropped Sammy off at home, where my mother and the Judge promised to feed her and tuck her into bed, then got back in my car to go to work.

As the rest of the city emptied out, heading to South County and Saint Charles, I crossed Forty against traffic and drove back over to the Northside. My task was to find Devon Walker's girlfriends.

This was it. I'd spent almost the entire day working on her brother's file. I was going to knock on a few doors, talk to these people, and be done with it.

As much as my heart broke for Tanisha Walker and her family, it couldn't be personal. I was a lawyer, I reminded myself, and I wouldn't do anybody any good going broke looking for a nasty kid that nobody besides his little sister wanted found.

◆ ◆ ◆

The streetlights came on as I pulled up to the first address that Tanisha Walker had given me. I got out of my car and looked for signs of life. It was a typical Northside home on one of the few blocks that were mostly intact. There was no extravagance. It didn't have arches or turrets. There was no grand Queen Anne–style porch wrapping around the front. Instead, it had a concrete stoop.

I walked up to the door and knocked, hearing a television on inside. I waited, then rang the doorbell when nobody came.

I was about to knock again when I heard some movement from behind the door. Then the door cracked open a few inches, still secured by a chain.

It was a heavyset woman, but I couldn't tell her age. Most of her face remained hidden behind the door. "One question," she said. Her visible eyeball looked me up and down. "Cop, bill collector, or preacher?"

"None of the above," I said. "Justin Glass." I hoped she'd recognize the last name, but she didn't. "I'm a lawyer. Got an office over on Fourteenth."

Her suspicion remained, so I told her about my client and her missing brother. "I think he was dating your daughter. At least, that's what Tanisha told me."

The woman closed the door in my face. I wondered whether that was the end of the conversation, whether she was going to return to her television show; but then I heard the chain fall away. I had passed the test—at least enough for her to open the door wide, if not to ask me in.

"Kids don't date no more. Always runnin'. And I ain't never heard of no Devon Walker, neither."

"Maybe a photo." I took one out of my pocket. Tanisha had brought it to our meeting. "He's the one on the right."

The woman leaned in, squinting at the photograph. After a few seconds, she nodded. "I seen him around plenty a while ago . . . not lately." She shook her head. "Didn't know who he was. Couldn't tell you where he is."

"When would you say was the last time you saw him?"

"Don't know." She glanced behind her. The commercial had ended and she longed to return to her television. Then she came back at me.

34

"Maybe last winter. Christmastime." She raised her eyebrows and put her hands on her ample hips. "Anything else?"

I knew from her expression and tone that our time had run out. "Well thank you," I said. "You know when your daughter's gonna be back?"

The woman shook her head. "No idea."

I gave her my card, told her to ask her daughter to call me, and thanked her again for her time.

Walking away, I heard the front door close behind me, followed by the chain.

I had no expectation that her daughter would ever call. I doubted that she would even get the message.

◆　◆　◆

The second girlfriend lived five blocks over from the first. Her house looked the same as the other, except it was lit and hopping. Every light was on. There were cars parked in front, people lingered in the street, and other groups gathered on the corner. Music came from somewhere, and three guys were on the porch smoking weed. More people were inside.

I wondered whether this was a party or just a regular night on the block—or maybe a little bit of both.

The palms of my hands started to sweat. My heart beat faster, and my adrenaline rose the closer I got to the front stoop. I wondered how I should start the conversation, but the boys on the front stoop made that decision for me.

"Fuck you want?" A tall kid with sagging pants and no shirt stood a step above me, looking down like he was ready to pounce. He was lean, with prison muscles—the kind you get when you work out in a cage, not a gym. "Come to arrest us?"

"Nope, not a cop."

"You look like a cop."

"Well," I said, trying to keep it friendly, "I'm a lawyer. Tanisha Walker sent me over here. She's looking for her big brother."

"Fuckin' lawyer drivin' that sad-ass ride?" The tall kid laughed and pointed at my Honda, and the other thugs on the porch joined in, all smirks and eye rolls. Once upon a time, there was an inherent respect for the older black men in the community, but not here. There wasn't anybody left to teach it.

"Is BeeBee here?" I thought it best to get to the point. "Tanisha told me that I should talk to BeeBee about her brother Devon."

"Well she ain't here." His words slurred together. "Nobody's here; ain't nobody knows nothing about D." He waved me off. "When D wantacomeback, hecomeback. So get the fuck in your shitty-ass car, negro, and get the fuck outta here." The tall kid took a step forward, and the others stood. They circled behind in support of whatever he wanted to do.

Getting into my "shitty-ass car" was an excellent idea. "Fine." As I took my business card out of my wallet, a few more curious people emerged from the house, and others looked out the windows to see what was going on. "If you see BeeBee, just give her this." I held out the business card, but the tall kid wouldn't take it. "Please."

Then the tall kid took my card. I had a small moment of hope, but that quickly went away.

"What I just say? You deaf?" The tall kid let the card fall out of his hand and down to the sidewalk. "Ain't nobody talking to you." He stared at me as he stepped on the card, grinding it beneath his foot. "Now get, 'fore I beat yo' ass."

◆ ◆ ◆

I managed to avoid getting killed at BeeBee's house. That, in hindsight, was a major success. I should have quit while I was ahead. A saner man would have gone home, but I made the unfortunate decision to stop by my office. That was when my luck ran out.

By the time I got over there, it was dark.

I found a parking space in front, because there was never a demand for parking in front of my office, day or night. I pulled into the spot, turned off the engine, and opened my car door. As soon as it was open, I heard yelling coming from the alley that ran behind the Fourteenth Street buildings.

Glass broke. Somebody screamed.

There was a narrow path to the alley between my office and the building next door. I pulled out my cell phone and dialed 911 as I ran toward the noise. When the operator answered, I slowed a little, telling her who and where I was, but kept going forward.

She wanted me to stop and wait, but I didn't.

Three kids stood over Hermes's brother in the back of the Northside Roastery.

Nikolas was on the ground. A broken computer monitor sat nearby. One arm was bent. His other arm tried to protect his head from another blow as he struggled to crawl away.

I didn't think anything through. No plan. I just had to stop it. "Police, get your hands up in the air." I held up my cell phone like it was a badge and put my hand on my hip like I was about to pull a gun. In the darkness and shadows of the back alley, I hoped that nobody could tell that none of it was real. I kept barking orders at them as I moved closer.

They didn't stick around. The trio took off down the alley, and within seconds they were gone.

"Nikolas." I crouched next to him, but anticipating another strike, he whimpered and tried to get away. "It's Justin Glass. You're going to be OK. Lie still." I lowered my voice, calm. "Lie still, Nik; help is coming."

I put my hand out. I tried to provide a gentle touch to reassure Nikolas that I wasn't a threat, but as I reached for him the alley flooded with flashing lights and sirens. I turned and was blinded.

Somebody yelled at me, but I didn't understand. "What?" I asked to a jumble of commands. Then a sickening flash of clarity as two police officers rushed toward me with their guns drawn: I was a black man, crouched over a downed white man in a dark alley. *This was how it ends.*

"I'm Justin Gl—" I managed before a thick white cop drove me into the pavement. He rolled off as the other drove his steel-toed boot into my side. Pain shot through me. I screamed and tried to turn away. "I'm the one who called—"

"I said freeze." Another kick to the side, harder and even more painful than the first. The bone cracked, and it felt like I'd never be able to force another breath inside me. Then a knee drove into my back as someone got on top. I thought my spine was going to snap in two. My face was pressed hard into the asphalt. I tasted blood as my arms were pulled back. Handcuffs were put on my wrists.

"I'm Justin Glass."

The officer leaned in close, still on top of me, breathing hard. "Don't care who the fuck you are, homey," he said. "You're under arrest." Then he grabbed my head, pulled it back a few inches, and slammed it down.

CHAPTER NINE

I was released from jail and into the custody of my father, United States congressman Arthur Glass. Buster, my father's chief of staff, and Lincoln were also there in the otherwise empty reception area.

Lincoln winced as he looked me over. "You look like shit, man."

"Thank you for stating the obvious." I walked toward them, limping. Fire shot up my side with every step. My lip was swollen, and my forehead was cut.

I knew that I had blacked out, but I wasn't sure for how long. When I woke up, the cops were in the process of pushing me into the back of a squad car. The trip to the jail was dizzying, and even now my head was in a fog. "Nikolas OK?"

"Probably saved his life," my father said.

"You're a certified hero." Lincoln smiled.

Buster, a short man who was built like a wrestler, took my arm and guided me to a row of seats along the wall. "Best if we all talk before we go out there." He nodded toward the exit, always handling the situation and playing the angles. "Every news outlet in the area is outside, waiting for you to say something."

I shook my head as I sat down. "I don't want to say anything." My throat was dry. "I want to go home, see Sammy, and get some sleep."

"Can't do that," Lincoln protested. "We got an opportunity here. We can introduce you to the people, create your brand, and lay the groundwork to make public safety and police accountability a big part of your campaign." He pumped his fist. "People have been waiting for this."

"My campaign?" I looked at my father for clarification, but he just rolled his eyes.

In addition to being a state senator, Lincoln had also taken it upon himself to lead and grow the Glass family's political machine. He cultivated family members and relatives to occupy various elected positions throughout Saint Louis and Saint Louis County. No position was too small or insignificant to get his full attention and support.

Every year, neighborhoods were filled with lawn signs touting the candidacy of somebody named Glass. The signs were all the same color, same font, and same logo. He had an army of volunteers ready to lit-drop, phone-bank, and work the polling places. It was meant to be intimidating, and it was. Saint Louis was a land of political dynasties, and ours was one of them.

"This is solid." Lincoln pointed at me. "People need to see what the police did to you, all banged up. Tomorrow you'll be clean and rested, and that's no good." He nodded, agreeing with his own plan. "Michael Brown, Eric Garner, Alton Sterling, Philando Castille, and now you."

"Hardly." I raised my hand, anger rising, but I wasn't sure whether I was angry at Lincoln or the police—or both. "All those guys are gone." I closed my eyes, trying to focus through the pain. "I'm lucky I wasn't shot tonight, but . . ." I faded. My breathing slowed. Every breath hurt. "I'm not doing the politics thing tonight or tomorrow or the next day. What part of that don't you seem to understand?"

"When we were little, you talked about it all the time." Lincoln put his hands on his hips. "You and me, just a darker shade of JFK and Bobby."

I shook my head. "That was a long time ago." I looked at my father for support. He provided none. He sat silently, a mixture of pride and sadness. He was proud that I was a survivor, but sad that even the son of a United States congressman couldn't just live. More than fifty years after the Freedom Rides and the March on Washington, his son had to fight to survive, just like he had to.

I turned my attention back to Lincoln. "Since Monica died, you've tried to recruit me for everything from school board to dog catcher, and every time I say no." I was frustrated now, lashing out. "They're just games. I can't do the games right now, maybe never."

At that moment, I realized how odd it was that my dad and Buster were actually there with me instead of in DC. I hadn't seen or personally talked to my father in about six months. When my foggy brain couldn't put any pieces together, I turned back to him. Quietly, I asked, "What are you doing here, Dad?"

He offered a restrained smile. "Retiring." My father looked at Lincoln and Buster, and then Lincoln jumped in to explain.

"Buster works for me now," Lincoln said. "We're transitioning, and I—"

"We've been waiting at the Judge's house for you to get home all night." My father looked at Lincoln with annoyance. "Nothing is set. We needed to discuss, plan for the future. I was about to give up and go to bed when we got the call. Your mother's been worried sick."

I clenched my jaw as I took a painful breath, remembering Lincoln's phone calls and my mother encouraging me to talk with him. Then I thought of my daughter.

"Does Sammy know?"

My dad's expression softened. "About my retirement, or you gettin' whupped?" A reserved smile came through, but his eyes remained sad. "Neither," he said. "Sammy's asleep." Then as an aside, he added, "She's such a good girl."

"I know." I thought about how much I wanted to hold her, feeling guilty. *What if I'd been killed?* Then I closed my eyes and centered myself. A migraine had started to form. The pain was now coming from my side and my head, forcing me even more off track. There was too much going on.

After a pause, I circled back. "So you're really doing it?" He'd threatened to retire numerous times over the past ten years, but he'd never done it. "You're not going to run again?"

"True." My dad looked up at the ceiling. "Forty years and I couldn't solve the world's problems. Time for somebody else to give it a try." Then my dad turned back to me, looking me over. "Lincoln is right, however. You do look like shit."

Then my father stood up, taking control. "Here's what we're going to do." It was clear that there wouldn't be any debate. "My son wants to go home and see his beautiful daughter, my beautiful granddaughter." He looked at Buster. "Go tell the cops that Justin is going to go out the back way—no cameras. The police chief will appreciate that, and he'll owe us. We also need them to find a nice car to take him home and a doctor to meet us at the house. And tell the chief that they shouldn't even think about transporting my son home in a squad car or some paddy wagon."

My father then turned to Lincoln. "Write up a statement, something like, 'We appreciate the community's concern, and we know that the police will conduct a full review regarding the incident tonight.'" He took a moment to compose the next part of the statement in his head and then continued. "Tell them Justin Glass was returning to his law office, heard noises in the alley, and went to help a neighbor in need after calling 911. We have no further comment at this time other than the Glass family is proud of his bravery."

My father looked at me and then turned and pointed at Lincoln. "And I mean that last part about no further comment. No ad libs. No off-the-record stuff about injuries or suggestions of racism. Nothing beyond the statement."

"But it was racism." Lincoln shook his head and pointed at me. "Look at him. It wouldn't have happened to a white guy."

"Of course I see what they did to him." My father's voice trembled. "Of course I know that, but I've been at this a lot longer than you. It doesn't matter. People will find the ambiguity, because they need to find the ambiguity. It won't get us anywhere."

"Especially if we don't try." Lincoln looked to Buster for support, and Buster looked at his old boss and his new, torn.

To Lincoln, Buster said, "Don't want to look like we're exploiting it." He searched for a compromise that Lincoln would accept. "And you don't want to light a fire that we can't put out."

Lincoln stared at Buster, obviously frustrated. "I thought that was your job." He shook his head and walked away. "You better get on the right page."

CHAPTER TEN

When I woke up, my mother was sitting in a chair by the window. She was drinking coffee and reading the newspaper, waiting. I closed my eyes again and let my head fall back into the pillow. My brain ground out a question. "What time is it?"

"About eleven o'clock." I heard her fold the newspaper. "Been asleep a long time," she said. "Buster's cocktail of painkillers and sleeping aids certainly did the trick."

I started to laugh, but it hurt too bad. "Not sure how he was able to acquire that stuff in the middle of the night."

I heard my mother stand and walk over to me. "You don't want to know how Buster does his job."

I opened my eyes and made an effort to push myself into an upright position, even though every muscle in my body resisted the movement. I grunted through it. The pain only stopped when I stopped.

I watched my mother lift a silver pot from my nightstand and pour coffee into an empty cup. "Cream?"

I nodded. A shot of fire raced up my side. "And if you could add a few more of Buster's narcotics into that coffee, that sure would be nice."

My mother smiled. "Absolutely." She brought the delicate china cup and saucer to me. "Here you are." Then she went to my dresser and picked up a pill bottle. She removed two and brought the pills back.

I took them from her. "You know I was just kidding about the narcotics." Then I put the pills into my mouth and swallowed. "But I'm also not going to turn them down." I looked at her. She was still a beautiful, sharp woman who could've done anything, but gave it all up for her children. I could tell that she was worried about me. "It'll be fine, Mom. Just wanted to do something stupid to let you know that you're still needed."

She laughed gently. "Boys always need their mothers, no matter how old they may get." She took a breath. "I think Sammy and your father would like to see you now."

My mother returned to her chair for the *St. Louis Post-Dispatch* that she'd been reading and brought it to me. "I'll send Sammy in first. She's concerned, although doing a pretty good job of hiding it."

"Sounds good, Mom." I looked down at the front page of the newspaper and saw a picture of me staring back. It was an old head shot, taken for the local bar association's legal directory. The headline across the top said, CONGRESSMAN'S SON WRONGLY ARRESTED AFTER SAVING FRIEND'S LIFE.

I scanned the article, which prominently featured the statement that my father had prepared in the jail's reception area. Near the end of the article were several quotes from unnamed sources. The first was a quote from somebody within the police department claiming that the arrest was a "black eye" for the police and that there was going to be "all political hell to pay for those responsible."

The last anonymous quote stated that I was a "community leader" who took on legal causes for "little or no money because of a commitment to service instilled at an early age."

Then I felt my body tense as I read the final paragraph of the article:

Justin Glass is rumored to be running for political office in the near future, and this incident will likely spur him into action. He has long been committed to addressing issues of police misconduct and eliminating racial disparities, which he may pursue as a state legislator.

I shook my head. "Lincoln."

"I know," my mother said as she walked out the door. "Your father is none too pleased with your brother."

◆ ◆ ◆

I smiled when Sammy poked her head through the doorway. "You should be in school." I said it with a hint of humor, but meant what I said.

"Daddy." Sammy waved the comment away, then changed the subject. "You're famous, newspaper and television. Bunch of reporters are out there in the street, even that woman from KMOV. Can I meet her?"

"Not today."

I held out my hand, and Sammy came over to the bed. She put her little hand in mine and sat on the edge. Her hand wasn't as little as it once was, and her weight was enough to cause the bed to sink on that side. My body rebelled against the movement. I tried to keep a straight face and hide the pain, but Sammy noticed.

"Are you gonna be OK?"

"Just a little sore." I patted her back. "It'll all heal soon. I'll be up and around, and then I can parent you proper."

She rolled her eyes. "Whatever." She leaned over and kissed me on my cheek. "You scared me."

"I know," I said. "But I'll always be here. Not going to leave you."

"Promise?"

"Pinky promise." I pointed my little pinky up in the air. Sammy wrapped hers around mine and we finished the ritual. I attempted to project the confidence and hope that I knew she needed, but I also knew that my eyes likely betrayed me just as my father's sad eyes had betrayed him the night before. Pinky promise or not, we lived in a harsh world. If it happened to me once, it could happen again, and I knew it could happen to her, too, and maybe she wouldn't be as lucky.

I noticed some movement in the doorway. "Looks like your grandpa wants to talk to me now." I nodded toward him, and Sammy turned to see Congressman Glass.

I patted her knee, then gestured to the door. "Why don't you go see if Grandma or somebody else can round me up some toast and orange juice? Then we can hang out for the rest of the day, maybe watch a movie."

Sammy smiled. She always liked the idea of helping her dad. "You got it." She jumped off the bed, which caused another shot of pain up my side, then ducked past my father as he came into the room and shut the door.

"Sorry to interrupt." He walked over to the window and picked up the chair that my mother had been sitting in. "Got a flight to catch back to DC in about an hour, so I haven't got long." He moved the chair closer to the bed and sat.

I picked up the newspaper that had been folded next to me. "Nice article." I was being sarcastic.

My father shook his head. "Reporters."

"Mom says you especially liked the dramatic conclusion."

"Lincoln." His face curled up in disgust when he said my brother's name. "The boy couldn't resist. I told him to keep his mouth shut. He promised that he would, then off he went, blabbing." He leaned back, put his hands behind his head, and closed his eyes, signaling the end of the discussion. He'd had a moment to vent, and now it was done.

My father was controlled like that. He never allowed himself to get too wound up.

I waited as he prepared himself to move on to other topics. Eventually he said, "So about that retirement." His tone was more defeated than triumphant. "Can you hear me out?"

I could tell that there was something weighing on him, but knew better than to move forward too fast. "Maybe." I smiled. "I'm on a lot of painkillers at the moment. I could fall asleep at any moment or howl at the moon."

"Bet you're right." My father's lips curled into a tight smile; then he took a deep breath and sat up straight. His eyes locked on me. "Been thinking." He was serious. "You know I've been kicking around the idea of retirement for a long time. Somewhere along the line I lost the energy to do it, but I stayed on. Kept running every two years. Kept raising money. Kept going through the motions. Know why?"

"No."

"Well I've been waiting for you." My father lowered his head, as if he were making a horrible confession. "Parents aren't supposed to have favorites, Justin, and I love both you and your brother, Lincoln, very much. But this isn't about parent and son. It's about a legacy. It's about merit, and it's about all those people out there who depend on us to help them out, to be their voice."

My father looked away from me and shook his head. "Sounds corny as shit." Then he came back to me. "Sounds so naive, out of step." He took his time. "But politics ain't a game to me. Never been a game, but too many people think it is." He gestured to the outside. "Buster, Lincoln, everybody. That's why our community is in such trouble. That's why Congress is so dysfunctional. It isn't politics that's the problem. It's the people who get into politics."

"Guess I'm not following you."

My father looked down at his feet. Then he decided to come out and say it directly. "I came back to Saint Louis last night to tell Buster and Lincoln that I want you to run for Congress. I want you to be my replacement. Always have. You'll have my full and public support."

I froze as I considered the ramifications. "But, Lincoln . . ." I thought about the years he'd spent toiling in the political trenches, attending meetings, collecting favors, courting support. "He's earned it."

"You think I don't know that?" My father stood up. "Your mother said the same thing. Of course I know that. Lincoln's worked hard, but to what end? *Building the brand.*" He said the last part harshly. "Lincoln and Buster both"—he shook his head—"they've lost sight of the mission."

My father pointed at me. "Those two want you to run for Lincoln's state Senate seat. Been planning it for a long time. That's what they expected us to talk about last night. Transition." He pointed at the paper. "Lincoln wanted to say that stuff to help you run for his Senate seat, but I told them this morning that'd be a waste of talent."

He waited for me to say something, but I remained silent, so he continued. "You understand what government should be, not what it is. You're authentic. You've got the head on your shoulders to write the civil rights legislation for the twenty-first century. You'll know better than anyone how to help these poor kids find a path out and up. I'm out of answers, Justin. I'm out of ideas. You're the one."

I lifted my palms up to him. "Dad," I said. "I can't do that right now." I thought about the darkness that had clouded me since cancer took Monica. My struggles as a single parent. My depression. I could think of a hundred reasons why being a United States congressman was a bad idea, but I couldn't get them out of my head. The words wouldn't come. Part of me, perhaps, wanted to keep the option of that childhood dream available. Up until now I had just avoided it.

Finally, I managed to ask, "So Lincoln knows all this?"

"Like I said, I told him this morning." My father pointed at the newspaper. "His nonsense with the reporter was a perfect illustration of why he needs some more time to grow up. Let this pass."

"He's plenty old enough," I said. "He's older than you were when you were elected. More experienced, too."

My father stood and put his hands on his hips. He wasn't going to argue anymore. His decision wasn't going to change. "Gotta catch this flight, son. I'll let you be." He walked over to the bed and held out his hand.

I took it and we shook, and then he leaned over and gave me a kiss on my forehead. It was probably the first time my father had done that since I was a little boy. "I can't make you do it," he said. "But you need to know that you've got more potential in you than you're letting on. I know what you're capable of. I know you can do great things, so just take a few days or weeks to consider. And I mean it—this isn't some silly job in Jeff City with a bunch of hicks. This is the real deal. A national platform, an opportunity to make a difference."

My father took a deep breath, and then he walked toward the door. As he went into the hall, he turned around. "I fought the battle over segregated lunch counters and the right to vote, but this is different." He pointed at me, lying injured in bed, my face swollen and cut. "The Whites Only signs have been taken down, but they're still there. This is your fight now."

My father turned away, took another step, then stopped and looked back again. "Lincoln and Buster will fall into line. It'll ruin their transition plans, but everybody'll fall in line when you decide to run. Just you see." He pointed at me. "Promise me you'll consider it."

"Dad." I shook my head. "Now *you're* sounding like Lincoln, pressuring."

"Promise me."

We stared at each other. My father's eyes were focused, passionate. I had so often felt like I'd been a disappointment, and I couldn't disappoint him again.

"Fine," I said. It wasn't convincing, because I wasn't convinced, but it was enough for him to leave. "Better go catch your plane."

CHAPTER ELEVEN

It took a week before I was without constant pain, but I wasn't going to fall back into the hole. The incident may have broken my body, but it strengthened my commitment to Sammy. Even though I wasn't working, I forced myself to get up, fix Sammy breakfast, and get her off to the bus. She wasn't happy, but recognizing the circumstances, she didn't protest too badly.

After watching her leave through the small window next to the door, as I'd done every morning, I carefully walked back through the kitchen, past the breakfast nook, to my toy room. If I moved too quickly or bent my upper body too far, the pain would return.

I hadn't always had a toy room. Grown men aren't supposed to play with toys, but I needed a safe place to heal after my wife died, and this was it: a small space with a record player and a stack of New Orleans jazz records (not the avant-garde New York kind); shelves of comic books, model cars, and figurines; and a maple worktable where I could carve my own villains and heroes out of clay.

I bent down and pulled an old Fats Waller record out of its sleeve, and then I put the record on the turntable, lowered the needle, and set it in motion.

Monica Glass was the love of my life.

She was my best friend. I've always known that a person can love many people, but I'm not convinced that I'll ever be able to fall so madly and completely in love with another.

A shell had formed around me since she passed away, and I couldn't allow myself to be that vulnerable ever again, not with Annie, not with anybody. I went to some dark places after she passed, and it almost broke me.

After Monica's funeral, I couldn't sleep at all. I couldn't talk about anything real. I was angry and irritable. I alienated clients and friends. I missed deadlines at work. Eventually I lost my job at a respectable midsize law firm downtown. I stopped paying bills. Our house went into foreclosure, but I didn't care.

After a year and a half of being a prisoner of my own mind, I was pulled out by my daughter.

Sammy crawled into my bed after a night during which I had abused my body with various chemicals. She snuggled up to me, in a way that only a child can fit alongside a parent, and waited, probably for hours, for me to wake up. Then, when I opened my eyes, she gave me a present.

"What's this?" I asked, still in the fog.

"Open it." She nodded toward the box wrapped in dark-blue paper.

I did as she had directed. I opened the package and saw that she had given me a model kit of Superboy. It was an original, manufactured by Aurora in the 1960s. It was an action scene involving a green monster in a cave. Superboy and his dog, Krypto, had the monster cornered.

I studied the box, smiling. Then I started to cry.

"You like it?"

I nodded. "Very much."

"Grandma said you liked reading about him as a kid. I found it on Cherokee Street a couple of weeks ago."

I put my arm around Sammy and gave her a hug.

"Happy birthday." She looked up at me. She was right. It was my birthday, and I had forgotten. That was how bad I was. "Can we do something today?"

Her eyes were pleading. We hadn't gone anywhere or done anything in so long. I had ignored her. It was just too painful. When I had looked at her, all I could see was Monica. Sammy's presence reminded me of her mother's absence. We had been a team, the three of us, and then her mother was gone.

I told Sammy that we would. I wiped the tears away from my eyes. "We'll go someplace special." Then I took her to Crown Candy for the first time, and we sat in my booth. When we moved into the carriage house a few weeks later, Superboy and Krypto were the first things on the shelf.

◆ ◆ ◆

The blinds were open as I carved the block of clay into smaller pieces. The time traveler that I had created needed opposition. Every good guy needs a bad guy. I decided that his nemesis would be wealthy, like an aristocrat from the 1920s with a top hat and an overcoat, and that he would also travel back and forth in time.

Morning sun came through the window. It lit the room in perfect light, and I worked the clay as my mind wandered.

Lincoln had not come to see me over the past week. My mother told me that he needed time, and I wondered what I would say to him when he did show up.

I thought about why my father wanted me to carry on his legacy, and why I had been so hesitant to embrace the idea. Part of my reluctance was surely an acknowledgment that Lincoln, despite his ambition and sometimes questionable tactics, had stepped forward when I had drifted away. My brother *wanted* what our father had to give and had positioned himself to receive it. Yet I had received the offer, not Lincoln.

And it was a fact that taking the position would solve some, if not all, of my problems.

I'd have money. I'd have a purpose, and Sammy and I could leave Saint Louis. We could find distance from the memories of my deceased wife that haunted every corner of the city.

Maybe I'd fallen so low that the darkness had convinced me I wasn't worthy of a lot of things in life: depression had rewired my brain. Maybe I *should* seriously consider it. I'd promised my father that I would, so why not?

Another hour passed, and then my cell phone rang. The screen said that the call was coming from Annie. It was the first time that she'd reached out since I was beaten and arrested. Each night as I tried to fall asleep, I wondered whether she would call or pay me an unexpected visit, but it hadn't happened.

I touched the screen to answer. "Madame Mayor." I pretended that I wasn't hurt by her absence. "It's been a while." There was noise in the background. She was breathing pretty hard. I figured that she was walking to a meeting and probably late.

I asked, "Interested in coming over tonight?"

She didn't answer. There was only background noise.

"You there?" I asked.

"Yes," Annie said, but she didn't answer my question. There was another long pause, and then she asked whether I'd heard from Lincoln lately.

"Why do you ask?"

"No reason," she said. "Just wondering if you two had talked recently." There was another pause, hesitation in her voice. "Listen, Justin, I've gotta go now, but I'll see you later." She was vague about where and when. "We need to talk." There was a beep, and then she was gone.

It was a strange exchange.

I set down the phone, wondering whether we had gotten disconnected. Then a few minutes later the phone rang again. I figured that it was Annie, calling back. Perhaps she had found a more private place to talk.

"Hello," I answered, but it wasn't Annie. It was Sergeant Schmidt.

CHAPTER TWELVE

I drove west on Highway 44, out of the city, through the dense first-ring suburbs, and eventually into a land called West County. It was noted for big lots, low taxes, and rich schools. I drove another twenty miles, and the subdivisions gave way to forest.

A large blue sign on the side of the road announced a new **HIGHWAY IMPROVEMENT PROJECT** courtesy of the governor. Then the highway was reduced down to one lane by the construction. Yellow lights flashed. Men held signs instructing me to slow down. There were orange pylons, huge trucks, and piles of pipe and rebar piled along the side of the road.

I was getting close.

My stomach tightened.

Then I saw it.

Yellow police tape wrapped around a pine and connected to another tree about a hundred yards farther west. There were three ambulances, four police cars, and a dozen officers. A helicopter circled overhead. I thought it all might be a little too much, but then I figured that finding a dead body was a relative novelty in this part of Missouri.

I pulled over. As soon as I got out of the car, a deputy sheriff spotted me and held up his hand to halt me. I nodded. I wanted him to know that I wasn't going any farther until we had a chance to talk. The car ride had stiffened me. The pain in my side was back, and I didn't feel like getting into another confrontation with the cops.

"Area is closed." He kept walking toward me. The deputy's chest was puffed. His teeth were gritted. "You gotta move along."

"Sergeant Schmidt from the Saint Louis Police Department sent for me." I nodded toward the woods. "He back there?"

The deputy was about to yell at me. Then he realized what he had just heard and stopped—delayed reaction. The deputy was mad, in a way that only cops can get mad. Cops hate people who mess with their protocol and make them think, and it didn't help that I was black. The deputy had just issued me a clear command to leave, and now he had been forced to back down.

"I'll radio it in." The deputy took a few steps back but did not turn. His eyes studied me, filled with suspicion. He pressed a button on top of a box attached to his belt and spoke into the radio attached to his shoulder. Noise came back at him, which I couldn't understand. Then he barked questions into his shoulder. "Got a guy here who claims he's supposed to meet up with some Saint Louis cop." His voice dripped with skepticism and disdain.

Static came back along with a mumbled response from dispatch.

"Says there's a Sergeant Schmidt here to meet with him."

More static, and then there must have been a response that the deputy didn't like, because I saw his lips tighten and his eyes roll.

To the person on the other end of the radio he said, "Fine." Then the deputy walked back toward me, still skeptical. "The sergeant will be out here in few minutes." He pointed at my car. "Wait in there."

◆ ◆ ◆

I sat and listened to the radio. I switched between KMOX and Saint Louis Public Radio, wondering if and when they were going to report the discovery, but there was nothing. The media didn't know yet, or didn't know enough to report.

I thought more about it and then considered the possibility that maybe they didn't care. Maybe Devon Walker and his short, tragic life didn't warrant any news coverage. Perhaps the only people in the world who cared were me and his little sister, Tanisha.

I waited for another ten minutes and then decided to call my mother. I didn't know how long it'd take, and I wanted her to be home when Sammy got back from school.

We talked.

My mother wasn't too happy to hear about my field trip, but in the end, she promised that she would take care of Sammy. As I hung up the phone and fiddled with the radio, Schmitty emerged from the woods just below where I'd parked.

He ducked under the yellow police tape and began walking up the small hill to the side of the road. I grunted as I got out of the car, paused to catch my breath and allow the pain to subside, and started walking toward him. We met halfway.

"Sergeant." I held out my hand. "Always in the middle of things."

We shook. "Never thought I'd be calling you for help, but"— Schmitty paused and looked back at the woods—"figured we owed you a heads-up after kicking your ass the other night."

I looked at him sharply. "Not funny."

"Nope, not funny at all, but at least they didn't shoot and plant a gun on you." It could've been a joke, but I didn't think it was.

Schmitty wiped the sweat from his forehead, and we began to walk back to the small break in the woods where he had emerged. "I also figured you'd be getting the call soon enough about this," he said. "Thought you might be willing to share any information with us, maybe do me a favor with the vic's family."

I shrugged. "Don't know how much help I'll be, but I'll tell you what I know."

When we got to the police tape, Schmitty ducked under the yellow line and then held it up for me to follow. It hurt to bend, but I tried to hide the pain.

As soon as we were in the woods, the temperature seemed to drop fifteen degrees. The trees were tall, nothing but shade. Even though it was now the end of August, there were no signs that fall would ever come.

Schmitty walked ahead, pointing around us. "Got the area secure. Tech did the initial run through, pictures and all that. The forensic chick from the university just left, but I'm wondering if we need to expand the scope."

This confused me, but I didn't say anything. The scene looked plenty big for one dead body.

We walked another fifty yards and then stopped. Schmitty pointed at the ground. "See that?"

I looked down. My eyes had adjusted to the darker space, and I saw a small tire track in the dirt about three feet away. There were two little yellow flags marking the spot.

I looked up, and when I didn't say anything, Schmitty filled in the blank. "Wheelbarrow." He turned and started walking again. "We figure he killed them pretty quick, as soon as they got out of the car or truck or whatever he was driving." Schmitty looked around. "Already dead when he got them back here. Must've loaded them into the wheelbarrow and took them into the clearing."

"Why are you saying *them*? Thought you just found Devon Walker."

Schmitty shook his head. "Afraid not."

We rounded a small outcropping of rock, and then I saw the clearing. At least nine bodies were partially excavated from the dirt, each marked with little yellow flags.

Schmitty pointed. "Your kid is over there, on the far side." Schmitty wiped his nose and then waved away the gnats circling his head. "He's one of the fresher pieces of meat."

◆　◆　◆

We walked around two bodies. "Takes about a month to go from flesh to bone, unless they were buried in the winter." Schmitty paused for a moment, waiting for a question like a tour guide in a museum. When I said nothing, he continued narrating what we were seeing. "Think these were some of the early ones." He pointed. "Removed the clothes and buried them naked. Also yanked out the teeth, so dental records won't help."

He stopped so I could look, then started walking again. "Later, I figure the perp stopped doing that, maybe too messy or maybe it took too long, or maybe he just got more confident." He pointed at another two bodies. "With these he started leaving the clothes on and they got to keep their teeth."

Schmitty stopped in front of a wheelbarrow and shovel. "This is what we think left that track back there." He smiled. "Know what you're thinking. Brilliant police work back there, right?" He emitted a little laugh, then picked one of the tech's flashlights up off the ground. "Guy had a system." He took a pair of glasses with orange lenses out of his pocket. "I say *guy* because it's almost unheard of for a woman to do something like this. Women aren't this cold. They kill for money or freedom, not this kind of stuff."

Schmitty handed the glasses to me and then pointed the flashlight at the wheelbarrow.

As I put the glasses on, I realized that it wasn't a normal flashlight. It was a black light, and it bathed the inside of the wheelbarrow in a blue light.

Big and small splotches appeared all over its surface.

"See that?"

I nodded.

"Dried blood." Schmitty turned off the black light, and the splotches on the wheelbarrow disappeared. "That's some of the only good news we found out here." He set the tech's light back on the ground, and I took off the orange glasses. "Should be able to get some DNA and maybe make some matches. Might even find some of the perpetrator's DNA. Who knows? Depends on how hard the victims fought."

I handed the glasses back to Schmitty. Then he led me to an area about ten feet from the other bodies. "We think this one is yours."

I looked down at the body.

It didn't look like much. A dead body deflates over time. What remained of Devon Walker was not so much a body as a pile of clothes and bone, caked with mud.

"How'd you get the ID so quick?"

"Utilized an old police trick." Schmitty looked toward the heavens and placed his hands together in prayer. "Divine intervention combined with dumb luck." He picked up a long stick and pointed to a pile on the side. "See that?"

I knelt and looked a little closer. "Jeans?"

"Correct," Schmitty said. "But more specifically, it was what we found in the back pocket of those jeans that helped us out." He backed away. "Because of budgets, a lot of schools in the city don't bus themselves anymore. The era of the yellow school bus is over. They issue all the high school students these plastic cards for the city bus. We pulled the card from the back pocket and could still make out the barcode numbers." He shrugged. "Made a call to the school, they looked up the number, and that's how we got the name."

"Might not be him, though," I said. "Wasn't exactly an academic."

Schmitty nodded. "True. We'll run the DNA and other stuff, but still, it feels right. A lot of kids just show up for the first day of school to get the bus card and never come back, and he's been missing for the right amount of time for the condition of the body."

"Doesn't explain all this." I looked around at the other piles of bone surrounded by flags.

"Nope," Schmitty said. "Sure don't explain it all, but having one of them ID'd sure helps." He crouched down again, near the side of Devon Walker's body, and pointed. "See that?"

"I think so." I edged closer, looking. It appeared to be a narrow band of white plastic.

Schmitty and I stood back up. "Those are disposable handcuffs," he said. "One loop. Heavy-duty nylon. Zip it on. Impossible to get off. You can buy them at any army navy store. Police use them in riot situations or when they're making multiple arrests during a raid." He turned back and looked over the field of bodies. "They all had them. Hands secured behind their backs." Schmitty started walking back the way we came. "Like I said, the guy had a system."

He led me away from the scene and toward the road. "Now as for you, his family probably don't like the cops too much, so we were hoping you could help us get some information about what Devon was doing before he disappeared, new people he was hanging with, rivals, anything."

"I can try, but it means more time and probably getting the mother and grandmother to talk. Nobody has been able to tell me too much so far." I dodged a branch from a tree, then asked an unrelated question. "Who found them?"

The tree cover over our heads started to break, allowing the Missouri heat to come back. "Hiker found them," he said, "doing that geocaching stuff."

Schmitty stopped at the edge of the trees, before the full sun came down, put his hands on his hips, and caught his breath. If we were going to continue talking, we might as well stay a little cooler in the shade. "Anyway, the current theory is that our perp couldn't bury the newer bodies deep enough because of the rock in this area. So the oldest ones were in the deepest holes."

Schmitty wiped the beads of sweat from his forehead. "Some critter found Devon, or who we think is Devon. Kid got dug up, and that's how the hiker found him. He called the cops. The local sheriff checked it out, and then this morning we were cleared by the medical examiner to poke around a little more. That's when we found the others."

Overhead, there was the sound of a helicopter. Schmitty stepped out into the break. I followed him, and we looked up at the helicopter and then at the cluster of vehicles down the road.

"Media bastards." Schmitty shook his head. "Now we're in for it."

CHAPTER THIRTEEN

One of the many mysteries of Saint Louis is its absurd traffic patterns. It doesn't matter if you're going into the city or leaving the city or cutting across the city. Even with more than half the town's population drained away, traffic is jammed up in every direction.

And so I found myself crawling across the county border into Saint Louis. An exit came up ahead. It wasn't the one I wanted, but I took it. I'd rather go twenty miles an hour on a side street than sit in traffic for another thirty minutes. I cut across the highway, took a couple of turns, and found Taylor Avenue heading north.

It wasn't bad scenery at first, filtering through the neighborhoods. There were a few churches, some nice cafés, and the Central West End's beautiful brownstones.

Then I crossed an imaginary line, and everything dimmed. Cafés were replaced with dirty fast-food restaurants. Churches went from majestic to pop-up, and the brownstones devolved into a mix of questionable housing, pawn shops, and dollar stores.

I checked the address on my notepad again, took a couple more turns, and returned to the cluster of houses on the edge of nothing. Tanisha Walker's little brother was in the same place, sitting in the dirt, alone in the front yard.

Yuppies and new urbanists always talk about the need for green space. Well on the north side there was plenty of green space, just not the right kind.

I walked past the little kid, but I didn't stop. At the door, I knocked and waited. Nobody came, although I could hear noise inside. It sounded like live voices, maybe a radio in the background. I knocked again, louder. This time the stronger, faster movement of my arm hurt.

There was life from inside. "Who is it?"

"Justin Glass." I waited a moment for a response, but nothing happened. "Tanisha hired me to look for her brother."

"Don't know nothing about that." There was a little more commotion, another voice—too muffled to understand—joining the conversation.

"If you could just open the door so that we could—"

An argument had started beyond the door. It grew louder, and I stopped talking because nobody was listening to me.

I turned and looked back at the boy, who I hoped was named Deon, not Dice. He watched me with the same intensity as his sister. He didn't smile or wave. He just watched as I stood alone on the porch, waiting for it all to play out inside. Then a deadbolt turned. A chain was unhooked, and the door opened.

Tanisha stood in front. Behind her was a well-worn older woman with her skinny arms crossed tight before her. She didn't like the look of me. That much was clear.

I took a step back from the door. "Tanisha, wondering whether I could talk to you and your mom."

Tanisha cocked her head to the side. "Find Devon?"

I nodded. "Maybe."

Tanisha turned and looked at the older woman behind her. "It's OK, Mama. See?" She touched her mother's arm, reassuring her. "He's just my lawyer."

We sat around the kitchen table. I was on one side. Tanisha and her mother were on the other. Auntie and Grandma had materialized and lingered behind them, shooting me suspicious looks. A half dozen kids of various ages came in and out. The radio continued, now joined by a television in the background. Not another man to be seen.

"I don't know if you know this, Ms. Walker, but Tanisha came to my office a few weeks ago and asked me to help her find Devon."

Tanisha's mom leaned back in her chair. "First I heard of that."

"Well she's a persistent young lady." I looked at Tanisha and nodded, then looked back at her mother. "It wasn't too much trouble to help out," I lied. "Called a contact down at the police station. There wasn't much information, at first, but then I got a phone call today."

Tanisha's eyes widened, excited.

"In jail, ain't he?" Tanisha's mother locked her arms across her thin body again. Her arms were mostly bone and bruises with a few needle marks.

"Afraid not, Ms. Walker." I took a breath, trying to keep my upper body still while thinking about how best to phrase it. "They're going to be running some tests, but the police think they found his body in a wooded area about an hour from here."

Tanisha's face tightened, but her mother's expression didn't change. I continued to tell her everything I knew. There were no tears or anger. No wild sobs or whispers, just acceptance, like she'd known all along this conversation was coming her way, in one form or another.

It was a safe bet, with a young man like her son.

Maybe the tears came later, maybe not.

◆ ◆ ◆

I didn't stay too much longer. I warned them that the police would be stopping by, and I encouraged them to cooperate. I told them that the police were going to need more information about who Devon was hanging around with and whether they knew anybody who might've done it.

"I already told you everything." Mrs. Walker wasn't interested in talking to the police, and she certainly didn't want them to drop by. The idea that she might cooperate with the police was crazy. "Only cause more problems than I already got."

"Well I just thought I'd let you know." I turned and stepped off the stoop, unsure of how to say good-bye. "Thank you for your time, Ms. Walker." As I walked past the little boy in the front yard, I pointed and turned back. "Is this Deon or Dice?"

The mother didn't respond, but Tanisha answered. "Dice."

That's too bad, I thought.

◆ ◆ ◆

As I pulled into the driveway at the Judge's house, I called Schmitty and filled him in on the conversation. Then I slowly extricated myself from the car. It had been a hard day, and my body wasn't happy. I walked around to the back of the house. My mother was in the kitchen working on a late dinner. She was washing and chopping vegetables. Everything smelled like garlic.

I took in the aromas. "Now that's a nice way to come home."

She picked up a handful of onions and carrots and tossed them into the Dutch oven on the stove. The vegetables sighed as they hit the hot oil. "Do my best."

"Sammy in the library with the Judge?"

"Always." My mother set the timer and then picked a bowl off the counter. She emptied the chopped green and yellow zucchini within it into the Dutch oven with the onions and carrots. She stirred it a few times, lowered the temperature, and turned back to me. "Long day?"

I nodded as I walked over to the refrigerator. I removed a beer and opened it. Then I started to pull out a barstool from underneath the kitchen island, but thought better of it. I remained standing and watched my mother fuss over the vegetables. "That boy I was looking for was found, but not in a good way."

"What do you mean?" My mother turned. She saw the expression on my face. "Oh." She nodded. "Understood."

"Probably nine or ten bodies buried near Castlewood State Park." I took a sip of beer. "One of the bodies was the boy I was looking for. Not quite sure what I'm supposed to do now."

"Up to you."

My mother often said stuff like that. It was both maddening and reassuring at the same time. She picked up a big salt shaker and added some salt to the vegetables, then turned the heat down even further to let them sweat. "I think you did a wonderful thing, helping that little girl out, but you probably have other cases."

I laughed. "Unfortunately, I don't, really." I put my beer down and started picking at the label, thinking about money and the fading hope that I was going to be able to afford an air conditioner. "Sammy say anything about school?"

My mother shook her head.

Then I asked, "Talk to Dad?"

"I did." My mom set down her wooden spoon and walked over to me. "He's wondering what you're going to do."

I shrugged. "Lincoln's the politician, not me. I don't need a pity job."

"Your father didn't choose you to follow him out of pity." My mom put her hand on my shoulder. "He made the decision because he respects you, and, as I recall, you once fancied yourself a politician."

"Things change."

My mother shook her head. "Not as much as you think."

"Lincoln is furious."

She nodded. "Feels betrayed. Thinks you may have known all along."

"Hope you corrected him."

"I tried." My mother pursed her lips. "But you know Lincoln. He and Buster had some big plans, even thinking about the Senate after being a congressman for a few terms."

"Well," I said, "he's got every right to be mad."

My mother started to speak, but the timer went off. She walked back over to the oven, and peeked at the garlic chicken roasting inside. "You know that I'm not the pretty little housewife that keeps her opinions to herself and lets the men think all the big thoughts."

I smiled. "Never were."

"But I do know it's your father's decision, not mine." My mother lifted the chicken out of the oven and set it on top of the stove. The smell of garlic in the room became stronger. "Love both you and Lincoln. You're both wonderful. You're both different, and that's fine."

Then my mother turned to me. She looked me directly in the eye. "But you need to seriously think about this. You have a lot to offer, and you've got a daughter in there that believes you can do or be anything." She paused. "Wouldn't it be nice to serve our community, fight the good fight, and pay the bills?"

She came back to me and put her hand on my cheek. "Just think about it. That's all. Think hard about it. Lincoln will be fine. There will be other opportunities."

CHAPTER FOURTEEN

I heard a car pull up and park in the alley as I tucked Sammy into bed. "Good night." I wanted to lean over and kiss her on the forehead, but my body wouldn't cooperate. Even after a fresh round of pills, the pain wasn't fully dulled. "Anything else you need to talk to me about?"

Sammy shook her head. "Nope."

"OK." I took her hand and gave it a squeeze, then started for the door. As I turned out the light, Sammy said that she loved me.

I stopped. "Love you, too, sweetheart."

"Glad you're moving a little better today."

"A little bit," I lied, but I was really thinking about what I couldn't tell her about my day, where I'd been and what I'd seen. A grove of bodies with no explanation.

I held the railing and walked carefully down the steps to the door of the carriage house, and I peeked through the small window beside it. Annie was waiting on the darkened doorstep, scrolling through her e-mails and texts on her cell phone. Never a wasted minute for the mayor.

I set aside my annoyance and opened the door. She came inside, and as I leaned in to kiss her, she moved away, walking past me.

"OK," I said. "Guess there's no time for that lovey-dovey stuff tonight."

"Got that right." I followed her through the small entryway and into the kitchen, where she opened the refrigerator and found a bottle of beer. "Want one?"

"Already had a couple with dinner, so I'm fine." I studied her from just inside the room. "*You*, on the other hand, don't seem so fine."

"No." Annie opened a drawer, found the bottle opener, and removed the cap. "Not fine." She looked at me and then away. In the light of the kitchen, I could now see that she'd been crying.

"Tell me about it." I walked over to the little kitchen table and sat. At first Annie didn't follow, but eventually she collected herself enough to be within a few feet of me.

She settled into the chair across from me and closed her eyes. There was a silence that seemed like forever, and then she looked me in the eye and asked a question. "What the hell are you doing?"

"Right now?" I shrugged. "Trying to figure out where you're coming from. Not a kiss. Not a hello. Not even a 'How's your day?' You call me, wanting to meet up. I say OK. You don't follow up. I hear nothing, so . . . now you're here, obviously mad."

Her face turned hard. "You know exactly what I'm mad about."

"No." I held out my hands in surrender. "No, I don't. I've been in bed for a week or so after being attacked by your cops, and then today I had the pleasure of seeing a whole lot of dead boys and telling the sister and mother of one of them that nobody has any idea what happened, except that the person who did it used plastic handcuffs and liked the solitude of nature." Her expression didn't change, and that fired some more anger in me. It was a spark that I hadn't felt in some time. "That what you're looking for?" I shook my head. "If not, I haven't a clue, Madame Mayor. You're the one who pretty much dropped out of my life the minute I suggested we might want to talk about—"

Annie held out her hand, cutting me off. "You're running for Congress."

Now I regretted not having another beer.

I should have known this mess of my brother's and my father's would get back to her.

"I was asked *by my father* to run for Congress." I tried to minimize it, but that didn't work.

"And you told him no, absolutely not?"

I wavered. "Not exactly, and please keep your voice down." I looked up. "My daughter is up there."

Annie shook her head. "Unbelievable," she said. "So Lincoln was right." Her hand curled into a tight ball. "That's a pretty big deal, don't you think?"

"Yes, I do." I nodded. "But I've never told Lincoln or my father or anyone else that I'm running. My dad asked me, and I think it deserves consideration, out of respect." I started to get more agitated. "I have a right to think about it. It's something that I haven't thought about for a long time, and I'm tired of you hacks pushing me around."

"I'm a hack now." Annie pursed her lips. "That's what you think of me—that I'm a political hack."

I waved it off. It wasn't personal. "I think you're all a bunch of political hacks—Lincoln, Buster, you—all of you." OK, maybe it was personal.

She set her jaw. "Let's stay on topic. Look me in the eye and tell me your father is not giving you his endorsement and you're not going to run as some outsider with a famous name."

"This is crazy." I stood up a little too fast. A fresh shot of pain ripped up my side. "Maybe you should leave before you really do wake up my daughter."

"I'm not leaving until we talk about this."

"That's the problem." I folded my arms across my chest. "We ain't talking. You're just attacking me for some unknown reason."

"Unknown reason?" Now Annie was on her feet. She put her beer down on the table. "You don't think this affects me? You don't think that a congressional campaign by you will impact me?"

I shook my head. "No, I don't. It's a family thing. Nothing to do with you."

"Well," Annie said. "Your brother doesn't share your view. He says if you run, he'll take me down. He says he'll find another candidate, maybe he'd run against me himself." She looked up at the ceiling, hands on her hips. "Our secret is not as big a secret as we think, Justin." She looked back at me, tears pooling in her eyes. "People know, and your brother will make sure everybody knows about it when I'm running for reelection next year."

"He said that?"

Annie blinked, and a solitary tear rolled down her cheek. "He and Buster." She turned away from me, staring out the dark window. "Stop this," she said. "Please."

CHAPTER FIFTEEN

The next day, I returned to the law factory. Despite my absence, it had remained in constant operation. Criminal charges were brought. Lawsuits were filed. Agreements were made. Nothing had changed upon my return, although I may have changed a little.

The hallway outside the courtroom was as crowded as ever, filled with people who were at some stage of "growing into their guilt." This refers to a concept very similar to the five stages of grief developed by Dr. Elisabeth Kübler-Ross: First, a criminal defendant denies; he claims to be innocent. Second, he gets angry at the system, lashing out at the cops or the judge or his attorney. Third, he bargains, searching for a plea deal that will keep him out of jail or prison. Fourth and fifth come depression, and, ultimately, acceptance.

The system lurches forward. I could argue that some of them are actually innocent, which may be true, but the law factory doesn't work like that. It isn't about guilt or innocence. The system is about keeping things moving. It grinds a person down—innocent or guilty—until he or she submits.

With fresh cocktail of painkillers working through my body, I set my stack of files on the hallway bench without too much trouble. I took the first file off the top and then called out the name. The crowd quieted down. I called out the name again.

"That's me." A large white woman raised her hand. She was leaning against the wall about fifteen feet away from me. I waved her over, and we began our brief consultation.

A half hour later, I had worked through most of the stack. It really didn't matter whether I needed more time. The judge wanted to get started, and so it began.

Judge Saul Polansky processed twenty-two cases in an hour and half, working out to a little more than four minutes per case. That's an average of 240 seconds per file, which is not bad.

About half were plea agreements. Three were set for trial, and the remainder were no-shows triggering arrest warrants.

The final case of the morning was Cecil Bates, the client who was having trouble moving out of the first phase. Though absent this morning, he was still claiming his innocence and had left messages throughout my recuperation about various legal theories and constitutional violations associated with his arrest.

The clerk called his name. "File 65-MD-14-358217, *State versus Cecil Bates*."

Judge Polansky nodded toward the prosecutor, and the prosecutor stepped forward.

"Yes, Your Honor. Since Mr. Bates had proper notice of this hearing and has failed to appear, I ask that a warrant be issued for his arrest and bail be set at five hundred dollars."

The judge looked at me.

"I'd ask that another notice be issued for this hearing instead of a warrant. I've been in pretty regular contact with Mr. Bates, and I'm surprised he's not here this morning." I had to make the argument. I had to ask for it, even though everyone knew that the request would be denied.

It was frustrating.

Giving Mr. Bates and the other low-level offenders another opportunity to come to court voluntarily could potentially save the taxpayers money, because we wouldn't have to pay for the arrest, transport, processing, and incarceration of somebody who wasn't a real threat to public safety. But it was easy to issue a warrant, and, more importantly, it put the clock on hold.

All judges and judicial districts were measured by, and their performance evaluated solely upon, how quickly they processed cases. The State of Missouri required that 80 percent of all petty misdemeanor and misdemeanor cases be concluded within sixty days of charges being brought. While *on warrant*—as Cecil would be, should a warrant for his arrest be issued—the clock stopped. If Judge Polansky gave Cecil Bates another chance, the clock would continue to tick, and his own performance would be called into question.

So Judge Polansky denied my request and issued a warrant for Cecil Bates.

I nodded, turned back toward the table, and started to gather up my files. I heard Judge Polansky say my name and looked back. "Yes, Judge?"

"Moment to chat?"

I was a little stunned. Nobody ever wanted to chat with a criminal defense lawyer, especially a public defender.

I nodded. "Sure."

The judge smiled. "Good. My clerk will lead you back to my chambers." Judge Polansky then stood and walked out the back door.

◆ ◆ ◆

He wanted to gossip.

My mother often talked about how isolated her father had felt after being appointed to the federal bench. His friends wouldn't call him by his first name, and his drinking partners soon became very limited. Judge Polansky appeared to be no different.

"Please, have a seat." Judge Polansky gestured for his law clerk to leave and close the door. "Read the paper this morning, and I couldn't resist."

"Resist what?"

"Asking if it's true." He blushed, a little embarrassed. "Whether you're going to run for Congress." I didn't respond, so Judge Polansky filled the silence with a series of declarations. "Kiss Saint Louis good-bye. Guaranteed paycheck. Escape from this hell hole, and you'd be a million times better than your brother."

I thought about Lincoln and then about Annie and the threat. "Not sure I'm cutthroat enough for Washington. Don't really aspire to it."

"But you've paid your dues." Judge Polansky shook his head. "Working out there for nothing. You've more than earned it. Plus representing one of the Lost Boys doesn't hurt."

"Lost Boys?"

"That kid," he said. "The one who was found in the park. They're calling him that—all of them—the Lost Boys. Nobody really knows who they were and how long they've been gone."

"I didn't know they had a name."

Judge Polansky shook his head. "You obviously don't watch television."

"Not really." I checked my watch and then looked back up. "Try to avoid it if I can."

"Or read the newspaper?" Judge Polansky picked up a copy of the current *St. Louis Post-Dispatch* from the top of his desk and handed it to me.

On its cover were pictures of Devon Walker and two other boys, as well as six boxes with large question marks. Across the top of the page, the headline read, MANY LOST BOYS REMAIN A MYSTERY.

I tried to play it cool, even though the whole thing made me feel uneasy.

I read the first few sensational sentences about the problem that the police were having in identifying the majority of victims and understanding why they were killed, then tried to hand the newspaper back to Judge Polansky. "Very subtle journalism."

"You can keep it." Judge Polansky smiled. "Read it *all*." He pointed toward the bottom of the page. "Says you're pretty much a saint, and the free plug for your congressional campaign was pretty nice, too."

CHAPTER SIXTEEN

The line outside my office was not welcome. If I sold shoes or televisions, a line of people waiting for my doors to open would've been a happy sight. For a lawyer, not so much.

I took my time driving by, taking in the scene. Most appeared to be mothers or grandmothers. Many of them holding photographs, several crying. A dozen young kids ran the street.

I circled the block to the alley and parked behind the Northside Roastery. Nobody answered when I knocked on the coffee shop's back door, but it opened when I turned the knob so I went inside.

"Hermes?" I took a step into their back storage area. "Nikolas?" I took another few steps. The back door closed behind me. "Hey, Hermes. It's me, Justin. Justin Glass."

"The famous celebrity is here." Hermes came around the corner with a big smile on his face. "You looking like rock star. Fans waiting to touch you."

"I don't feel like a rock star."

"Come." He grabbed my shoulder and guided me past the boxes and bags of green coffee beans to the front of the shop. "I get you something to drink."

"Thanks," I said. "You doing OK?"

Hermes hedged. "Doing OK. I had some bad feelings."

"Another premonition?" I played along, but Hermes was serious.

He pointed to a little shelf underneath the cash register. "Got me a gun for protection now." He tilted his head from side to side, considering whether he should elaborate. "Makes me feel a little better."

◆ ◆ ◆

I sat at a table near the window and watched the people coming and going. There was a mix of emotions, but mostly a realization that this wasn't going to change. This was the new normal, and I was at the center of the storm.

Hermes knew I was overwhelmed, but he didn't want to overstep. "Mind if I sit a moment?" He pointed at the chair across from me.

I nodded, still fixated on the crowd as Hermes sat down. He told me that he had a cousin who was going through a divorce and looking for work. She needed some money, and I clearly needed some help. I'd never met her. Didn't know her qualifications, but Hermes dismissed my concerns. "She take care of everything. Very smart. Be here in thirty minutes."

Who was I to argue?

It took her forty minutes, but I didn't mind. I hoped that all the people standing outside my law office would give up and leave, but instead of shrinking, the crowd only grew.

Hermes went to go make another coffee drink for me, and then the bell above the coffee shop's front door rang.

I looked over and saw a woman who had to be either Hermes's cousin or seriously lost.

Her name was Emma Tadic. She was a compact woman with serious curves. Emma arrived in five-inch heels, large hoop earrings, and a black "business" suit. The suit consisted of a jacket and the tightest, shortest dress I'd ever seen. "You must be Mr. Justin Glass." She walked over to me and held out her perfectly manicured hand. "Pleasure to meet you." Her speech was clipped by her Eastern European accent.

We shook hands.

Hers were soft.

"You must be the cousin."

She nodded. "Hermes told me you needed some help." On first sight, it might've been easy to dismiss her as an airhead, some man's mail-order trophy, but there was intelligence behind her eyes. Wheels were turning.

I nodded toward the street. "Probably saw the line."

"I did. All want to be your clients?"

"Probably," I said. "I figure their sons are missing, and they want me to find them. Never thought there'd be so many." I shook my head, remembering that first conversation with Schmitty about it being common for kids from the Northside to just disappear. As an aside I said, "They probably can't pay me anything."

A sadness came through me, and sadness seemed to wash over Emma, too. She went someplace far away in her mind, perhaps remembering all the people in her country who were "lost" during the years of civil war.

Then she came back to the present. Her face hardened. "What do you want me to do?"

"I don't know." I shrugged. "Maybe just get rid of them?"

Emma shook her head. "Disrespectful to get rid of them without even a short talk." She looked me up and down, assessing. "Especially when you are running for Congress." She looked around the coffee shop. "And you cannot hide all day like a little rabbit, either."

"Hiding actually seems like a pretty good option." I smiled, but she didn't smile back. Maybe passive-aggressiveness wasn't as valued in Bosnia as it was in the Midwest.

She folded her arms across her chest. "Do you have a computer?"

I nodded.

"Just give me your office key. I'll handle them." She held out her hand for the key.

I reached into my pocket, found my key ring, and removed my office key. "What are you going to do?"

"Do you care?" Emma took the key, turned, and started walking toward the door without waiting for my answer.

As Emma left the shop, she stopped at the door and turned back to look at me. "You pay twenty dollars per hour, cash, every week. That's the deal."

◆ ◆ ◆

Emma was somebody I couldn't afford, but I'd figure that out later. Maybe I'd do an advance on a credit card or something.

With her taking over the office, I got in my car for some privacy and called Schmitty.

When he answered, I asked, "Is there a reason that you're sending these people to me? Punishment? Revenge? Spite?"

Schmitty laughed. "I'm not sending anybody to you. Heard you've got a crowd, though. They want you. I'd have thought you'd be happy."

"Why would I be happy to have a bunch of people who don't have any legal claims? They don't even have money to pay me to tell them that there's nothing that I can do."

"Politics, my friend." He waited a beat. "This is great press for you and your campaign." Schmitty had obviously read the article about me and my purported intention to carry on my father's legacy in DC. I thought about who could be the unnamed source. I didn't think it was Buster, since he now worked for Lincoln, which really only left my father. Even though he said that he'd give me time, the old man knew how to pull the levers.

Schmitty continued. "Got it on good authority that there's going to be another front-page story in tomorrow's newspaper about you. Profile piece. Big picture of that line of people standing outside your door right now. A headline, something like, JUSTIN GLASS: FINDER OF LOST BOYS."

"Schmitty," I said, "I don't have any intention of running for Congress."

"That's what they all say." Schmitty laughed. "I note, my friend, that you did not unequivocally rule it out. You stated that you do not presently have any intention of running for Congress. Tomorrow, however, is another day with possibly different intentions."

I closed my eyes. "That's crazy."

"Of course it's crazy," Schmitty said. "The world is crazy."

"But it buys *you* some time. That's why you're happy about it." I thought about the angles that Schmitty and the politicians were playing. "Using me to get these mothers and grandmothers out of your hair."

"That could be an added benefit, like a bonus," Schmitty said. "But the truth is these folks won't talk to us. They don't trust the police, but they trust you. You're a Glass. You can help."

"So a few weeks ago, your colleagues in blue beat the crap out of me, and now you want me to do your investigation for free."

The anger that I had felt weeks earlier rushed back. I was expected to play along. They had minimized and dismissed me just as they'd been minimizing and dismissing concerns about their relationship with the community for years. Neighborhood beat cops transformed into a militarized force.

"It's not like that, exactly." Schmitty started to get defensive, but knew he couldn't lose my cooperation. He stopped himself, allowing me to correct him.

"It's exactly like that," I said. "You've got about nine black kids— kids that have been missing for a long time—and you weren't out there looking for them. You've done nothing."

"We didn't know about them."

"You knew about Devon Walker," I said. "His sister filed the report, remember?"

Schmitty wasn't going to get sucked into the argument, because he knew that he wasn't going to win. "Let's be practical. The world is the way it is. Neither you nor I can change it overnight, but we do have to get this case figured out. We need the families. The families have the information, but even when we try, they don't let us get anywhere. That's why we need you. They're choosing you."

There was silence in the conversation as everything sunk in. Just like I wanted to walk away when Tanisha first came into my office, I wanted to tell Schmitty that I wasn't going to work on an investigation that they should've been doing from the beginning. And, just like when Tanisha first came into my office, I couldn't say no.

I asked, "Have you at least got the rest of the bodies identified?"

"Getting closer," Schmitty said, and I wasn't sure whether he was lying. "I can get you a list of possibles, if you keep it confidential. See if any of their parents show up at your door."

"What about Devon Walker?"

"Nothing much more that you don't already know."

I rolled down my window, trying to get some fresh air, maybe catch a breeze. I decided to push him again. "Are you sure you don't have anything else for me?"

"Well." Schmitty hesitated, then continued. "All these kids got records."

"So you think we got kids in gangs killing other kids in gangs?"

"No," Schmitty said, pausing. "Maybe we should meet and talk. I don't like doing this over the phone."

CHAPTER SEVENTEEN

The dog park was a relatively recent development in the evolution of Lucas Park. In the 1980s and 1990s, the only dogs in the park were strays, and the only people in the park were homeless, looking for a quiet place to satisfy various physical urges.

Now the small park, nestled behind the Saint Louis Public Library, had been miraculously transformed into a space where the downtown condo owners and yuppies took their dogs to go to the bathroom. It's what the politicians called progress.

Schmitty was already there when I arrived.

He sat on a bench across from a new children's playground set. There were no kids playing, and nobody else was in the park, either. It was too hot. A sheen of sweat had already formed on Schmitty's broad forehead.

I sat down next to him, and Schmitty handed me a large, thin envelope. I opened the envelope to find information about the young men who still hadn't been identified, including photographs of the decomposed bodies, clothing, and personal items.

Schmitty watched me as I thumbed through the packet. "The parents we can find have been contacted," he said. "But these families tend to move a lot, and most aren't excited about talking to the police. There's a better chance they'll come to you or the media before us."

"I don't really want to be the guy who tells them."

"Fair." Schmitty nodded. "But you might not have a choice. If you think you've got a match, just play it straight. Check it out, and if you want to give me a call, I'll send somebody over to break the news."

"So what about the investigation?"

His body stiffened. He turned and looked me in the eye. "Repeat this to anybody, and I'll hang you. Understand?"

I nodded, deciding it wasn't the right moment to educate Schmitty about why it may not be a good idea for a police officer to threaten to hang a black man. Cultural competency lessons were better left for another day. "I get it," I said. "Understood."

"My theory—and it's just my theory—is that this wasn't gang-bangers taking each other out. It's got nothing to do with drug dealing or even some lonely serial killer or whack-job in the projects."

"So what is it, then?"

Schmitty rubbed his chin, hesitant to say what he was thinking out loud.

Eventually he said, "They're too cold, the murders. They're too calculated, too smart."

"What do you mean?" I wanted to keep Schmitty talking. "Regular people are smarter than they used to be. Plenty of stuff on the Internet. Watch any police show and anybody would have a pretty good idea about DNA and police investigations."

"Possible." Then he came back around. "But we knew all these kids. Too damn well." He pointed at the envelope. "They were all regulars in the juvenile system. They weren't misunderstood artists or kids on the edge. Every one of them had done really bad things from an early age, and they were well along in the prison pipeline. No doubt in my mind or anybody's mind. They were on their way, leaving a long trail of victims in the process."

"So what? You're thinking there's a vigilante?"

"If I was a betting man?" Schmitty nodded. "That's where I'd go—one of the neighborhood watch people, or the victim of a crime, or someone who knew somebody who got hurt by one of these guys . . . that's a possibility." Schmitty's voice trailed off. "But honestly, there's too many for that. Unless you're a complete psychopath, which maybe the perp is, you'd be satisfied after one or maybe two. And carrying off this many without fouling up and getting caught . . ."

I nodded, understanding where Schmitty's theory was going. "That leaves you with the professionals."

"Afraid so." He stood up. "We should be looking hard at the cops that patrol that area, but I doubt we'll be looking too hard in that direction. The chief doesn't want that. He told me today that he's not sure we'd be able to recover, if it's true. He'd lose his job for sure, and he loves going to all those fancy police conferences and sitting on those panels discussing new police tactics that we never actually implement."

Schmitty put his hand on my shoulder and squeezed; then he walked away.

The message was clear. If somebody was going to look in that direction, it was going to be me.

CHAPTER EIGHTEEN

I drove slowly past my office, stunned that the line of people was gone. I drove around the block a second time, looking in the alleys and vacant lots for any sign of them. I was sure, if I stopped the car, they would reappear.

Working up the nerve, I parked the car, got out, and ducked inside my office.

Emma Tadic looked up from her computer. "Your office stinks." Her long fingernails clicked away at the keyboard as she spoke. "But I do my best. Tomorrow I will bring some proper cleaning supplies."

I nodded. "Thank you." Then I noticed that the temperature in the office was a comfortable sixty-nine degrees. "You got the air conditioner to work?"

"No." She stopped typing and looked up at me. "Called my brother. He bring a new one." There was silence, and then she said, "Don't worry about the money. I got a good deal for you. You pay him later."

"I appreciate it." I ran the financial calculations in my head. "But I'm really not sure—"

Emma raised her hand, cutting me off. "I do not work in a sweat lodge. Don't worry about the money." Then she opened the drawer to her desk. She removed a fat envelope. "Take a look."

I took the envelope from her. Inside there was probably $2,000 in cash. "What is this?"

"I tell them we don't even open a file unless they pay two hundred dollars. That will get them an initial consultation, and then we decide if we take them as a client or if they have a claim." Emma took the envelope back from me. "So fifteen families had some money to get started," she said. "Some pay a little and bring the rest later. Some pay full. Others not pay, but may be back as well."

"But these are poor people, Emma." I shook my head. "I never charge for a consultation. I'm not sure I feel right about—"

"Enough." Emma dropped the envelope into her desk drawer and slammed it shut. "You have bills to pay, including my salary. A lawyer has to see who is really serious, right away. I make no other promises to them."

"But that's not how I've—"

"You go do some work now. I will get these files set up and then we will schedule the interviews for tomorrow."

I started to argue with her again, but this time I was interrupted by a phone call. I took the cell phone out of my pocket and looked at the caller ID.

It was Sammy's school.

CHAPTER NINETEEN

Vice Principal Jimmy Gieser's office smelled like rotting flowers. There was a bike helmet in the corner, and my guess was that there was a pile of sweaty clothing somewhere in the room along with the cheap air freshener that he was using to cover up the smell.

"I don't really want to have this meeting with you, Mr. Glass." He put his hands on his desk and leaned forward. The vice principal was young. He had probably worked a few years and then got the magic ticket out of the classroom. He was also nervous. "I have the utmost respect for your family. You really should know that, nothing but respect for your family."

"But . . ." I knew something was coming, but I wasn't sure what it was.

"There's a new district protocol. I've been looking the other way for most of the year—given that Samantha is obviously bright and has excellent test scores—but our school has to submit a report by the end of the month of all the kids who have missed over fifty days this calendar year."

"Fifty days?" This shocked me.

He nodded. "She missed forty days last spring, then there was the summer break, and now she's missed almost every day of the current school year."

I did some calculations in my head, and it didn't come close to adding up. I had allowed her to stay home a few times, but . . . Had there even been fifty days of school to miss? Another quick set of calculations. "You're saying that my daughter has missed about half."

"Actually more than half." He looked down at the printed spreadsheet in front of him. "I'd say your daughter has missed about eighty percent this calendar year, starting January 1." He handed me the list of absences.

"Eighty percent."

I looked down at the dates. One stood out. It was the day Tanisha Walker hired me to find her brother. The day I came to pick Sammy up from school and thought I had missed her. She'd lied. Sammy had told me that she'd ridden the bus.

I put the spreadsheet back on the desk. "Why the hell didn't you call me?" My voice had raised.

Gieser shrunk a little from the challenge. Busied himself with flipping through more sheets of paper. "I don't want to get into an argument here, Mr. Glass." Keeping his eyes averted, he passed another piece of paper to me from his file. "But it looks like we did call. We called often, but you never called us back."

He handed me a call log, a list of the dates and times as well as the name of the school secretary who had called my house. I tried to find a call listed that I could dispute, but the school wasn't making it up. I had to admit to myself that there had been a lot of calls, and I hadn't returned a single one.

I had been in my own head, struggling with the darkness. It took so much energy just to get up in the morning and be somewhat present during the day that returning phone calls wasn't a priority.

I handed the list back, defeated. "What do you want from me?"

"Right now I can keep your daughter's name off the list if you enter into a performance contract."

"A performance contract?"

He shrugged as if nothing was in his control, which was probably true. "That's the superintendent's new protocol. We sign a contract, which essentially states that you will ensure that your daughter attends school, every day and every class. If you sign the contract, you're off the list."

I folded my arms across my chest. "And if I refuse?"

"If you refuse, your daughter goes on the list and we send it to the city attorney. Then he files a truancy petition with the court, alleging that your child is in need of protection."

"What if I tell you that she's getting bullied?"

"That's for the city attorney to figure out." The young administrator held out his hands again, powerless. "This is what I'm told to do. I don't control what they do."

"What if I sign the contract, and my daughter misses more days of school?"

"As I've said, then we send you to the city attorney and they file a petition." He sighed. "The performance contract gives you a second chance." He leaned forward, stressing the importance of what he was about to say. "It's an opportunity to keep this private."

I nodded, understanding what he meant and the ramifications. Regardless of whether I ran for Congress or not, I was from a political family, and political families keep these things private.

CHAPTER TWENTY

It was dusk by the time I got back to the house. My cell phone rang as I pulled into the back drive. It was Emma. She gave an update on what happened after I left, and told me I had a full day of work tomorrow. She had set up Lost Boys interviews one after another from nine until five. She didn't want me to be late.

"Sounds painful," I said.

She didn't care. "It's money. We need the money." Then she hung up.

I got out of the car, wondering how a woman I had met and hired just that morning had somehow become my new boss.

I walked through the backyard up to the main house. The door was unlocked, and I went inside. "Mom?" There was no answer, so I walked through the mud room and the empty kitchen. "Anybody around?" Then I heard giggling coming from the library.

The door was open a crack. I looked inside through the narrow slit but didn't open the door. I didn't want to interrupt.

Sammy was sidled up to the Judge. One of his arms circled around her. They were both smiling and talking about a picture in one of the old man's books. She looked so happy in this moment, and yet I knew it was just a moment. I knew that things weren't right.

She was hurting, and I'd been so self-absorbed that I hadn't noticed. I knew she missed her mother, like I did, but I didn't know school had gotten so bad that she'd lie to me. I wondered where she spent her days. What did she do for six or eight hours a day by herself?

My weight shifted and the floor creaked.

Both of them stopped talking and looked toward the sound, and I was forced to open the door and reveal myself. Both looked disappointed. "Sorry," I said, stepping inside. "It's getting late. Time to go."

She stuck out her lip, but she knew that I was right.

"Run along now." The Judge kissed her cheek and then patted her back as she got off the couch.

"See you tomorrow, Judge." Sammy waved good-bye.

"Of course." The Judge smiled back, and then Sammy and I walked out of the library.

"Grandma left a plate of dinner for you in the fridge."

"That was nice of her." At the mention of food, I realized how hungry I was. "I'll grab it and take it back to our place." We walked from the hallway into the kitchen.

I found a plate of meatloaf, mashed potatoes, and green beans in the refrigerator, secured beneath plastic wrap.

"Do your homework tonight?" I asked as we continued to the back door.

"Yes." Sammy answered a little too quickly.

"Great." I opened the door and we went outside. "You can show it to me, tell me what you've been working on."

"Why?"

"Because I want to see it." I got the carriage house key out of my pocket. "I want to see how you're doing."

"Since when?" She sounded defensive, but I didn't blame her. I hadn't ever asked to see her homework, but now things were different.

"Things change," I told her. "Conversations with Vice Principal Gieser will do that." I opened the door to the carriage house, and Sammy walked inside, her head bowed. She'd been caught.

◆　◆　◆

I took refuge that night in the toy room among the figurines and play-things of my youth. An old Artie Flake record spun on the player as I sat at my worktable. My time traveler was almost done. There was, however, some trim work on the clay base. Paint needed to be applied. Then there were the other figurines. Every good hero needs a cast of supporting players.

Monica looked as dazzling as ever. Her framed picture sat on the edge of my table, and we talked about Sammy and the Lost Boys. I didn't tell her much about the family drama and Annie. Some things needed to be kept close, even if I was talking to a memory.

The record played through to the final song. The music was slow and simple. A light brush on the snare kept time. An upright bass carried the tune, and Artie Flake sang the tale:

> Won't you come down to Saint Louie.
> Won't you be my pretty baby.
> Won't you come down to Saint Louie.
> This town's got me crazy.

It was well past midnight when I turned off the lights and closed the door. I walked through the kitchen, then started up the stairs. My mind was now too dull and my body too tired for the worries that had stacked up over the past week to interfere with my sleep.

That was the magic of the toy room.

I got to the upper landing, thinking only about brushing my teeth and laying my head down on my pillow. Then there was a noise in the alley. It sounded like a few empty bottles rolling across the cobblestones.

I turned out the lights and stood at the edge of the window. Whatever calm I had felt seconds before was gone. I scanned the alley, not sure what I was looking for and even less sure about what I was going to do about whatever I might find.

I waited.

My heart beat faster. Adrenaline.

It took some time for my eyes to adjust to the darkness, but even then there wasn't anything to see. No cars drove by. Nobody emerged from the shadows. I saw nothing, but I knew there was someone out there.

CHAPTER TWENTY-ONE

The next morning didn't go as planned. Emma had scheduled family interviews with a half dozen new clients, but I got a call from the city prosecutor as I arrived with Sammy at her school.

"Hold on." I covered the phone and looked back at Sammy. She had her backpack in her lap and was staring at the front entrance. "You gonna be OK?"

She looked at me and nodded. "I'll be fine." She didn't sound convinced. She reached out toward the handle, but hesitated.

"It'll be OK." I nodded. "Love you, Sammy."

"Love you, too, Daddy." She opened the door and got out.

I didn't pull away, even though the volunteer running the school drop-off lane waved me forward. I watched her go up the large walkway to the entrance of the school, and then I waited until she was inside. The whole time I was half expecting her to run away.

"Mr. Glass?" It was a faint voice. The prosecutor was still on the line.

I put the cell phone back to my ear. "Sorry about that." I pulled away from the curb. "What's going on?"

◆ ◆ ◆

Cecil Bates was in jail, scheduled to appear on the morning detention calendar, and the prosecutor wanted to cut a deal. No probation. No additional time to serve hanging over his head. Credit for time served with a minimal fine that everybody knew would never be collected.

It was a good deal, but it wasn't because the prosecutor thought she had a bad case. She wanted to dump it. A trial would be a waste of resources.

I called Emma and told her to reschedule the interviews. She cursed, but I told her that I didn't have any choice. That was the life of a solo street lawyer. There weren't associates or other partners available to bail you out when there was an unexpected court hearing. The meetings had to be rescheduled, and I had to drive down to the City Justice Center and convince Cecil to take the plea.

The building was new—built in the last twenty years, when every major American city built a new jail and a new sports stadium downtown.

Constructed of polished stone and glass, it was meant to look like a mid-rise office tower. The cameras, metal detectors, cops, and lack of windows on the sides of the building, however, gave its true purpose away.

I found a parking space off Tucker at a surface lot behind city hall, then crossed the street. The last time I had been down at the jail was the night that one of Saint Louis's finest kicked my ass.

I went up the steps, pushed through the revolving doors, and checked in through security. They directed me to the courtrooms on the second floor, and, from there, I was hustled to the back by the deputies.

Ten guys sat on a bench along the wall. I saw Cecil sitting at the end. He appeared to be about half the size of the other defendants in orange. That old *Sesame Street* song popped into my head. Cecil Bates was not like the others. Cecil Bates was doing his own thing.

I called Cecil toward me so that we could speak in semiprivacy. Leaning in, I said, "They offered a nice deal this time." I relayed the details to him—no probation and no additional time.

Cecil shook his head. "Didn't do it. Ain't gonna say I did." He folded his arms across his chest. "Done lots of stuff, but didn't do this."

I rolled my eyes and shook my head. "We aren't playing games here. This is it."

"I know." Cecil's face hardened. "Ain't my first rodeo, you know?" He held his chin high and puffed out his chest. "Ain't pleadin' to nothing I didn't do."

◆　◆　◆

The judge handling the detention calendar looked like a gigantic black buzzard peering down at us from the bench. His bald head had turned a splotched red. His sharp nose shot out from his face like a beak, and his beady eyes examined Cecil.

He gave a look of both hunger and disgust.

"Not taking the deal?" His face tightened even further. "Don't get much better than that." He swung his buzzard head toward the prosecutor and then back to us.

"I've explained the prosecution's generous offer to my client, Your Honor." I took a breath. "But he's been clear with me from the beginning. Mr. Bates would like to take this matter to trial. He is not pleading guilty. If held, he'll be demanding a speedy trial."

The judge leaned back. "Lots of people say that, but then when the time comes, they plead. They all plead, but not before disrupting the lives of potential jurors, the witnesses, and the court." He folded his arms across his chest, and we waited in silence. Finally, he looked at the clerk. "Set this matter on for trial in fifteen days, back with Judge Polansky. Bail is set at fifteen hundred dollars."

"Your honor, Mr. Bates doesn't have ten dollars for bail, much less fifteen hundred dollars."

My argument was ignored.

The gavel came down, and Cecil went back to jail.

So far, the prosecution of Cecil Bates for allegedly drinking an alcoholic beverage in a public space had cost the good taxpayers of Missouri over $2,000 for booking, incarceration, prosecution, and defense.

And we hadn't even had a trial.

CHAPTER TWENTY-TWO

I arrived at my office in the late morning. Thankfully there was no line outside my door. It looked quiet.

I drove around the block and then came through the alley in the back. After I parked the car and got out, I noticed that the dumpster was full.

The dumpster was never full.

I walked a little closer.

There were three trash bags piled next to it, a table with a broken leg, and a lamp without a shade. Inside, the dumpster was filled with other pieces of old, broken office furniture.

Every piece piled in the dumpster was mine.

With the discarded lamp in hand, I opened the office door. "Emma." I didn't wait for a greeting. "Want to explain what the—" My voice fell away.

A family sat in the front waiting area, staring at me. They sat on a new brown leather couch. The mother was flipping through a magazine, and the kids were in mid-squirm. "Good morning," I said to them as my eyes scanned the completely redecorated room. The office was beautiful, clean, and bright.

I held my finger up in the air. "I need a moment to talk with my paralegal." My eyes locked on Emma Tadic, sitting at a new oak desk with brass trim. "Perhaps you and I could talk in private?"

I walked back toward my office, and Emma followed.

She shut the door behind her as I walked around my new desk and sat down in a high-backed, leather chair. "Ms. Tadic . . ." I closed my eyes, wondering what I had gotten myself into.

Not knowing where to begin, I tried to keep it simple.

"I don't believe that I asked you to throw all my furniture into the garbage, true?"

"No." Emma didn't seem to care, nor was she offering to explain. She looked at me like she had better things to do.

So I tried a different approach. "The office looks very nice. This is all beautiful, but I can't afford any of it. I don't know what you're thinking, but I'm not that kind of a lawyer. I do street law. I work for the public defender. I have trouble making a small lease payment every month."

"No worries." She smiled. "I got this from my uncle. He runs a furniture store down on Market and Beaumont. You can pay him later."

"But I don't have the money now, and I don't think I'll have the money later, either."

Emma dismissed my concerns. "Then he'll take it back when he needs it."

"But I don't feel right about—"

"Nonsense, he knows what you did for my cousin Nikolas. He knows what you do for me." She tilted her head to the side. "And, of course, he knows your family. It's always good to have friends in high places, he says."

"I understand, but all this stuff is a waste." I ran my hand along the smooth oak desktop. "I don't need it, and my clients don't care."

"Yes, you do need it, and your clients definitely care." Emma rolled her eyes at my naïveté. "People buy the sizzle, not the steak. You know that. You don't want to admit it, but it's true. Plus"—she put her hands on her hips—"I do not work in a dump. Are we now done?"

I didn't have the energy to fight her. "I guess so."

"Good." Emma nodded. "I have a new client you need to meet this afternoon. Retainer is paid, but you need to go over the agreement with him and get it signed. First appearance tomorrow, suburban guy with a simple DWI. Just don't plead him right away. Keep him on the hook a little, let him sweat it out. He'll be more appreciative of your work if you fight a little, maybe challenge the traffic stop."

If she ever allowed my practice a quiet moment, I needed to ask Emma where she'd learned everything she knew about retainer agreements, client management, and running a law practice. "Thanks," I said as she stepped forward and handed me the file with the name of the new client printed neatly on the front. "You also need to meet with that family out in the waiting area right now and get them out of here. The kids are driving me crazy, and you have two others in about ten minutes."

I nodded, trying to process all the information. It had been a long time since I was part of a functioning law office, and I wasn't sure how I felt about it. "Anything else?"

"You do civil?"

Thinking back to my days as a young lawyer and husband, before it all fell apart, I said, "I *used* to do civil."

"Good." She nodded. "I told them, yes. They want you to work on a real estate deal for some affordable housing near the convention center. Part legal and part political."

I held out my palms, trying to slow her down. "I'm not sure about—"

"I say ten-thousand-dollar retainer, up front. You charge three hundred fifty dollars an hour and one hundred fifty dollars an hour for paralegal—that's me. They say no problem."

The money stopped me cold. I ran the calculations in my head. Even if it was a simple deal, I'd make more on that single file than I did working for the public defender in three months.

The room was silent.

Emma waited for me to say something, but I didn't. So she pushed forward. "Any questions?" She tilted her head, setting the big hoop earring on one side swaying back and forth.

Resigned, I quietly told her that I had nothing more.

Emma offered an understanding smile and nod. Then she turned and opened the door.

"Ms. Tadic," I said before she left. "How?"

She glanced back, smiling. "I answered the phone." Then she turned back and walked into the reception area. Before the door closed, she said, "Being on the front page of the newspaper also doesn't hurt."

CHAPTER TWENTY-THREE

By the third family interview, I was exhausted. Talking to people was my job, but these were more confessionals than anything else.

I heard about abusive boyfriends, drug use, working two jobs, evictions, intermittent homelessness, and couch-crashing. It was the harshness of living on the edge.

The disappearances in the first two interviews followed a progression. The same pattern as Tanisha's brother, Devon Walker.

When the boys hit puberty, their attendance at school worsened. They began hanging around with other boys who'd spend their days smoking marijuana, committing petty crimes, and hustling.

They joined a gang, but not in the way that a person joins the Rotary Club or the Masons. It wasn't even as formal as jumping into the Bloods or Crips. These gangs were more like loose affiliations, with names that teenage boys might think are cool, but actually revealed that they were still kids: Egan's Rats, Shaw Boys, Money Over Bitches (MOB), Saint Louis Crime Family, Bottoms Gang, Black Mafia.

They'd disappear for a weekend or even a week, dropping in for food or money or just to hide. The crimes got increasingly serious. Probation officers and cops became regular fixtures in their lives.

And then, one day they were gone.

I listened and took notes, and then, eventually, we had just one more for the day.

Emma brought me a cup of coffee and set it and the file on my desk, then leaned in. "You do this last one"—she patted my shoulder and whispered—"then you run to the jail before four o'clock. The DWI retainer agreement is on my desk."

Emma left as Deonna Villa and her sister came into the office.

I pointed to the seats in front of me, introduced myself, and took a sip of the coffee, hoping the caffeine would bring me back to life. "And which one of you is Deonna Villa?" I looked back and forth until, eventually, Deonna identified herself. "Well I apologize for the wait." I nodded, forcing a smile, and she nodded back. "Been a long day, but I'm sure it's been a longer day for you."

Neither said a word. They sat on the edges of their chairs. It was as if I were the doctor and they were the patient waiting for the diagnosis, which wasn't too far from the truth.

"You haven't been treated right." I paused. "If your kid was blond with blue eyes, this would've been on the news a long time ago and there would be a real investigation. But now, at last, people are paying attention." I put my hands together, an unintentional moment of prayer. "You don't trust the police, and I'm not here to argue with that. As I've told the other families, I can't make any guarantees about finding your son. I'm not a detective. I'm a lawyer. The best thing that I can do is gather your information, and then I'll make sure that the Saint Louis Police Department is aware and starts really looking for your son." I paused. "Do you understand that?"

Deonna nodded. "I'll do anything to get him back."

"I know you would." I opened her file and read the preliminary information that Emma had gathered. "Your son's name is Brendon, and it looks like he's been missing for a year. True?"

"Yes, sir." Deonna reached out and took her sister's hand. The mere fact that somebody was asking her about her son had almost pushed her to tears.

"You've filed a missing person report, but the police haven't contacted you."

Deonna's face hardened. "Never." She looked at her sister. "They ain't never called."

"So I have some pictures of the boys that the police haven't been able to identify." I paused. "The pictures are the remains. After months, maybe years in the ground, there isn't much left, but maybe you'd recognize an item of clothing or something else." I opened a three-ring binder. It was filled with the documents and photographs that I had gotten from Schmitty; each missing boy was separated by a tab. "And I'd like you to look—" I was about to push the open binder across the table but stopped. "You OK?"

Deonna closed her eyes and gathered herself. "Think so."

"I'm doubtful that your son will be in here or that you'd be able to tell by the pictures, but I have to ask you to look." I handed the binder across the desk to her. "We just need to rule it out."

Deonna took the binder, and then she and her sister looked at the first set of pictures. Both shook their heads. Then they turned to the next tab and looked at the second set of photographs. Again, no match.

Deonna looked up at me. She was struggling. I could tell she wanted one of the pictures to identify her son, Brendon, even though she would never want him to be dead. The need for closure was that great.

She turned the page, working through the binder, staring at some photographs longer than others. Tears rolled down her cheeks and dropped onto the laminated pages.

"Ain't him." She closed the binder and looked up. "These ain't him."

I nodded. "Just because you don't see anything doesn't mean he hasn't been found. The police have all their DNA and ran it through the system, but there was nothing on file that matched a name. So the only way we can make an identification is through a family member. We'd like to get a quick sample from you to see if there's a match. Is that OK?"

Deonna agreed to provide a sample, and I took the binder back from her, closed it, and put it to the side. "I'll make an arrangement to do a DNA test. Just to see. It's pretty quick."

◆　◆　◆

I arrived at the self-described Justice Center ten minutes before the front desk clerks left for the day. Instead of going up the elevator to the courtrooms, I went through the metal detectors and took a left down a hallway, through a waiting area, and up to a person sitting behind a window of bulletproof glass.

"Afternoon." I removed the thin file from my briefcase, reading the name printed on the top. "Here for . . . Stanley Kantor." I took out my card as well as a check for the maximum bail amount that can be levied in a DWI case. "My paralegal made arrangements for me to post this bond on his behalf and have him released to me with a court date."

The clerk let out a heavy sigh, looking at the clock. "Little late for this, dontchathink?"

"Apologies." I slid the paperwork and the cashier's check through the slot in the window.

The clerk, being unable to refuse my request, took it. She examined every page, looking for an error. She needed a technicality to give her a basis to reject it, send me on my way, and go home early.

She found none.

"Have a seat." She pointed at the rows of chairs, mostly empty.

A half hour later, Stanley Kantor was released. He was ecstatic to be out of jail. He couldn't stop thanking me. He didn't know that he would have been released the next morning, regardless of whether he had hired me or had any attorney at all.

The police can only hold somebody for seventy-two hours without charging them, and the prosecutor's office was so backed up with work that DWIs got a low priority.

But, with bail money and a private attorney, the Saint Charles businessman didn't have to spend an extra night in jail. He got to go home to his family, while old Cecil Bates was held. That's how it worked.

CHAPTER TWENTY-FOUR

It was after dinner by the time I got home. The carriage house was dark, but there was life in the main house.

I found Sammy, my mother, and the Judge sitting around the table eating ice cream from the Clementine's Creamery on Lafayette Square.

"Looks good." I squeezed Sammy's shoulder and pulled up a chair. "What's the flavor?"

"Mine's the Malted Milk Ball." Sammy stuffed a spoonful into her mouth. "Grandma and the Judge got the naughty kind."

"Bourbon Kentucky Pie." My mother smiled slyly. "Made with real bourbon. The Judge made me get it."

"True." The Judge laughed. Then he switched to his official voice so he could make a formal declaration. "A good bourbon, frozen and creamed with an appropriate number of pecan pieces, is always a fair and just selection."

"And it is so ordered by the court." I loosened my tie and leaned back. It had been such a busy day, and yet, satisfying. It was as if the black storms had rolled off, just a little bit, and I could see some sunlight in my mind.

I looked at Sammy. "Get your homework done yet?"

She stuck another spoonful of ice cream in her mouth and said something at the same time.

"What was that?"

"I said, not yet."

I nodded, looking at the Judge and my mother and then back at Sammy. "Well that needs to be done before you go to bed tonight." I pointed at her bowl of ice cream. "Finish that up, and then it'll be time to go back to our little abode. You can finish your homework, and then I'll be checking. Don't be rushing through it."

Sammy feigned a pout, but there was a twinkle in her eyes.

She was happy I cared.

The Judge, in his younger and harsher days—before he had fully embraced the role of great- grandfather extraordinaire—used to tell my mother, "Rules equal love. If you let your children run the show, then you really don't love them."

Perhaps the Judge was right.

◆ ◆ ◆

My mother led me toward the sunroom as Sammy went back to the carriage house to work on her homework. Just as the library was an oasis for the Judge, the sunroom was where my mother spent her time, knitting and simultaneously reading three or four books. She opened the nine-panel French doors and then flipped a switch. The dimmed lights grew brighter, and I followed her to the couch.

"I'm worried about you and your brother." She sat down and patted a spot next to her. "Heard from him?"

I hesitated, thinking about the threat he'd delivered to me and Annie. "Not really," I said. "I know he's mad. I know he wants me to step aside, and Buster is helping him out."

"Buster." Mother's eyes narrowed. "Always willing to do the dirty work. Have you told your father what you're intending to do?"

I shook my head. "Should, but I haven't." I leaned back. "Never asked for the job. Never really wanted it, but when Dad asked me to do it . . ." I got quiet, and I remembered standing next to him as a boy. My father speaking in front of an adoring crowd chanting his name, and me soaking it in. "It felt good to be acknowledged by him, especially since Monica passed and everything sort of fell apart for me."

My mother put her hand on my shoulder and I continued.

"Initially, I thought it's kinda like that old saying, 'Don't want to go, but always nice to be asked to the dance.' Thought it was an honor to be asked by Pop, and it made me feel proud. But, after a few days of being polite, I'd planned to tell him that Lincoln was the guy he really wanted. Then I kept thinking. Never made the call. And then . . . I don't know . . . a couple weeks . . . maybe I should."

"I talked to your father this morning." She was looking at me with concern. "He's officially announcing the retirement in two weeks. Doesn't want to rush you, but he's done, Justin. He's tired. I'm not even sure he's going to do that lobbying nonsense. He wants to come home. He knows the city is hurting."

I nodded, but I didn't have anything to say.

My mother rubbed my back, like she used to do when I was a boy. "Maybe I should get Lincoln over here," she said, "and you two can talk about it, you know, as brothers."

I looked up at the dark oak beadboard, studying the hundreds of lines running parallel across the ceiling. Then I stood up. "Maybe," I said softly. Then I leaned over and kissed my mother on the cheek. "Just give me some more time. Pieces might be starting to fall into place."

CHAPTER TWENTY-FIVE

It took another week, but I made it through all the Lost Boys interviews. There were no more discussions about running for Congress with my mother or anyone else. Ignoring the topic hadn't postponed my father's retirement or made the issue go away, but it was nice to pretend.

My law practice was actually making real money for the first time in its history. I got Sammy to and from school on time every day, and made sure she did her homework every night. The dark fog that had hovered in my head and slowed my brain for so long lifted a little.

I woke up with energy on this morning, and after breakfast, I arrived at my office a little after eight thirty. Emma Tadic was already there. The coffee was made, and she had a list of issues and potential clients that she wanted to discuss with me.

"Need a minute," she said, "or you want to do this?"

I sat down at my desk and waved her inside. "Now's as good a time as ever."

Emma nodded and sat down in the chair across from me. "Prosecutors called about Cecil Bates. They want a continuance for the trial. An officer is on vacation and unavailable to be a witness."

I shook my head. "Tell them no, unless they release him from jail. Otherwise we'll go to trial."

Emma nodded, and then she started talking about other potential clients.

She went through brief backgrounds, as well as the charges. We rejected two and kept one. Then Emma turned to the final potential client on her list. "He told me he was beat up by the bouncer pretty bad. Charged with disorderly conduct, so he wants criminal representation on that, but then he also wants to sue the nightclub. Don't know about the damages, but he sounded pretty good, kind of a two-for-one. Do the criminal for free and then take a cut on the civil."

I nodded and then realized something. "When did you talk to him?"

"Last night. This morning." Emma thought for a moment. "Called at three or four, whenever they released him from the hospital."

"You were here in the office at three in the morning answering the phone?"

Emma laughed. "No," she said. "I have the calls forwarded from here to my cell phone in the evening. Otherwise we miss them. They find somebody else."

The thought of having a twenty-four-hour answering service had never occurred to me, and I knew nothing about how phone calls could technologically get forwarded from one to another.

"I think you're overqualified for this job," I said.

"True." Emma thought for a moment. "My boobs fooled you." She shrugged. "Not the first man to underestimate me."

I nodded, admitting that the tight, short skirts and the big hair were, for lack of a better description, distracting. "I think you also deserve a raise."

"You're right, again." Emma smiled. "Twice in one morning. Not bad."

Schmitty and I had met at the Northside Roastery. I handed the spread-sheets over to him, and he looked at them. After flipping through the first few pages, he looked up. "Been busy."

"I know." A little bell rang at the counter, and Hermes waved at me. I nodded back at him, and then to Schmitty I said, "Cream?"

"A little."

"Keep reading." I pointed at the spreadsheets, and then I got up and walked to the back of the shop to pick up our drinks. The coffee shop was empty, as usual, but Hermes didn't seem to mind. He was all smiles.

"How's Nikolas?"

"Better every day, Mr. Glass." Hermes glanced over his shoulder to the little room where Nikolas did his work. "He's at the computer again. So that's good. He says to ask you if you need anything."

"I'm good for now." I placed a few dollars in the tip jar, then picked up the two steaming cups of coffee.

"Emma working out OK?"

"You already know the answer to that." I walked over to a little table with sugar and cream and started to prepare the drinks. "Emma's been great."

Hermes nodded. "She was a good lawyer."

I stopped. *Emma's a lawyer.* I knew she was more than just a quick learner. Now it made sense.

"Back home," Hermes clarified. "In Bosnia, she was a well-known lawyer. Women's rights. Human rights. My cousin, she was the first that had to leave when the troubles started."

"Emma never told me." I felt bad, when I also realized that I'd never asked.

"She doesn't talk about what happened to her." He paused. "Makes her sad. Makes me sad." He shook his head. "Nobody recognizes any of our degrees here, but . . ." Hermes went a little distant again and stopped talking, then shrugged. "We're alive."

"Thanks for telling me."

"Suppose I shouldn't have," he said. "It's not good to brag, but if you can't brag on family . . . who to brag on?"

"Exactly." I picked up the cups of coffee and took them back to the table. I put one down in front of Schmitty and sat down across from him. "See anything?"

"A little." He pushed the papers aside and looked up. "More interested in what you see."

"Well I've interviewed about thirty families. There are more, but we prioritized."

Schmitty grinned. "Meaning that you focused on the ones who could pay."

"Of course." I smiled. "But if the family was associated with one of the kids identified and found in the woods, we interviewed those folks, regardless." I leaned across the table. I found the one-page summary sheet with a star drawn in the corner. "This is the one that just has the information about the known Lost Boys. The ones we know were found with Devon in the woods."

Schmitty looked at it.

"See something in common?" I pointed at the last column on the sheet that identified the boys' probation officers.

"Six out of nine." Schmitty thought for a moment. "Don't know what the caseloads are like." He rubbed his chin. "Could be a coincidence. Could be some other explanation, geographic assignment or something."

"Could be." I leaned back. "Or maybe not."

CHAPTER TWENTY-SIX

Schmitty set up the meeting for eleven o'clock at Kendrick's Chili on Broadway. I wasn't expecting much, but I was curious. I hadn't ever met someone who was so universally hated.

According to Schmitty, Jimmy Poles was a wiseass, but not the funny kind. His face rested in a snarl. He was always on high alert to snap out an insult or release a high-pitched whine when asked to do his job or otherwise exert energy.

Poles was never asked to go out for a beer after work or invited to lunch by the other probation officers, yet he somehow found out about any such gathering and weaseled his way to the table. That was Jimmy Poles. People couldn't say his name without shaking their head in dismay.

He was, however, union. Poles couldn't get fired for annoying the hell out of everybody. The best his supervisors could do was keep a calendar. The calendar counted down the days until his retirement: 8,478 on the day that I met him.

Some of my families had never seen or heard of Poles, even though their missing sons were supposed be on intensive supervised probation with him. A high-risk juvenile was to be seen by their probation officer at least once a week. Poles fell far short of that standard.

To the family members who had actually spoken with him or met him, most didn't know his name. He was simply a skinny white dude with a crew cut and an attitude.

One mother had told me, "He walked up in here like he was the master. Didn't matter that it was my damn house."

◆ ◆ ◆

Twenty minutes late, Poles walked in the door. I recognized him immediately from the descriptions I had heard during the interviews.

I raised my hand, and he shot me a look. Poles made it clear that his presence was not voluntary. His supervisor had forced him to come, after the supervisor's supervisor got the call from above.

He came over to the table and then folded his long body into the chair.

I held out my hand to introduce myself. "Justin Glass. Thanks for coming."

He hesitated, staring at my hand for a moment. I could tell that he was contemplating whether he should touch it at all. He decided to shake my hand and said, "I know who you are."

Smiling, I tried to soften the mood. "Could be good or could be bad, depending on what you know."

His eyes narrowed, and then he looked off to the side with a smirk. Whatever he was thinking, he didn't share it with me.

We sat for a moment in silence. Poles drummed his fingers on the tabletop. Then he said, "Well let's get on with it." He looked at me flat. "What do you want to know?"

"Tell me about yourself."

Poles didn't say anything, and then he barked, "We on a date?"

"No, but right now I think you know some things about all these missing kids." I leaned forward, holding his stare. "So I'm hoping you can help me out. Being a prick isn't really going to benefit you much in this situation."

Poles lifted his hand, making it clear that I should stop talking. "I'm here because my boss told me I had to come." He shrugged. "Didn't say anything about talking about my life or being Mr. Warm and Fuzzy."

"Wasn't expecting Mr. Warm and Fuzzy." I leaned back. "Just hoping for smart." I signaled to the waitress from across the room. She came over and I ordered a chili dog, a bag of chips, and a Diet Coke. She turned to Poles, and he shook his head, refusing to order. Then she walked away.

"So"—I turned back to Poles—"you want to talk about these kids, or let me assume the worst about you?"

I opened my folder and then pushed the photographs of all the young men who had been assigned to Poles and were now missing.

Poles quickly flipped through the stack. "Don't have much to say," he said. "I got a big caseload, and they all pretty much look the same. Don't leave much of an impression, you know, other than they're a waste of everybody's time."

"Lost causes?"

Poles laughed. "Beyond lost causes." He pointed at me, getting angry. "You all expect us to be miracle workers. We're not. None of these kids want to change. None of their families want to change."

"None?" I raised an eyebrow. "You're saying there's never been a kid who wanted a better life."

Poles got silent. Then he said, "No." He shook his head. "Not that I met. Not really."

◆ ◆ ◆

The rest of the interview wasn't any more helpful than the start. Poles offered no real information related to any of the Lost Boys. He claimed ignorance, and part of me believed him. The other part, however, wondered whether he was really the one.

He fit the profile: loner, angry, narcissistic, and knowledgeable about police procedures and DNA. There was also something about his attitude. Although he was combative, he had this look in his eye. It was like he might've been enjoying himself.

Poles knew I wasn't a cop. He knew he wasn't in any real danger. So why not play with me?

Neither Poles nor the chili dog was sitting with me very well as I returned to my car. As I pulled out into the street, my telephone rang. I looked down at the tiny screen and saw that it was Emma.

"What's going on?"

"Where are you?"

"Downtown." I stopped for a red light and watched as a half dozen cars paraded by. "Just finished my meeting."

"Good," Emma said. "Stay down there. You've got court in an hour, and then I've got two more clients you need to meet at the jail and post bail for them."

"Court?" The car behind me honked. The light had turned green. I acknowledged them with a wave and then jerked the car forward. "I didn't think I had any appearances today."

"Well now you do," Emma said. "The crazy one."

I paused, thinking. "Could you be a little more specific?"

"Bates."

"Cecil?"

"That's the one," Emma said. "Emergency motion for a continuance."

CHAPTER TWENTY-SEVEN

Judge Saul Polansky called our case last. He wanted to make me wait. Punishment for clogging up his calendar.

The judge's personality had changed since the last time we'd seen each other. He didn't want to chitchat and gossip. He was irritated. He wanted to go home and didn't appreciate an "emergency" motion being added to his calendar.

I sat in the back of the courtroom for two hours. The law factory processed a half dozen misdemeanors and a couple of gross misdemeanors as my cell phone buzzed. I knew better than to answer my phone. There was a clear "no cell phone" policy in the courts. The judge was already annoyed with Cecil Bates, and I didn't want to give him another reason to yell at me or my client.

At four o'clock, Cecil Bates was led into the courtroom. He was thinner than when we had last seen each other. His face was drawn, and Cecil looked even smaller than usual as he stood next to the large bailiff sporting a bulletproof vest under his uniform.

The judge pointed at the prosecutor. "It's your motion."

The prosecutor nodded. "Yes." Then she looked at me and my client. "As you know, Your Honor, Mr. Bates has refused to plead guilty."

Bates bolted straight. "'Cuz I ain't guilty." He pointed at the judge. "And I ain't pleading guilty to nothing I didn't do."

Judge Polansky's face turned red. "Mr. Bates, you will remain quiet and not interrupt these proceedings, or I will find you in contempt."

I put my hand on Cecil's shoulder, trying to calm him down.

"Understood?" The judge cocked his head to the side.

The judge waited, and eventually Cecil nodded his head. "Yes, sir."

"Good." The judge turned back to the prosecutor. "Go on."

"Mr. Bates has asked for a speedy trial. The court has granted that speedy trial request and set a date. Unfortunately, Your Honor, our office learned recently that the arresting police officer will be on a family vacation and out of state during the scheduled trial."

"And?" Judge Polansky was getting bored.

"And, we promptly asked counsel for Mr. Bates for a continuance, and he refused."

The judge turned to me.

"That's not exactly accurate, Your Honor." As a lawyer-actor, I offered a dramatic sigh before continuing. "I agreed to the continuance if the State would agree to let my client out of jail pending trial. They refused that request, and so I refused to agree to the continuance."

The muscles in the judge's neck visibly tightened, and his hands balled into tight little fists. Then he closed his eyes. Judge Polansky asked, almost in a whisper, "What is wrong with you two?" When neither the prosecutor nor I responded, the judge continued. "Last time I checked, this case is about drinking alcohol in a park." He opened his eyes and stared at the prosecutor. "Not exactly the crime of the century. You'd agree?"

The prosecutor stammered, mumbling something about Cecil Bates's failure to appear at the last hearing and the quality of life in downtown Saint Louis.

"And you"—Judge Polansky turned to me—"you can't negotiate a plea, can't control your client, can't find a resolution to a simple motion for a continuance." He picked up his gavel and slammed it down on the bench.

The sound echoed throughout the courtroom. I thought, for a second, that the gavel may snap in half.

"I'm done with this." Judge Polansky stood up. As he left the courtroom, he said, "Motion for continuance granted. The defendant is released pending trial. That's it for me today. I'm going home."

CHAPTER TWENTY-EIGHT

It took until mid-September for the sporadic shooting pain and tenderness to be completely gone. Life was busy but falling into a routine. A late-night phone call from Schmitty, however, changed the rhythm that Sammy and I had developed. I had to figure out how to balance everything, and I decided to wake her earlier than normal, holding off as long as possible. It wasn't ideal, but there wasn't much choice.

I opened the door to her room. "Sweetie." I walked over to the window and lifted the shade. The sun was rising, but still low in the sky. Then I walked to the bed and kissed her on the forehead. "Daddy needs you to wake up now."

Sammy rolled over but didn't show many other signs of life.

I tried rubbing her back, which only elicited a groan. "Come on now." I returned to the door and flipped the light switch. Sammy pulled the sheet over her head. "I need you up so we can talk."

Then she stated the obvious. "I'm tired."

"I am, too," I said, "but I have to go. Are you listening?"

Another groan came from under the sheets.

I sat on the edge of the bed. "You know that case I've been working on? The case with the missing boys." I paused, waiting for Sammy to say something in response or acknowledge that I was not simply talking to a lump of bedding. "They found something, and I have to go help them figure it out."

This got Sammy's attention. She slowly pulled the sheets down, so that I could see her face. With eyes half-closed, she asked, "Right now?"

I nodded. "Need you to be a big girl and get ready and take the bus this morning." I thought about all our progress and that it was about to unravel, but I didn't have a choice. "I can't drive you today."

Sammy looked away. She was calculating. "When are you coming back?"

"Tonight." I reached out and found her hand. "You'll do fine. You've been doing great." It sounded more like I was trying to convince myself more than her. "Your mama would be proud of you."

She nodded but didn't say anything.

"I've already talked to Grandma. She's going to have a big breakfast for you at the main house and make sure you get off OK. Understand?"

"Yes."

"Good." I leaned over and kissed her on the head, then I checked my watch. "Gotta go now, but I'm not leaving until I see those feet on the floor." Then I stood up and walked over to the doorway. "Come on now. You can do it."

Another groan, and then she said, "Fine." Sammy pulled her sheets down and swung her legs over the side of the bed. "Good enough?"

I shook my head. "Nope." I smiled. "Need to see you standing on the floor and walking in the general direction of the bathroom or your dresser."

"Dad." Sammy was exasperated, but was also milking it a little now, enjoying the attention. "OK." She stood fully, took a few steps away from her bed, and held out her arms. "Happy?"

I laughed. "Totally."

◆ ◆ ◆

Castlewood State Park was just over forty minutes outside the city, depending on traffic. It was easy to see the park's large trees and a distant rolling hill from Highway 44, but it took some effort to figure out how to get to it. The interstate, built for trucks, speed, and sprawl, offered no logical exit ramp for the park, and then, once I'd left the highway, the roads followed the terrain rather than anything resembling a logical grid.

At last I drove in a large loop over the Meramec River to Big Bend Road, then wound back along Kiefer Creek to the meeting site, where the road ended in a large trailhead parking lot. Police had put up a wooden barricade at the entrance. A highway patrolman stood in front.

The Highway Patrol is the most formal of all law enforcement agencies. He addressed me as *sir*. He confirmed my identity and reason for being there, then pulled the barricade aside.

◆ ◆ ◆

Schmitty and three cops stood around a picnic table examining something. As I approached, Schmitty noticed and gestured for me to join them. I squeezed between him and one of the other officers and looked down. There was a large map of the park. It had two marks. The first mark was the location of the original crime scene. Somebody had written the number nine next to it, representing the number of bodies recovered, including Devon Walker's.

The second mark was still in the park but across the river, not too far from where we now stood. There was no number written next to this mark yet.

"How many?" I asked.

They turned. No one answered my question, deferring to Schmitty.

"Three more, at least." Schmitty put his hand on my shoulder. "Justin Glass, let me introduce you to officers Johnson, Cole, and Bilcik."

"Morning." I nodded. "Sorry to hear about this."

"Ain't that the truth," Schmitty said, gesturing for me to follow him away from the others. He walked toward the trailhead and then onto a path leading into the woods. "Techs are still working the scene. They think that they've located another body, so that would bring it up to four, but nobody knows whether this site is as compact as the other one or whether the other bone fragments belong to a deer or another animal."

I followed him farther into a grove of oak and hickory, and Schmitty continued. "When I heard about the first one being found by the construction crew, I was hoping it was an old, unmarked native gravesite—not too uncommon around the river—but when they pulled the second and third one up, figured it wasn't a coincidence, not with how close we are to the other site." Schmitty stopped when we got to a line of yellow police tape. "Then, when I saw the bodies"—he took a breath and spoke on the long exhale—"knew for sure it was the same deal."

"Hands behind the back with plastic ties."

Schmitty pointed at me. "Bingo."

We ducked under the police tape, and he led me farther into the woods. "Little farther." Schmitty pointed. "Construction guys were building a couple yurts out here. Kind of a new thing. Not quite camping, but not as expensive as the traditional cabins, either. Construction crews were digging holes for the footings and a pit toilet. That's when they found it."

We entered a clearing. There was an ATV and a small trailer loaded with building materials, as well as a yellow Bobcat excavator. Two crime scene techs circled the site taking photographs, and I noticed a couple of mounds of dirt with little orange flags sticking up.

"So this is a nice field trip and all," I said, "and I mean no offense here, Schmitty, but why do I need to see all this?"

"Didn't need you here only to see." He put his hand on my shoulder and guided me over to the excavator. "I needed you here to talk."

Standing on the other side of the Bobcat was the Saint Louis chief of police, Max Wilson.

"Justin Glass," Chief Wilson said, holding out his hand. "We haven't met, but of course I know who you are. Thanks for coming."

We shook. "Long way for me to come for a conversation."

The chief shook his head. "Too many eyes and ears in the city." Chief Wilson gave me a look. "You already know that."

It was the way he held my eye that gave me pause. It was like he knew things. Maybe he was referring to Sammy, or maybe to me and the mayor, but the chief wasn't going to say it. Perhaps it was all in my head—or maybe not.

"OK." I put my hands on my hips. "You got me in the woods. Now what?"

"You know that family you talked with and got the DNA sample?"

"Deonna Villa?"

"That's it." Chief Wilson nodded. "Came back a match."

Schmitty picked up where Chief Wilson was headed. "Now with these." He looked at the mounds of dirt and orange flags. "It'll hit the news again, and you'll have more families coming out of the woodwork. I want to get DNA swabs of everybody who's come to your door, even the ones that you reject."

"Why don't you get them yourself?"

"Because they're not coming to us. They're still coming to you," Schmitty said.

"They trust you," added Chief Wilson. "I saw the spreadsheet. It was nice work. Better than anything we've got."

I folded my arms across my chest. "But I don't have the time to do your job." A dozen kids had disappeared, and the police hadn't lifted a finger. Even now I wasn't sure what they were doing, except hoping that people would get tired of the story and forget it. "Don't get me wrong," I said. "My heart breaks for these families, but I need paying work. I've already sunk too much into this."

"Come on," Schmitty said. "It'll be good for you. A favor for us."

"A favor, huh?" I looked at them, skeptical. "More like favors, plural, and I want to know if you have any other suspects besides Jimmy Poles."

"You know, officially, I can't tell you that." Chief Wilson looked at Schmitty and then back at me. "But we still don't have much."

"We got a dozen dead kids, and you don't have much." The challenge went unanswered. "So how hard are you actually looking?"

"We're looking hard," Chief Wilson said. "But it's a tough case."

"Right." I turned and walked a few feet away from them. Part of me wanted to be done with them, let the whole thing go, but I knew that the families would come regardless of what I told Chief Wilson or Schmitty.

Chief Wilson allowed for some space and silence, then walked over to me. "We could be very helpful to you and whatever endeavors you may pursue. You want more legal work? We can make that happen. You want to run for something? I've got a thousand people, between the officers and civilian support staff under my command. They'll put up those signs, make those calls, and attend a rally in the rain if I tell them to do it."

I rolled my eyes, hopefully reminding Chief Wilson who I was and who was in control. "If I help, it's because it is the right thing to do. And if I were to do it, and I do mean *if*, you'd need to have the tech there at my office during the initial response. If you want these families to call and make an appointment, it's not going to happen. It needs to be right there or maybe train my paralegal, Emma, how to get the DNA sample."

Both Schmitty and the chief smiled.

Schmitty clapped his hands together. "Good. We can do that."

"And I want to know what you're doing. You need to tell me how you're following up on the information that I give you."

Schmitty looked at Chief Wilson, who nodded, and then looked back at me. "Done."

"Good." I checked the time. It was still relatively early, and I'd be able to make it to the office and get some real work done. "Then that's it."

"Not exactly," Chief Wilson said. "You mentioned that probation officer, and I heard you talked with Poles yourself."

"I did." I was surprised he'd brought this up, but I wondered whether this was the real reason they'd called me out to the woods so early in the morning. "Didn't learn much, other than he didn't want to talk with me."

"Well that's not a surprise." Chief Wilson looked at Schmitty and then continued. "I don't want you doing any of that type of investigation anymore. Just focus on the families."

"Are you kidding?"

"No," Chief Wilson said. "I know Sergeant Schmidt was trying to be helpful when he arranged that meeting, but I want you to leave that sort of thing for the real investigators."

"The real investigators? You mean the ones that hadn't noticed that a dozen kids had gone missing?"

Chief Wilson stayed calm. "This is a high-profile case, and I want you to be safe."

I shook my head. "Safe?"

"And I don't want you to do anything that is going to jeopardize the investigation."

"I won't jeopardize the investigation."

"Well this is sensitive business," Chief Wilson said. "Poles was placed on paid administrative leave."

"And why's that, exactly?"

"Can't say too much," Schmitty said, "but he has used the government's computer system inappropriately and accessed files he shouldn't have accessed."

"Related to these kids?"

Schmitty shook his head. "Not exactly, but it's important that you be discreet about him. I think what the chief is trying to say is that we don't want people jumping to conclusions. We don't want you telling people that he may be a suspect."

"But he is," I said. "The only suspect, as near as I can tell. Why don't you tell me what you found? Tell me what you know."

Wilson ignored my question and didn't offer any further information on Poles. "It's a tense time." His face turned grave. "I know you can feel it. The hot weather isn't helping anybody relax, either. I don't want a media firestorm before we know what's going on."

"Things *could* turn violent." Schmitty put words to what Chief Wilson had implied.

"You guys don't get it." I looked back over the crime scene. "Things have already turned violent." I looked at them, thinking about laying on the ground with blood in my mouth as a white police officer cracked my ribs with his boot. Being cooperative and respectful didn't make me safe. It didn't change the color of my skin. "Things have been violent for years—not just this, but everything." I started to walk away, then stopped and turned back to them. "But you're right. When this breaks open, it's not just young black kids who are going to get hurt."

CHAPTER TWENTY-NINE

I arrived at the office after one o'clock. My cell phone had been off. It was a deliberate decision, although somewhat irresponsible. I needed the quiet. I had meetings with clients all over town. Cases and tasks were waiting to be prioritized, and I had to make sense of all the mounds of dirt and little orange flags representing missing sons that the police didn't want to find.

But even with no phone calls and no radio, I didn't make much progress during the drive. My mind bounced from one case to the other and then back again. I tried to focus, but my thoughts drifted to Sammy and my brother and my father and my future.

I knew I was on the edge.

Things were going well, but it was now getting too complicated, and when it got complicated, things inevitably fell apart for me. Depression is like that. I was smart enough to know when I was about to be kicked down. I just didn't know what was going to do it, and I certainly didn't know it was going to happen the moment that I walked in the door.

Emma was on the phone at her desk, writing down a message. She looked up at me, and I waved as I went through the reception area toward my office. She held up a finger.

I stopped.

Without a word and with the phone still pressed against her ear, she pointed at the chair behind me. I turned and looked, and then I saw my daughter.

Sammy's eye was swollen shut. Her lip was cut, and when she saw me, she started to cry.

◆ ◆ ◆

I had failed.

My job was to protect my daughter from harm. I was supposed to love her, nurture her, and shield her from the ugliness that pervaded our brutal and broken world.

Some may argue that we shouldn't shelter our children. We should let them see and experience the sins that are all around us. By keeping the children unaware, they say, we are preventing the development of their defenses.

I disagreed.

We have our whole lives to experience the ugliness. We have our whole lives to grapple with the reasons for society's misplaced priorities. Trying to give a child a childhood was nothing to be ashamed of.

And now my little girl was broken.

I walked Sammy back to my office. "Sit down in my chair, sweetheart." I guided her behind my desk. "Going to talk with Emma for a little bit, and then I'm going to get you home."

I watched as she sat down in my chair. She wiped the tears off her cheeks and tried to be brave.

I promised her I'd only be a minute or two, then turned and walked out of the office. I closed the door, because I didn't want Sammy to overhear the conversation, and then said to Emma, "Sorry I had my phone off." I shook my head in disbelief. "Didn't expect this."

"Not a problem." She shrugged as if it wasn't a big deal, but her eyes were filled with sympathy. "I go pick her up. Knew you were coming back."

"What happened?"

Emma took a shallow breath. "Not sure." She bit her lower lip. "They almost didn't let me take her—not on some preapproved list—but I wasn't having any of it."

I looked back toward the office where Sammy was waiting and lowered my voice. "And she didn't tell you what happened?"

"Didn't ask, and she didn't offer."

"OK." I tried to compartmentalize. I forced the sight of my daughter and what she was going through to the side. I needed to organize my thoughts and give Emma some direction before I left for the day. "We should be getting calls about the Lost Boys again. The police found more at Castlewood, so it's going to be in the media."

"Do the same as before?"

"Yes and no. We need DNA samples from everybody who comes in, even if we don't interview. We're also supposed to circle back and get samples from everybody else who has called or come to us. Saint Louis PD is giving us a tech or some training in how to get the DNA swab. They say it's easy."

Emma picked up a notepad. "Anything else?"

My mind wandered to Sammy and all the questions that I had for her, but I forced myself back into the conversation with Emma. "Talked to this probation officer named Jimmy Poles. There's something there that Schmitty isn't saying. Poles is now on leave. Hoping you could try and dig up something on him."

"Like on the Internet?"

"Whatever you can find." I shrugged. This was out of my depth. "Maybe some background databases that we can pay to search . . . court actions, past addresses, relatives, stuff like that. Cops are always protective of their own, and Schmitty doesn't seem to think they're going to press him. The chief is worried about whatever's going on with him going public."

Emma made some notes. "I'll try."

"And we have to connect with Cecil Bates. Try and convince him to plead. The judge isn't too happy with us at the moment."

"And the new clients?"

"New clients." I smiled just saying it, more in muted bemusement than anything approaching happiness. "I have no idea. Put them off. Can't do anything more today, maybe not even tomorrow." I thought about Sammy and felt the darkness again, a black tar seeping down and through my head. "I don't know."

◆ ◆ ◆

Back home, Sammy was tucked into her bed. I snuggled the blankets up a little higher than normal. The ice pack sat on the nightstand, wrapped in a kitchen towel. "Want to talk about it?" I leaned over and kissed her forehead, careful to move slow and act soft.

She shut her eyes and turned her head away. "I want to sleep now, Daddy. Please?"

"Fine." I rubbed her leg. "But we'll have to talk about it at some point."

"I know."

"Love you, tiger." I turned and walked to the door. As I turned off the light, Sammy told me that she loved me, too.

I shut the door, walked out into the narrow hallway, and went downstairs to the kitchen. My mother and the Judge were waiting for me. It was rare for them to come to the carriage house. Their presence was a product of their concern.

My mother looked at me as I approached. "Anything more?"

"No." I sat down at the table with them. "It was the other girls at school that had been giving her trouble . . . I can guess that, but nothing about what led up to it."

"The bullies." My mother took a sip of tea. Her hands held the cup so tightly that I thought it might shatter. "Sammy told me about them. Tried to reassure her. Told her they were harmless. Told her to talk to the teachers. Maybe I was wrong."

The Judge shook his head in disgust and then pushed himself away from the table. "Public schools, one step removed from the—"

I held out my hand. "Lower your voice," I said. "And it's not the time—"

"It most certainly is the time." The Judge wasn't a man to be quieted by anyone. He sat more erect. "Had concerns for quite a while, but I've kept my mouth shut out of respect for you and at the urging of your mother to mind my own business. But this is my very special little great-granddaughter."

"Judge, I appreciate what you're—"

The Judge looked at me and I stopped. Even though I wasn't in his courtroom, the Judge had that power. He had presence. The way he stared at me was an order to stop speaking, not a suggestion, and I didn't want to know what would happen if I disobeyed.

"Thank you." The Judge nodded. "This afternoon I made several phone calls to some excellent private schools. I explained the situation, and the directors assured me that Sammy is welcome at any time. They are ready to arrange for tours, and I have the personal cell phone numbers for all of them, when Sammy is ready."

I looked at my mother and she looked away. I wasn't going to get any support from her. Even if she didn't like her father's politics or approach, I could tell she agreed with the Judge.

My head bowed and I closed my eyes. In a whisper, I said, "Please don't think that I don't appreciate how much you love Sammy, or that I'm ungrateful for how much support you've given us these past few years." I didn't look up. I couldn't look at them. "I simply can't afford those schools."

It was a shameful confession, even though my mother and the Judge were fully aware of my financial situation. Saying the words seemed to push me even further into the dark places in my head. Not only could I not protect my daughter, I couldn't provide for her.

My mother's hand touched mine, and she leaned in toward me. She put her head on my shoulder. "That's why we're here, son. That's why you have family."

"You're not poor, Justin." I felt the Judge put his hand on my other shoulder. "We have plenty of resources to do this. We *want* to do this. What kind of family would not support you? We've got money to cover whatever tuition there is. If you refuse to take it, consider the money a loan. Take it out of your inheritance when I kick the bucket. Who cares?"

I didn't know what to say. I looked up at both of them with tears in my eyes, and then there was a knock at the door.

CHAPTER THIRTY

The video's sound was bad, but the picture was clear. Light from the school's hallway window flashed as the crowd of kids shifted and swelled. It was a mob, and in the middle was my little girl. There were screams. There were shouts, but the most haunting sound was laughter.

The laughter turned my stomach. It echoed, hollow and distorted through the iPad's tiny speaker. If I had closed my eyes, it could have been laughter from a birthday party or flying on a swing, but it was not. The laughter came from kids reveling in the violence.

Sammy was on the ground. The major blows had already occurred. A girl came from the top of the screen and kicked her in the back. Another pranced toward her and palmed the back of Sammy's head and pushed it toward the floor. Then the sequence repeated with variations.

Sammy swung and kicked blindly, unsure of who the next attacker would be or where the next strike would occur. Her shirt was ripped and pulled up.

Her pink tween training bra was exposed.

All the while, laughter and taunts echoed in the school hallway.

A teacher entered the fray, ordering the students back into their classrooms. A school resource officer ran to Sammy, kneeling beside her, and then the video cut out.

The ticker below the video indicated that it had been viewed 1,348 times. Below the ticker was a thumbs-up image. Four hundred eighty people had clicked that they liked it; just fifty had clicked that they did not.

The video was titled "Lil Rich Bitch Gets Stomped."

Schmitty turned the iPad off. "We contacted the website, and they say it'll be down within an hour." He looked beyond me, at my mother and the Judge at the kitchen table, and then back at me. "Sammy doing OK?"

"Not really." The knot grew in my throat. I tried to compose myself. "Thanks for coming, but"—I looked down at the iPad in his hand—"this is a little below your rank, isn't it?"

"You and your kid are not below my rank." Schmitty forced a smile, and I could tell that there was something more.

"And?" I pressed.

"And I wanted you to know that this is out there." He spoke softly. "No calls from the media yet, but it could happen. The district attorney is thinking about charging, but there's some complications."

"Complications?"

"It's high profile, Justin. You're high profile right now. Most people are thinking you're our next United States congressman. We're just now getting out from under the police wrongly arresting you. Plus we got the Lost Boys story about to explode again, and now we got your kid beat up in one of our public schools."

"So?" I was in no mood to debate the poor reputation of Saint Louis public schools or my political career, such as it was. "My daughter was hurt. I don't have any comment on any of this."

"Well that's sort of the problem," Schmitty said. "The girls in that video say that your daughter was bullying them. They say that she's been antagonizing them all year, and that she threw the first punch before this video starts."

"That's ridiculous." My anger boiled.

"I know it's ridiculous, but we're reviewing the school security videos now. That should help." No doubt seeing the agitation on my face, Schmitty spoke in soothing tones. "The girls are being held down at juvie. But their families are demanding that we arrest your daughter, too."

The muscles in my neck seized up as I spat out the words. "She was on the ground getting punched and kicked."

"I know." Schmitty raised his voice to match mine, then turned down the volume again. "But these aren't rational people. They got dollar signs in their eyes. When they heard it was your daughter, they got an attorney who's making noises about a civil lawsuit against the school for not protecting their kids, and another against you, against your daughter."

Now my entire body was locked up tight. My hands balled in fists. "You should go now."

Schmitty nodded. "That's fine, but I needed you to know what's going on." He put his hand on my shoulder and leaned in. "And you need to know that we got you on this one. Chief owes you. I owe you. But know, too, that we got no control over these girls and their welfare moms. No control over them."

CHAPTER THIRTY-ONE

Before I did anything the next day, I flipped through the entire morning paper. There was no story about Sammy and the incident at school. Then I turned on my laptop computer.

I typed Sammy's name into the search engine, quickly scanning the results. There was nothing. I ran a search using the school's name and then typed an increasingly abstract combination of different words.

It wasn't out there yet.

Instead, the discovery of three more Lost Boys was the dominant story. It was the top headline on the front page of the *St. Louis Post-Dispatch*. I read the first few sentences of the article and then decided to set it aside for a moment.

I needed coffee.

I walked over to the kitchen counter, scooped some freshly ground beans from the Northside Roastery into the filter, filled the machine with water, and waited for the magical brown liquid to start its slow drip into the glass carafe.

It was quiet in the house. The sun had barely peeked above the horizon. The garden was peaceful, and the low morning light gave it a look of anticipation. The plants knew the heat was coming and wanted to enjoy the day while they could.

Sammy was still asleep, and I figured that I had at least an hour more to myself.

The night before, my mother and the Judge had left shortly after Schmitty. The Judge had told me that we would "revisit" Sammy's choice of school in the near future, which meant I half expected him to come through the door with a schedule of campus visits at any moment.

The coffeemaker beeped twice, meaning that it was done, and I filled my cup.

There were no more excuses.

I had to figure out a plan. I couldn't be an observer of my own life. I had to take control, or what little I had left would be washed away. Sammy needed an engaged father. My clients needed a real lawyer. My own father deserved an answer. And Tanisha Walker needed to know what happened to her brother.

I walked back to my toy room. I turned on the lights, walked over to the worktable, sat down, and removed an empty sketch pad from the drawer.

This was the first time I had ever used the room for anything besides solitude. The toy room now had to become a place I worked and made decisions.

I turned to a blank page and began to write. It was a list of all the things that I needed to do to help Sammy find a new school. Dealing with the parents of the bullies was secondary. Then I started writing a list of everything I needed to do for work; a list of thoughts, ideas, and facts about Tanisha Walker's brother and the other Lost Boys; and finally a structure to make a decision for my father and about my future.

I wasn't going to run away. I was going to run toward it, whatever *it* may be.

CHAPTER THIRTY-TWO

It was shortly before noon when Sammy finally emerged and came downstairs. She had eaten a short stack of pancakes, three scrambled eggs, and four sausages in her room. "Didn't realize how hungry I was."

"Well," I said, picking up her dirty plate and starting to the sink with it, "you didn't really eat much yesterday." I saw her begin to retreat, and so I tried to keep her engaged. "Talked with my mom and the Judge last night. They'd like you to come over there and hang out, maybe watch a movie. I'm going to the office real quick, just to check on some things, and then I'll be back."

"That's fine, Dad." Sammy sighed. "You don't need to babysit me."

I walked back over to her, pulled out the kitchen chair, and sat down. "I know I don't need to babysit you." I touched her knee. "But I want to be with you, and we do need to talk."

Sammy wouldn't look me in the eye. "I didn't start the fight." A tear rolled down her cheek.

I wasn't going to push it, and I wouldn't tell her about the video, Schmitty's visit, or the crazy parents. "It's just important that we talk about what happened and then about what's going to happen."

"You're sending me back there?" Sammy's sadness flipped to anger. "I'm not going back there."

I held her gaze. "Let me be clear," I said. Worries about money and debt were gone. They had to be. Sammy was smart enough to pick up on doubt. She needed strength. "You are not going back to that school ever again. Understood?"

I saw her body relax and she nodded. "Understood."

"Trust me," I said. "We'll take our time and find a new school for you. Don't worry. There are lots of places to go to school."

◆ ◆ ◆

As I crossed the highway over to the Northside, there was a group of about twenty protesters congregated near the top of the exit ramp. They were chanting and holding signs. How many more Lost Boys were out there? Why hadn't they found the killer? They wanted to hold the police accountable. They wanted answers.

That's how it begins. The initial shock was gone, and now people were getting angry.

I kept driving to my office, wondering how many would be waiting for me there, but there wasn't a line. Two women were smoking outside my office door. I resisted the urge to drive past and parked directly in front of my office. I turned off the old car's engine and, when it had rattled to a stop, forced myself to get out and walk toward my office.

The old me would have blasted past the mothers without so much as a nod when they looked my way, but that day I started taking control and even channeling some of my brother's charm.

"Good morning, ladies." I forced a smile and moved ahead. "I'm Justin Glass and I appreciate you coming here, filling out the screening forms, and speaking with my paralegal." I checked my watch. "But I have a meeting now, so I need to get inside and get to work." I reached out and touched one of the women's shoulder. "Thank you for coming here."

Then I stepped past and into the office, still forcing the smile. Three adults and three kids were crammed in the reception area. "Good afternoon, everybody." I smiled and greeted them, then continued walking to my office. "Emma, can I see you?"

She was already standing. "Of course." She picked up a manila folder, a notebook, and a pen and followed me inside, saying to the people waiting, "It'll be a moment." She closed the office door behind her. "Pretty smooth, Mr. Glass."

I slouched down into my seat. "It's exhausting being nice."

Emma pulled the extra chair away from the wall and moved it closer, then sat down across from me. "Preference as to where we begin?"

"Surprise me."

"How about Mr. Bates?"

"Cecil Bates." I smiled. "Perfect."

"He's coming in for a meeting next week, Monday. I think you have to be there for that."

"OK. Morning or afternoon?"

"Early afternoon." Emma laughed. "In the morning he'd be hung over and by late afternoon he'd be drunk, so scheduling it was a tough call."

"Hard decision," I deadpanned. There was a pause, and then I started to laugh, too. It wasn't even that funny, but I needed to laugh. It just came up and out. To the people waiting outside, I probably sounded like a madman. Then I shook my head, got control of myself. "Figure out something to do for him, Emma. I don't know. Anything. If he wants me to fight, I'll fight."

"OK." Emma wrote the instruction down. "I also got a bunch of interviews with families set up." Her face turned sour. "But there's no money in them. We lose on every one."

"I know." I thought about Schmitty and the chief and keeping the community together and Sammy, and then, ultimately, Tanisha and all the families that came to me, the ones who chose me. "We have to do it," I said. "It'll die down, eventually."

"Maybe." She nodded. "I'll call you if there's something interesting."

"And the Poles research?"

Emma handed me the manila folder that she had brought from her desk. "Definitely questionable."

I opened the folder and flipped through the various reports, spreadsheets, and screenshots taken from websites. "Where'd you get all this?"

"Nikolas helped out."

I looked up at her. "All public information?"

Emma didn't answer. Her silence was its own confession.

CHAPTER THIRTY-THREE

I pity most of them, although I'd likely be among the last people they'd want pity from. The racists on the edge of society were so fragile. The assumptions and lessons they'd been taught for generations now under attack from all directions, they had to feel what little they had was in danger of being taken away. Racism had become the last defense of a way of life that'd been dead for over a century.

But Jimmy Poles was different. I had no pity for him. He wasn't on the edge. He wasn't fragile. He had a good-paying and stable government job. He graduated high school and finished college at Mizzou. He wasn't living in a trailer park on the fringe of the Ozarks, isolated. He lived in a rambler in the suburbs.

There was no argument that he was being left behind by the modern world, but there he was with an AK-47, a Confederate flag, and a picture of Hillary Clinton riddled with bullet holes.

His Facebook page was a stream of racist pictures and videos. One was a collage containing portraits of every president—but at the end of the list, instead of an official portrait, Barack Obama was portrayed as two cartoonish white eyes peering from a black background. There were images of Michelle Obama as a monkey and then hundreds of racist comments about newspaper articles and current events.

It turned my stomach.

Perhaps the worst part was that I knew exactly how Jimmy Poles would respond when confronted about his online and off-line activities. He'd smirk and dismiss me as politically correct. He'd talk about his right to free speech. He'd talk about defending the Constitution from both foreign and domestic threats—people who looked like me, of course, being the domestic threat.

But was somebody like that a killer?

"He's single. Doesn't appear to be dating anybody." Emma leaned over and pointed to a printout of a chat room set up for fans of a local country music radio station. "Then there's this."

Poles had posted a long statement about the Lost Boys. It was entitled "A Different Point of View."

> JPOLE18361: I work with these thugs every day. And I think we should all give him a round of applause. Shake his hand. We should lift him up as a great leader. For the cost of a few ounces of lead, he saved the taxpayers millions of dollars. Everybody knows where these kids were headed. The liberals will never admit it. But it is fact. He saved us all a lot of work. The guy put a lot of sick dogs to sleep.

◆ ◆ ◆

After work, I went home and dropped my briefcase off in the carriage house, then walked through the garden and up the short path to the main house. I was only outside the comfort of air conditioning for less than a minute, but the brief time outdoors resulted in a nice coat of sweat.

My mind was still on Poles when I opened the back door. My mother was in the kitchen. Dinner was already done, simmering in a pot on the stove. She was now baking cookies, but from the look on her face I knew that the cookies were just a pretext. She was actually waiting for me, wanting to intercept me before I got too far inside.

"Justin." She forced her face to soften, and then her eyes glanced back to the other room. "How was the office?"

"OK." I walked over to her and gave her a quick hug. "How's Sammy?"

"Fine." My mother scooped some dough onto a cookie sheet. "Watching a movie upstairs, eating popcorn. Not saying much."

"I'll go check on her."

"Wait."

I knew it was coming. "OK." I stopped, curious. "What's going on?"

My mother looked around, making sure that we were alone. "Annie and Lincoln are here."

"Both of them?"

My mother didn't respond at first, then added, "Buster, too."

"Buster." It came out louder than I expected. "After everything, Lincoln brought that snake." My mood had flashed from blue to red. "Gonna pop that—"

"Justin." My mother held out her hands. "Think of Sammy. Calm down a minute before you go in."

"What do they want?"

"Your father's coming into town this weekend." My mother's voice got quieter. "I think you know what they want."

◆ ◆ ◆

"Get him out of here." I pointed at Buster, who was standing on the far side of the parlor with Lincoln. "Can't hardly look at him. Can't believe you brought him here."

150

Buster stood up a little taller. The wrestler's hands had turned into fists. He was ready to fight, if necessary, but Lincoln patted him on the back and guided him toward the door.

Annie watched from a chair in the corner. I couldn't figure why she'd conspire with two people who were ready and willing to destroy her career. I looked at her with disgust. "You invite him?"

"Of course not." She looked at Lincoln and then back at me. "I'm here because your mother called me this morning. She was worried about you." She looked over at Lincoln. "She was worried about what you were going to do to your brother."

"My mom's a smart lady." I watched as Lincoln leaned out the doorway, whispered something to Buster, and shut the parlor door. To him, I said, "A phone call would have been nice." I turned away, shaking my head. "When is an ambush ever a good idea?"

I stared at the large painting on the main wall of the downstairs parlor, a dramatic image of a farm on a hill by Saint Louis artist Joe Jones from 1936. It was as if the land were lifting the farmstead up to the gods as a sacrifice, just as a storm rolled in.

I lost myself in the painting, allowing myself to calm down.

Lincoln and Annie waited me out, until finally I said to Lincoln, "I guess I have to listen to you now." I kept staring at the painting. "But I'm only doing it for Mom and Dad."

"You gonna sit down with me or what?"

I took a breath and turned around.

Lincoln was now on the couch. Annie was still in her corner chair.

"Suppose I will." I walked over and sat in the chair across from Lincoln, still cold to the situation. "You called the meeting."

Lincoln looked at Annie and then back at me. "Brother, we gotta—"

I held up my hand. "You gonna *brother* me right out the gate? That's your approach? Where have you been for the past month? Sending Buster out to follow me—probably him in the alley. Blackmailing

Annie. How about you start with an apology?" I pointed at him. "Apologize."

"Ain't nobody send Buster out to follow you, OK?" Lincoln looked at Annie. "OK?" When neither of us said anything back, he sighed. "I apologize." He waited a moment, checking on my response. "How's that?" Lincoln waited another beat and then backtracked. "But I didn't tell Buster to do anything." I started to interrupt, but Lincoln talked over me. "That's why I brought him. That's why he was here, and you can call him later if you want. He'll tell you."

I dismissed it, even if it was true. I wasn't going to let my brother go that easy. "He'll say whatever you want him to say. You're unbelievable."

Lincoln rolled his eyes. "You want to talk or not?" He held out his hands in surrender. "I'm here in good faith. Here to work this through. You want to yell at me, go for it. Get it all out. I got all night." He looked at Annie again for confirmation, but she remained silent. "But we gotta work this out now."

"Everything's on your schedule, huh?"

"No," he said. "It's on Dad's schedule. He set it, not me." Lincoln waited for me to disagree. When I didn't, he continued. "Here's the deal, brother—straight talk." Lincoln edged closer, becoming a bit more aggressive. "You two ain't no secret." He looked at Annie and then back at me. "You think the mayor doesn't get noticed in this town? You think you two can have an intimate conversation at a bar or a lovely dinner together on The Hill and nobody's going to notice?" He looked at us like we were two teenagers that had been sneaking out at night. "People know. With or without Buster doing or telling anybody, people know." He nodded. "That's the truth, and it's a problem."

To Annie, Lincoln said, "It ain't gonna be broke in the traditional media, but they're waiting. Come election time, a blog will do something and then the newspapers and television will cover it through the back door. The story will purportedly be about the blog post and the identity of the anonymous blogger, but it'll really be about you. First woman mayor is an adulterer. The end. You're done."

Lincoln turned to me. "And you don't get much more of a pass, big brother. You can play the lonely widower card, but I don't think there's gonna be much sympathy. They're building you up now, so there's a bigger fall. Folks are already sniffing around Sammy's school. We got truancy issues, and now there's that fight."

With that I stood up. "Leave her out of it."

Lincoln stood up, too, matching me. "It ain't me." We went chest to chest; Lincoln looked to Annie for confirmation and then back. "This is politics. It's blood sport now. There's no control. There's no privacy. People are out there destroying politicians for fun. Anybody with a computer and Internet access can write whatever they want for the world to see." Lincoln closed his eyes and shook his head, calming himself down. "You and Dad haven't been in the trenches like me. You're up in your ivory towers, but those big save-the-world ideas got nothing to do with the way things are now. That's what I'm talking about. That's real. Sorry to be the messenger."

Lincoln sat back down, allowing the exhaustion with the situation to roll over him. "You two laugh and scoff at me, thinking that I'm some huckster out there selling the Glass name. But what you don't understand is that all that stuff I do is meant to protect us, and you're fooling yourselves if you don't think we need it. Dad came up in a different era. He hasn't had a real challenger in thirty years, but we're different. We're vulnerable. Maybe we win. Maybe we lose. But there are people out there who want to hurt us, marginalize us. It's not my imagination. Ain't paranoia."

I turned and walked back over to the painting. When I tilted my head to the side, I felt my spine crack. Everything my brother was saying to me was true, but I didn't want it to be true. I wanted the world to be different . . . better.

Finally I said, "I know, Lincoln." I swallowed hard. "I've been thinking about it. Thought real hard about it this morning, and I know I can't do it." I took a deep breath. "I know I don't have the stomach for it, the fund-raising and the back-room deals." I shook my head. "But it's nice to pretend there's an answer. It's nice to be asked."

I walked back over to my chair and sat down. "Sammy's in trouble. I'm in trouble." I looked my brother in the eye. "For a moment, I thought maybe a fresh start in DC might be the answer to everything." A soft laugh. "Ideas of grandeur didn't hurt my ego none, neither." I looked at Annie and then back at him. "But I'm out. Maybe known it for a long time, maybe from the beginning, but now I'm telling you . . . I'm out."

Then I turned to Annie. "What do you think?"

She shook her head, sad. "I don't think much of anything." Then she looked down at her feet. "Maybe I should quit, too."

"Hold on." I pointed at Lincoln. "We have a world-class fixer in the room. He's probably got a half dozen plans ready to go." I looked at Lincoln. "Am I right?"

Lincoln smiled, grateful. Then he nodded his head. "Things just have to be handled, that's all. We have to think them through . . . together."

CHAPTER THIRTY-FOUR

Lincoln and Annie didn't stay for dinner. Buster had been waiting outside, and they left as soon as I agreed to Lincoln's master plan. The rest of us ate, and when we were done, Sammy snuck off to the library with the Judge, as usual, while my mother and I did the dishes.

After the final pot was scrubbed and dried, I walked from the kitchen to the library, where Sammy sat with the Judge on the couch. They'd finished *The Iliad*. They had now moved on to a compilation of poems by Walt Whitman. I knocked on the door frame as I entered. "Time for bed, sweetie."

Sammy groaned.

"Have to talk to the Judge for a few minutes." I gave her my hand and pulled her from the couch. "Why don't you stop in the kitchen and have another cookie and some milk with Grandma. I'll be out in a few."

My consent to yet another cookie got her moving toward the door, where she stopped and blew the Judge a kiss before hustling away.

He smiled, then closed the book and put it on the end table next to the couch. "Everything going OK?" He gestured to the chair. "Have a seat and tell me what the great political mastermind had to say."

I sat down. "You must be talking about Lincoln?"

"Of course," the Judge said. "I'm sure he had a plan."

I nodded. "Always." I thought for a moment and then added, "Not a bad one, either."

"I'm sure it entails you giving up your father's congressional seat." The Judge was always skeptical of Lincoln's motives.

"Yes," I said, "but the seat was never mine to begin with."

The Judge scoffed. "You don't believe that, do you? Your father, in a rare moment of insight and wisdom, picked you, and that's the end of it. Lincoln could bluster and whine, but he's smart enough to know the rules." He folded his arms across his chest, signaling his opinion was final. "You win."

"I appreciate that, but it's more complicated."

The Judge raised an eyebrow. "The good mayor?"

I shouldn't have been surprised that the Judge knew, too. Seemed like everybody knew.

"That's part of it," I said. "Sammy is another part . . . school issues."

"You have the name and your father's support. That's all you need."

"Maybe." I nodded. "But politics hasn't been my thing for a long time."

"You say that now." The Judge shook his head. "So that means the state Senate seat is out, too?"

"I don't know," I said, which was true.

The Judge looked at me, knowing the haze that I'd been living in and continued to struggle with, then he set it all aside, ready for a new topic. "Assume you had other reasons that you wanted to talk."

"I do." I leaned back, thinking about Sammy. "I told Sammy that I wasn't going to send her back to her old school, so"—the words caught in my throat—"I am going to need your . . . help."

The Judge looked at me with kindness. I knew it had more to do with his love of Sammy than me, but it was the first time he'd ever looked at me like that. "Of course." He nodded.

I half expected him to snap out of it and revert to his old self, bashing public schools and government regulation, but he didn't. He didn't make me feel guilty or sign a contract with a repayment plan. He just gave me a sympathetic grin. "Anything else?"

It took a moment, but my mind shifted to Devon Walker and all the bodies in Castlewood Park and my conversation with Chief Wilson. I remembered promising to help the families, but I didn't remember agreeing to heed his warning about doing my own investigation. I didn't see any harm in doing a little more independent field research. "Wondering if you know any of the judges who work down in juvenile?"

"In the city?" The Judge raised his eyebrows. "Most of them have long retired, but I think I know a few that are active."

"There's a probation officer I want to talk to somebody about, hear from somebody who works with him."

The Judge thought about it a little more. "Danny Bryce would probably be your man. He's pretty passionate about all that stuff."

The name rang a bell for me. "The Missouri Miracle?"

The Judge nodded. "That's the one. He's the judge they put on all the legal panels to talk about juvenile crime. He's written quite a few law review articles about intervening early in a juvenile's life and providing them with wraparound support. He started it in the 1990s and experienced significant drops in juvenile crime. Many jurisdictions copied it, wanting their own miracle."

"Can you make an introduction for me?"

"You can use my name if it'll help you get a meeting."

CHAPTER THIRTY-FIVE

They scheduled the press conference for ten thirty in the morning on Saturday to allow enough time for reporters to write their stories for the Sunday newspaper and television stations to edit the video for their midday and evening newscasts.

Theoretically.

But Lincoln understood the current disarray of modern journalism. He wasn't going to leave anything to chance. For community newspapers operating with either volunteers or somebody making less than minimum wage per story, he e-mailed an electronic draft of a story about his announcement for Congress. It was all in the package—quotes, photos, and headline. They didn't even need to send a reporter, just cut and paste.

He did the same for the political reporters at the *St. Louis Post-Dispatch* and the Associated Press. They'd probably get their own quotes, but the draft saved them time and made them happy.

For the television stations, Lincoln hired his own videographer. If no cameraman or reporter made it to the announcement, that wasn't a problem. His communications director sent the raw footage as well as edited versions to all the stations. Then, for the bloggers, thirty-second clips were posted on YouTube and Vimeo so that they could be embedded into their websites.

It was orchestrated perfectly.

My father spoke to the small room of fifty people, announcing his retirement. He got choked up a few times, and I swore that I saw him glance my way. He wanted me to be taking his place, but he understood my choice was final.

I stood next to Annie in front of a large GLASS FOR CONGRESS sign, and we watched my father introduce my brother. He gave Lincoln a hug and then receded into the background.

Lincoln smiled as family members, campaign workers, and some folks from the community whooped and hollered in the back of the room.

"I want to thank my dad for being a wonderful father, mentor, and example to me and my brother." He turned back, looked at our father, and nodded. "Thank you." Then he continued. "I also want to thank my brother and Mayor Angela Montgomery. They are my campaign cochairs, and some of my closest advisors."

That was the plan that Lincoln had devised for us. To the extent there were rumors about my relationship with Annie, we now had a legitimate and simple reason for our late-night dinners and meetings. We could say that we had been planning and coordinating his future campaign.

Neither of us liked it, but the move was smart. The direct connection to Lincoln gave Annie some assurance that her crumbling marriage and rocky personal life wouldn't come to light because of him. For Lincoln, saving Annie helped neutralize the one person who could've prevented him from achieving the next step in his career: me.

Standing on stage, I was a pawn. My brother, Lincoln, was the chess master.

He played us beautifully, Annie and me.

The Glass and Montgomery machines were now connected.

My heart sank a little as I exited the highway onto McKnight Road and then drove into a neighborhood with huge trees, large lots, and no sidewalks. This was no longer the city proper.

The Nathan Baxter School was on the left, set far back from the street. Beautiful buildings rose up from a distance on the school's fifty-acre wooded campus. They were all light tans and beiges. The campus could easily be confused with a small liberal arts college.

The small parking lot was dominated by fancy cars that cost more than I earned in a year. I parked my rusted Honda Civic next to an Audi, then I walked up the path. Ahead of me, I saw the Judge waiting on a bench near the entrance. He stood when I got closer. "How'd it go?"

I shrugged. "As expected." I stopped at the front door. "The torch was officially passed this morning."

"Surprises?"

"Nope, everybody stuck to the script." I opened the door, allowing the Judge to enter the school first. "At the end, some reporters asked questions. You could tell Dan Dooley is going to rant about dynasties and nepotism in his next column, but Lincoln knew it was coming. Jane Mix from the *Dispatch* asked Lincoln whether he knew who was going to run for his state Senate seat. She was looking at me the whole time she was asking."

"Bet she was." The Judge laughed as we walked through the bright and clean foyer toward the administrative offices and the director of admissions.

"Lincoln saw we were about to go off-message, so he simply smiled and told her that"—I paused for dramatic effect, transitioning into my best Lincoln Glass impersonation—"'Today we're all focused on everything that our father has accomplished during his many years of service and ensuring that his legacy continues for this district. I am honored to carry on that legacy.' Then one of Lincoln's lackeys ended the press conference before anybody could ask about the state Senate seat again."

"Still thinking about it?"

"Yes."

The Judge pressed for more. "Leaning toward it?"

"Yes."

"So what's changed?"

"Time," I said. After weeks of hedging and indecision, it felt odd to just come out and admit the truth. "The job might be interesting. I might be able to do some good." Then I gestured at the immaculate building that surrounded us. "And the extra money might be enough to pay for tuition at this school . . . or part."

The Judge smiled. "The prodigal son returns."

CHAPTER THIRTY-SIX

After visiting the school with the Judge and enjoying the rest of the weekend, I spent Monday morning hanging out at the Northside Roastery. In the past it may have been considered to be hiding, but today it was for the sake of productivity. There were too many things happening at my office.

I sat at a table near the front window, watching a steady stream of people coming and going. They were the mothers of the Lost Boys. Some of them were alone, but most had an auntie or grandmother with them. A small kid or two often trailed behind.

Hermes kept my cup of coffee filled as I switched back and forth between watching and working on my laptop. There were over a dozen e-mails from Emma, some related to routine office management, but also summaries of potential cases: an aggravated robbery, a divorce, and a domestic assault.

They didn't excite me, but it didn't matter whether or not they excited me. Where once I'd have let them slip away, now I didn't have that luxury. Emma needed to get paid, and if I really didn't want the Judge to pay for most—if not all—of Sammy's tuition, I needed to make some real money.

I took a sip of coffee, leaned back in my chair, and watched as an older man shuffled by on the other side of the street. He had two plastic grocery bags from Dollar Time. I knew what he'd think of a private school that cost three times what he probably had to live on in a year.

I slumped a little bit in my chair. Then I scrolled back through the e-mails describing the potential cases and, for each one, pressed "Reply" and instructed Emma to sign them up. I'd meet with them when they paid the retainer.

◆ ◆ ◆

Emma came into the coffee shop a little after four and sat down across the table from me. "Working from here now?"

I smiled. "Thinking about it." I shut down my laptop, closed it, and pushed it aside. "Quieter here."

Emma nodded. "That's good for you." She looked around the empty space. "Not so good for my cousin's bottom line."

"Looked like you were busy today."

"Interviews and DNA swabs." She shook her head. "Sad stories."

"Sorry I missed it."

I'd tried to sound empathetic, but Emma saw through it. "Yes," she said. "I bet you are very, very sorry to have missed the honor of sticking a Q-tip inside a stranger's mouth and swabbing their cheek."

"Buy you something?"

"Would be nice." She checked the chalkboard behind the register, then turned back to me. "A latte, skim milk."

"Done." I stood up and walked to the back of the shop in search of Hermes. "Anybody home?" I called finally.

"Yes, yes." Hermes emerged from the back.

"Emma wants a fancy, girlie drink." I got out my wallet and put a ten-dollar bill on the counter. "Skinny latte."

"Very good." He rang up the order. He had started to make change when I stopped him.

"Keep it," I said. "I owe you."

I could tell he wanted to decline the overpayment, but couldn't find a polite way to do it. "OK," he said, shutting the drawer. "I bring it out to you." He looked past me at Emma and waved to her. "Nikolas wants to see her," he said. "I send him."

Back at the table, I told Emma that Nikolas was coming out. "What's he working on?"

"Probably best if you don't know." Emma looked down and removed a file from her briefcase.

She wanted the conversation about Nikolas to be done, but I pushed. "About Poles? You're working on finding more stuff on Poles?"

"Really, no worries. Do not worry about it." Then she changed the subject. "I thought this was an interesting interview." She removed her typed summary as well as a few pages of handwritten notes. "Look at this." She pointed.

I did as directed. "A witness?"

"Perhaps."

I read her summary from the beginning.

It had been an interview with a mother and one of her sons—an eleven-year-old whose eldest brother, Thomas, had been gone for nine months. Emma had been careful to take down every word that the boy had said.

I looked away, thinking out loud. "Says he didn't see who did it."

"True," said Emma. "But he saw his brother get stopped, have a conversation with somebody driving a van, and then his brother got inside. Didn't ever see the driver, but his brother was never seen again."

"No plate. No make or model."

"Says it was dark blue."

I paused, thinking. "It's something," I said. "Don't know what, but it might be something."

After we left the coffee shop, I went to my office to read mail and prepare for the next day. We were both ready to go home, when there was a knock on the outer door.

I heard Emma talking to whoever was there, and then she ducked her head into my interior office and told me it was Cecil, and that she'd been able to smell the alcohol on him through the closed door. "Do you still want to meet with him?" We had had an appointment in the early afternoon, but he hadn't shown up.

I sighed, not really wanting to consult with a drunk client, but decided to go ahead. "I'd still rather meet and maybe talk him into settling now rather than going to trial."

Emma unlocked the door and let him inside. "Mr. Bates." She pointed toward my office. "Mr. Glass has been waiting for you."

"Oh." Cecil nodded and then looked around. "Suppose I may have lost track of the time."

"Well he's very busy, and we may need to cut our meeting short."

Cecil wobbled, looking from Emma to me and then back again. His eyes narrowed. "Well it ain't gonna take long." Cecil's voice faded and then came back strong. "'Cuz we got ourselves a slam-dunk defense."

The small, soft-spoken Cecil that I had met at the courthouse was now gone. The alcohol had transformed him. He sauntered into my office, removed his large backpack from his shoulder, and put it on my desk.

After a few seconds of searching the backpack's many pockets, Cecil removed a folded and slightly torn piece of paper. "Proof." He smacked it down in front of me. "Check it out, bro."

I picked it up and started reading. I took my time, hoping Cecil would sit down and calm himself. He didn't. Then I looked up at him. "Looks like a Freedom of Information Act request you've filled out—and, I presume, submitted?"

He gave a decisive nod.

I set the request down and then gestured to the chair. "Please." I pointed again at the chair. "Why don't you tell me about it?"

Cecil looked back at Emma, who had been standing in the doorway, then at me. "OK." He seemed a little confused, as though he'd either been expecting me to applaud his initiative with a round of celebratory drinks or kick him out of my office. My request to talk quietly appeared to have come as a surprise.

He sat down and tried to find a comfortable position.

"When did you send this in?"

"The other day." Cecil pointed at the piece of paper. "Told that woman about it, too." His head rolled back in the general direction of Emma and then rolled back to me. "Lady knows all about it. Gave her a copy when I sent it. We got 'em."

"So no plea agreement?"

"Hell no." Cecil looked up to the heavens and then back at me. "When we get this"—he pointed at the FOIA request—"we got the proof."

"Proof of what?"

Cecil folded his arms across his chest. "Proof of my in-no-cence." He smiled. "Did it all on my own. Went to the library. Told them ladies there what I wants to do, and they helped me get the stuff, make the copies, and send it in."

I looked over at Emma and then back at Cecil. "And what are we looking for?"

"Video. Video of me in that park. Video of my arrest." Cecil grinned. "Once you see the video, you see I wasn't drinking in no public place."

I refrained from reminding Cecil that he had approximately thirty prior citations for drinking in public and was, in fact, now drunk in my office. "So what if we get it back and it shows that you were drinking?"

Cecil laughed. "Ain't gonna show that." He shook his head confidently. "I was not drinking that day. Had no money. End of the month. Check didn't come yet. I can't drink when I'm broke."

"And how do you know there's video?"

"'Cuz that presidential debate, bro."

He'd lost me. "A debate?"

Cecil nodded. "When those candidates came up into town, they put all them cameras all over the place. The other days, I was in the park. Look up, and sees this little camera on the lamppost. That's when I realized I gots the proof."

"But even assuming those cameras were still running when you were there, these requests"—I looked at Emma and then back at Cecil—"the government is notoriously slow in responding to these things. In a month, you'll probably get a letter that says that they received it, and then who knows how long it'll take to get it back." I picked up the FOIA letter and read it through, hoping that this action would satisfy Cecil that I knew what I was talking about. "The truth is," I said, looking up again, "we don't have a year to wait. We don't even have a month. Our trial is next week, and the judge isn't going to give us a continuance for this. It isn't going to happen."

"Well then you get it some other way." Cecil was agitated now. "You my lawyer. You figure it out. I been doing all the work."

CHAPTER THIRTY-SEVEN

The next day, I arrived at the office early. A stack of files waited for review. When that was done, there were phone calls to return and meetings with potential clients all over the Saint Louis area.

The coffeemaker popped and gurgled as I raised the shade. The early morning light flooded my office, and my mind felt a lightness that I hadn't experienced for quite some time, maybe more than a year. The situation with Annie and my brother was done. I had made the decision that Sammy was going to private school—probably on the Judge's dime for now. I didn't know where exactly, but she wasn't going back to the place where she was hurt, and that's what mattered.

These things offered some clarity and satisfaction, at least before the rest of the world woke up and interfered with my dream.

I stared at the beautiful restored buildings across the street. Even though there was decay behind them, they were enough to give a man a little hope. There was nobody around at that time, and I could almost imagine a bustling business corridor, a Norman Rockwell painting with more soul. Maybe the Northside was ready to be reclaimed one block at a time.

The coffeemaker beeped. Reality returned.

I walked into the main reception area, poured a cup, and went back to my desk to work. When Emma arrived a few hours later, I had reviewed almost every file.

She sat down across from me. "Been busy this morning." She reviewed my pages of notes. "Impressive."

I brushed aside the compliment. "Every once in a while."

We discussed the paying clients first and then finished with a general discussion about the Lost Boys interviews.

"They're slowing down," Emma said. "Not as many calls, but it's hard to predict. You really should talk to the Turners."

"The Turners?" I couldn't remember the significance of that one.

"The boy who came in yesterday with his mother," Emma prompted. "He saw the van."

"The van." I nodded, remembering. "Makes sense."

Emma got up to leave. "Anything else?"

I thought for a moment. Then I wrote a name down on a piece of paper. "Can you look up the contact information for Judge Danny Bryce? Maybe see if you can set up a meeting."

I handed the sheet of paper to Emma and she took it. "What for?"

"I need to talk to him about Poles," I said. "My grandpa knows Bryce, says he works in the juvenile courts here, and we can drop his name to get in."

CHAPTER THIRTY-EIGHT

The rest of the day was a blur of security screens, metal detectors, and conversations through bulletproof glass. I prioritized the in-custody clients and then had a couple of meetings with people who were out on bail and awaiting their first hearing.

Two of them couldn't afford my retainer. One needed to ask his parents for the money, but was pretty sure he'd get the cash, and two others signed the retainer agreement and handed me cashier's checks for $3,500 each. That money would get them representation up to trial. If they wanted to go to trial, it'd be more.

It was late afternoon when I arrived at the police station. After some hassle with the front desk, I was awarded a badge and allowed to proceed to the elevator. The box took me up to the sixth floor, and Schmitty was waiting for me when the doors slid open.

"Afternoon." He held out his hand. We shook, and then he led me back to his office.

Once he'd closed the door and we were sitting across his desk from each other, Schmitty said, "My DNA guy says you've been busy."

I nodded. "But I'm still waiting for that big paycheck from the city."

"Be waiting a long time on that one." Schmitty leaned back. "Anything new?"

"Not really." I thought about all the things that Emma and Nikolas had found out about Poles in the dark corners of the Internet, but figured that Schmitty already knew. I also decided that trying to explain how I'd obtained the information would be more trouble than it was worth.

I talked about the interviews and gave Schmitty a copy of the new spreadsheet that Emma and I had prepared. "We added a column about whether they'd be willing to talk to you." I leaned across the desk and pointed at the column on the far right. "Figured you might want to send a detective out on a few, since the families seemed willing."

Schmitty flipped through the sheets of paper, nodding. "This is good."

"Mostly my paralegal," I said, then added, "There was a mother and a kid who came in recently—Turner is the last name. Kid thinks he saw his brother get into a blue van."

Schmitty's eyebrows raised. "Want me to send somebody over?"

I shook my head. "Not yet," I said. "It's all secondhand for me. I want to interview him myself first. Don't want to waste your time."

Schmitty nodded. "Anything else?"

"Don't think so."

"OK." Schmitty paused, looking uncomfortable. "We're starting to feel some heat now. That group of protesters by the highway is growing, and I heard that they're talking about shutting down the highway."

"I can't say I blame them."

Schmitty stared at me, and we sat in silence for half a second too long. Then he opened the bottom drawer of his desk. "Guess we better deal with this now." He reached down and pulled out a large brown accordion file.

I stood behind him and watched Schmitty push in his computer's open disc drawer, loaded with the disc he'd pulled from the accordion file. With a couple of clicks, the player whirred to life, and a new window flashed up onto his screen. Images jerked, then started to flow.

It was the security video from Sammy's school.

We watched for a moment, and then Schmitty forwarded the recording to a time that he had written down in his notes. "Here we go." He clicked again, and the video played.

It was shot from a distance. The camera was likely mounted high on the wall in the lunchroom. At first I didn't see her, but then I spotted Sammy sitting alone at a table on the far right. *Alone,* I thought. *My beautiful, smart daughter eats lunch by herself.*

I held my breath as I watched four girls surround Sammy. The video didn't have any sound. There was no way to know what was being said, but the body language wasn't friendly.

The crowding continued for a few minutes, and then Sammy got up to leave. *Good,* I thought. *Walk away.* Sammy made it through the wall of girls. She started toward the dish room window with her tray, but the others followed her. Words were still being said, but Sammy didn't respond. She kept her head down, returned the tray and silverware, and started walking toward the door.

Other kids in the lunchroom were now paying attention. They could sense the situation escalating. They stopped eating and watched. A few stood on their seats and said something, egging on the group hounding Sammy.

Then Sammy walked out the door.

"That's where this one ends." Schmitty leaned over and pressed the "Eject" button. The tray slid out, and he replaced that disc with another. "But this picks it up in the hallway."

The second disc started, and Schmitty pressed the button to forward it ahead. "We'll just jump to the right time." He checked his notes, the images flashed, and he clicked "Play." "Here she comes."

I felt my stomach turn and my hands go cold as I watched Sammy enter the hallway followed, half a second later, by a gaggle of girls. They made it about five yards when the leader—a big girl wearing some sort of purple outfit—edged closer to Sammy. It looked like she whispered something in her ear, and then Sammy turned and pushed her away.

That was when the fight started.

The big girl threw a punch, and it caught Sammy on the right side of her face. She raised her arms to cover herself. Then another girl ran forward and pushed her to the floor. Another one kicked Sammy's side. They circled her as Sammy got up, swinging blindly.

More kids, likely drawn by the commotion, streamed into the hallway.

Schmitty stopped the video. "It goes on like this until the teachers and school resource officer come to break it up." He pressed a small button and the disc ejected. Schmitty leaned over to get it and put the disc back in the file, but I stopped him.

"I want to watch it."

"But you can't really see what's going on from the angle of the security camera. Pretty much the same as that one on YouTube that I showed you before."

"I don't care," I said. "It's my daughter, and I need to see what happened."

He hesitated and then loaded the disc back into the computer. We watched the rest of the chaos play out.

When it was over, I slumped back down in my chair. "What now?"

He shook his head. "Unless you want us to, there's not going to be any charges. We could get a couple of the girls for assault, but the fat girl is claiming self-defense."

"Self-defense?" I shook my head in disbelief. "How's that self-defense?"

"Legally, it's not," said Schmitty. "But they've concocted a whole story about threats that Samantha had made toward them. They say that she was bullying them, and that your daughter was going to come get them with some older boys, so they all decided to stand up to her first before anything happened."

"That's ridiculous." I closed my eyes. "Sammy was surrounded." I said it more to myself than to Schmitty. The peace that I had felt that morning was long gone, and it took everything in my power to keep my cool.

I opened my eyes and saw that Schmitty was looking at me with a helpless expression. "I'm only saying what they told our investigator."

"And the beat-down. That was all in self-defense." My voice was louder than I intended.

"Of course it wasn't." Then Schmitty leaned in and softly repeated himself. "Of course it wasn't, but we gotta be smart. You've gotta be smart. With your brother on the ballot and you maybe making a run for something else, I hear, we should make this go away. No good is gonna come from this." He sat back. "A juvenile judge isn't going to do anything to any of these girls. Maybe some community service, and what does that do? Nothing. Just riles the crazy family up and makes your daughter relive it. Imagine your daughter being cross-examined by some asshole defense attorney." Schmitty stopped himself. "No offense."

I let the comment pass. "So you don't want to press charges against them?"

"No," Schmitty said. "I don't, and neither should you." He began to pack up the notes and police reports, pushing the few small stacks back into the brown folder. "We start doing that, then they start claiming special treatment, and then it's in the newspapers and we get pressure to charge Sammy. Best thing to do is to leave it alone."

"Leave it alone," I repeated dully.

"Good." He shrugged. "And you're not gonna send her back to that school, right?"

"No," I said. "I'm not sending her back there, but I'm sure those girls will soon find a different target. Can't be on top without somebody on the bottom."

Schmitty nodded. "Just like real life."

CHAPTER THIRTY-NINE

The rest of the week passed without anything unusual, except the continuing heat and humidity. Summer wouldn't quit. By mid-September, the heat was supposed to have broken, but it hadn't. When I arrived at the courthouse for Cecil Bates's trial on Monday morning, the temperature hovered around eighty-two degrees, and I could feel the sweat soak through my shirt.

Judge Polansky had scheduled five cases for trial on this Monday morning. Of course it wasn't possible to begin five trials at the same time. It was a hedge. He wanted to clear as many cases from his calendar as possible. Knowing that some defendants wouldn't show up and others would likely plead guilty the moment the jury was called into the room, he called five instead of one, thus potentially moving that many more widgets through the law factory in a single morning.

Sometimes it didn't, but usually the hedge worked.

The clerk banged down the gavel. "All rise," she said. "The Honorable Saul Polansky presiding."

Judge Polansky entered the courtroom from a side door, walked up a few steps, and sat in the large leather chair behind the bench. "Please have a seat." He turned to his computer—a relatively new addition to courtroom—punched a few keys to log in, and called up the cases on the morning docket.

To his clerk: "OK."

The clerk stood. "*State of Missouri versus Tyrone O'Neil.*"

Mr. O'Neil and his defense attorney walked from the back of the courtroom to the front as the prosecutor stood. When they were all situated, the judge instructed them to note their appearances for the record. Both complied, and then Judge Polansky asked the defense attorney about the status of the case.

"My client would like to plead guilty, Your Honor."

Judge Polansky allowed a smile to escape, ever so briefly, and then listened as they outlined the plea agreement, waived the defendant's right to a trial, and laid a factual basis for the guilty plea. The judge scheduled a sentencing hearing in three weeks and then moved on to the next case.

The clerk stood and called the next one. The parties shuffled into position, but this time the defendant had not arrived for trial, and a warrant was issued for his arrest.

Two more cases were called: another no-show and then a dismissal because one of the witnesses was refusing to cooperate.

Finally, the clerk called, "*State of Missouri versus Cecil Bates.*"

I looked over at Cecil and nodded. He nodded back, and then we stood and walked up to the front of the courtroom together.

We noted our appearances on the record as the judge pulled the file up on his computer. All the pleadings and other documents were now electronic. There was no paper record for the court, even though I had been unable to wean myself from the traditional paper files.

"OK." The judge looked at Cecil as would a parent humoring a precocious child. "I remember you." He glanced at his screen. "Charged with drinking in a public park." Then the judge looked at me. "What's the status?"

"My client would like to proceed with trial, Your Honor."

Judge Polansky could barely contain his annoyance. Going to trial meant that he couldn't call another five cases for trial that afternoon. The law factory would have to slow down.

Now conceding that my client was a lost cause, the judge waved the prosecutor, a young lawyer named Cynthia Curtis, and myself forward. "Approach."

Judge Polansky turned off the microphone as Ms. Curtis and I walked up to the bench. He leaned over. "What the hell are you doing?" His question was directed at Ms. Curtis. "You're honestly going to take a misdemeanor drinking in public case to trial?"

Curtis glanced at me. Prosecutors aren't used to being challenged. Usually the wrath of a judge is directed at the recalcitrant criminal, not the knight on the white horse. "Sir?"

The judge's impatience grew. "You dump cases all the time," Judge Polansky said. "What's so special about Mr. Bates? Why are we going to waste three days or more of this court's time on this?"

"Your honor, Mr. Bates is a chronic offender. He's got multiple convictions for drinking in public, public urination, aggressive panhandling—"

Judge Polansky raised his hand, cutting her off. "Exactly. So?" It was a rhetorical question. "He'll be back whether you go to trial or not. You're wasting resources. We could be taking some domestic assaults or robberies to trial. How about them?"

Cynthia Curtis knew enough to know that it was dangerous to argue with a judge, and so she played the only card she had left: she blamed somebody else.

She said, "The deputy told me that dumping the case would reward Mr. Bates for being an obstructionist. He wants a conviction and three months in jail. Get him off the streets, maybe give him a chance to sober up."

"That's your plan, huh?" Judge Polansky looked at me and rolled his eyes, but he was playing us both beautifully. He wanted the prosecutor to know that he wasn't happy with her and also wanted me to hear that my client was potentially facing some significant time in jail.

The judge leaned back. "Well I think you are both assuming a lot of things. This is my only case left for the morning, so I'll take a fifteen-minute break." Polansky looked at his watch. "Talk one more time." To Curtis: "Confirm with your supervisor that he wants to go down this stupid path." To me: "Confirm with your client whether he really wants to spend three months in jail." Then to the both of us: "If you're unable to come to your collective senses, we'll call up the jury in fifteen minutes."

Like scolded children, we both responded in unison. "Yes, Judge."

"And just so you both know." He pointed at me and then to the prosecutor. "Once this trial starts, I don't stop. We go until there's a verdict. I won't accept pleas in the middle of a trial. We go to the end."

◆ ◆ ◆

I met with Cecil in the hallway and did as I was supposed to do. "The prosecutor wants to set an example. Seeking three months in jail and probably a stay-away order, prohibiting you from all downtown parks."

"Three months and then I'm supposed to disappear?" Cecil shook his head. "Where they think I'm going to go?"

I responded half joking. "They're hoping that you go away, like to Kansas City or Chicago. That's what I think. Probably buy you a bus ticket if you want."

"Well that ain't gonna happen." Cecil looked down at the floor, shaking his head. "Don't want to go to jail for that long, neither."

"I know you don't." I put my hand on his shoulder. "But it's our word against the cop's, and I don't think those are good odds."

"You telling me to plead guilty to something that I didn't do?" Cecil looked at me, disappointed. "I'll plead guilty to something that I *did* do. Done it before. Do it in a heartbeat. But I ain't saying I did something that I know isn't true."

"I understand. Only telling you the odds and the consequences. That's what lawyers do."

Cecil looked up at me. "What about my video?"

"What about it?"

"What about it?" Cecil said, mimicking me. His mood had shifted. He was angry now, and the noise brought a deputy into the hall to make sure everything was OK.

I nodded toward the deputy to assure him that the situation was under control, then lowered my voice to Cecil. "I asked for it through discovery, and the prosecutor says that it doesn't exist."

"They lyin'."

"Don't know," I said. "But I can't make them give us something that they claim doesn't exist."

"Well try harder."

Judge Polansky came back onto the bench, still annoyed that he may actually have to preside over a trial. "OK." He looked at me. "Have the parties reached a resolution?"

I shook my head. "No, Your Honor. My client has decided that he would like to exercise his right to go to trial."

The judge looked at Cynthia Curtis. "And you have your witnesses subpoenaed?"

"I do."

Judge Polansky nodded and then gestured for his law clerk to make the phone call down to the jury room in the courthouse basement. "Then we'll bring the panel up, select a jury, and start taking testimony this afternoon."

Both Curtis and I agreed, trying to be respectful.

Then the judge asked, "Anything else we need to put on the record before we get started?"

I hesitated, but then decided that I didn't have much choice. "I do have one thing, Your Honor."

Judge Polansky smirked. "You do?"

"Yes." I looked over at Cecil and then proceeded. It wasn't necessary, but I wanted Cecil to know that he had been heard, in the hope that he'd be calmer in front of the jury if he knew that I had tried. "We made a discovery request for a video that my client believes is in the possession of the Saint Louis Police Department."

One of Judge Polansky's eyebrows raised. "Video?"

"Yes," I said. "I think this case would resolve if we had the video. I requested it through discovery and my client, separately, requested it through Missouri's Freedom of Information Act, but we haven't gotten it."

Cynthia Curtis stepped forward. "That's because it doesn't exist, Your Honor. I asked for it as well. The police have no knowledge of it, and it's not referenced in any police report."

"But there are cameras recording all the activities in that park," I said. "To the extent that the arresting police officer lost the video or never got it as part of his investigation, then I would like permission to question that officer about this critical piece of evidence."

"Your Honor." Curtis raised her voice. "As you know, a defendant cannot impeach a witness with evidence that doesn't exist. There is no video."

Judge Polansky sighed. "Everybody calm down." He looked at me. I could tell he was thinking, *Really? All this about a misdemeanor?* Then he sighed and issued his ruling. "The prosecutor is correct. Absent something more than what you've told me, I can't allow you to ask such questions." He looked at Cynthia Curtis. "She's an officer of the court"—he looked back at me—"as are you, and she has a duty of candor to this tribunal. If she says that the video doesn't exist, then we have to accept that and move on."

CHAPTER FORTY

It took the rest of the morning to select the twelve jurors.

In a murder or a felony assault, jury selection may take a week or more. In a high-profile medical malpractice or civil class action, a company may hire consultants or psychologists to craft the perfect questions to find the jury that is most sympathetic to their case.

Here, jury selection took about an hour and a half. There weren't any fancy questionnaires or trick questions. The prosecutor and I weren't getting paid by the hour. We just needed to get it done.

That meant we were focused on trying to get rid of three types of people: racists, vigilantes, and the anxious. The reasons to rid ourselves of racists and vigilantes were self-explanatory and straightforward. Anxious people were a little more complex. Usually their anxiety stems from the financial hardship that serving on a jury would cause by missing work or having to pay for childcare. Anxious people have a tendency to disrupt jury deliberations or, worse, go to the bathroom in the middle of trial and never come back.

Nobody wanted a mistrial.

Judge Polansky warmly thanked the remaining individuals who were finally selected to serve on the jury. Their numbers had dropped from a total pool of twenty to seven, six jurors and one alternate. "We are now going to break for lunch. The trial will begin in one hour. I need you all to be back in the jury deliberation room so that there are no delays. My clerk will have posted signs indicating where you should go."

The annoyance that Judge Polansky had exhibited all morning with me and Cecil was gone. He had made a shift, playing a new role for the jurors. It was now his job to be a kind and benevolent leader. Judge Polansky looked at the remaining jurors with the pride of a father, then his expression turned serious again.

"In the meantime, you are not to speak to one another about this case, the defendant, the lawyers, or the court. If a family member or friend asks you about this case, you may say that you are now serving on a jury, but you cannot talk about any details. Even saying that you are serving on a criminal jury may elicit a comment or further questions that could result in prejudicing you toward either the prosecution or the defense. It is best to avoid these conversations, as well as any television, newspapers, or Internet."

Judge Polansky took a deep breath, checked the clock, and added, "Finally, no Facebook, Twitter, Instagram, Tumblr, or any other social media." A few of the jurors giggled, and Judge Polanksy shot them a look of concern. "Seriously, you'd be amazed at the number of trials that have to be redone because a juror is live-tweeting the proceedings. It's insane. It's stupid, but it happens, and I feel like I have to tell you not to do it on the record."

Judge Polansky stood. "We will now rise as the jurors exit the room, and then this court will stand in recess until one o'clock."

The prosecutor, Cecil Bates, and I stood. We watched the jury leave the room. Then Cecil turned to me. His anger and bluster were gone. Seeing an actual jury did that to people. The courtroom was theater, and the formalities developed over hundreds of years had the ability to weigh down any person. I'd seen it many times. A juror or defendant would come in with an attitude, or joking about this or that. Then the veneer washed away, and they started to see the genius of the process, however flawed the process might be.

"I'm thinking it'll be OK now." Cecil nodded in agreement with his own observation. "Still know the odds, though. Ain't dumb."

I put my hand on Cecil's back. "We'll do our best."

"Can you call abouts the video request?" He asked it with the contriteness of a child, and I couldn't refuse. I'd follow up even though I knew the video was never going to be provided in time. The bureaucrats that ran the city were not in a hurry to help anybody.

"I'll give it another shot." Then I opened my wallet and took out a ten-dollar bill. It was against the rules of professional responsibility to give a client money, but I didn't care. "Take it."

Cecil hesitated, staring at the money. "I can't, Mr. Glass."

"You need to eat something." I reached out, took Cecil's hand, and placed the ten-dollar bill into his palm. "It'll help you feel better to get some lunch."

Cecil looked down at his hand and nodded. "No booze." It was a command directed at himself, not a promise to me.

I patted him on the back. "Definitely no booze."

We walked out of the courtroom together. No further words. Silence. He went left to the stairs, and I went right to a cluster of small conference rooms.

It was going to be a working lunch. I needed to prepare my opening statement as well as keep up with my practice. I had received three texts that morning, all of them from Emma. She had more appointments scheduled with, and phone calls to, potential clients. She'd also scheduled an interview with the young witness who might've seen his brother get into a van on the night that his brother disappeared, which I needed to confirm.

Then there was the search for Sammy's school. I had decided that we'd continue to visit schools for another week, maybe two, and then it was going to be time to make a decision. She couldn't stay at home forever.

The Judge had called to tell me that there were two school open houses. He also thought I might be interested in attending a fund-raiser for the Children's Defense League. He'd found the invitation when he was going through his mail.

Judge Danny Bryce was the keynote speaker.

CHAPTER FORTY-ONE

After lunch, I saw Cecil in the hallway outside the courtroom. He looked at me. "Any luck with the video?"

Shaking my head, I leaned closer so nobody could hear. "Afraid not, but we'll keep working at it." We walked back into the courtroom together and took our places. A few minutes later the bailiff rapped the gavel and ordered us to rise; then Judge Polansky came into the courtroom.

The judge waved us back down. "Please be seated." He sat, then said to his court reporter, "Off the record." Then back at us: "Don't suppose that either of you were able to reach an agreement over the lunch hour."

Cynthia Curtis stood, looked at me, and then looked back at the judge. "No, Your Honor. Since this is a misdemeanor, there really isn't much room to negotiate."

"Fine." The judge rolled his eyes. "A man can hope, can't he?" He turned back to his court reporter and told her that we were going back on the record. "Before we begin with opening statements, any objections or issues that we need to get on the record?"

Curtis and I responded with the same answer at the same time. "No, Your Honor."

"Then away we go."

◆ ◆ ◆

The prosecutor's opening argument wasn't anything special. It didn't need to be. The case was simple: My client was in a public park. A Saint Louis police officer saw him holding and drinking a bottle of alcohol. The end.

When Curtis finished, I stood and walked toward the jury. I introduced myself once again. "My name is Justin Glass, and I represent Cecil Bates in this matter." I walked to the edge of the jury box, making eye contact with each juror before I went forward with the rest of my opening. "But what the prosecutor just told you is merely their side of the story." I pointed at Judge Polansky. "You see, the judge will very clearly instruct you to keep an open mind and wait until the end of all the testimony and the receipt of all the evidence before making a decision."

I stepped away from the jury box, giving them space. "The government has the highest burden in our entire legal system—beyond a reasonable doubt—and they have the burden to prove every single element. So I ask you to listen to what they have to say, but wait and also hear the other side of the story. After the prosecution rests, we will be given an opportunity to present our witnesses as well."

The last bit was a gamble.

I wasn't sure if Cecil was going to testify or not. If I was being honest with myself, I hoped to keep him as far away from the witness stand as possible. We didn't, however, have many better options.

◆ ◆ ◆

The police officer was going to be the first and only witness for the prosecution. I checked the time, hoping that the State would not rest too early.

I wanted to talk more with Cecil about whether he truly wanted to testify in his own defense, and I also didn't want to be the defense attorney responsible for setting a world record for the quickest conviction by a jury in the history of criminal law.

Officer Butler waddled up to the witness stand. He was squat, a little over five foot eight and about thirty pounds overweight. The combination of his stature and the bulletproof vest made him look like a blue penguin.

He raised his right hand. The judge swore Officer Butler to tell the "whole truth," and then he squeezed into the witness chair.

"Could you state your name for the record?" Curtis picked up her pen and checked off the first question on her list.

The officer stated and spelled his name, and then Curtis went through the first four questions that every prosecutor asks a police officer in a criminal trial:

Are you a licensed peace officer in the state of Missouri?

How long have you been a licensed peace officer?

Where are you currently employed?

How long have you been in that position?

When she was done with the preliminaries, Curtis nodded. "Very good." By her patronizing tone, it wouldn't have surprised me if she had added "Good dog" and offered the police officer a treat.

Having checked the initial questions off her list, Curtis then opened the file. She took a moment and then asked, "Officer Butler, were you working at approximately six thirty in the evening on July 17 of this year?"

"Yes."

"And do you recall where you were on that date and time?"

"Yes, ma'am." Officer Butler nodded. "I was on patrol, going east on Market."

"Can you describe what you saw?"

"I can." Officer Butler turned to the jury and started to describe the scene. His tone was clipped. His language was concise, and he sounded a little bit like a general describing a battle. "A mall or long park runs east-west on the north side of Market. As I approached Fifteenth, a man caught my eye."

"And then what did you do?"

"I decided to park, get out, and approach the man."

"Why?"

"I was concerned. He was slumped over on a park bench. He looked like he was homeless, and I thought he might need medical attention."

Cecil nearly jumped out of his seat, and I put my hand firmly on his arm. I needed to keep him calm, and I also needed to scribble down every word that the officer was saying. None of that information was in his police report.

"Did you approach?"

Officer Butler nodded. "I did."

"And what did you see?"

"I saw a man on a park bench, possibly passed out, with an open container of malt liquor."

"Would you recognize that man if you were to see him today?"

Officer Butler nodded. "Yes, most definitely."

"And do you see him in the courtroom?"

"I do." Officer Butler pointed at Cecil. "He's the gentleman at that table, wearing a blue sweatshirt."

"Thank you." Curtis smiled, then turned to Judge Polansky. "Let the record reflect that the officer has identified Mr. Cecil Bates, the defendant in this matter."

Judge Polansky nodded. "So noted."

Then Curtis continued. "And then what happened?"

"Objection." I stood. "I believe that what occurred after this point is not relevant and will confuse the jury."

Judge Polansky didn't even wait for the prosecutor's argument. "Overruled." He looked at me with disdain. My interruption was not welcome.

Curtis encouraged the officer to continue.

"Thank you." Officer Butler then turned to the jury. "I walked up to Mr. Bates. At that point, I knew who he was because most of the cops that work the downtown area are fully aware of Mr. Bates and his problems."

I was on my feet. "Objection, Your Honor." I put my hands on my hips. "The answer is nonresponsive and this officer is—"

Judge Polansky cut me off with the wave of his hand. "Stop," he said. "Objection is sustained. The witness's statement is struck. The jury is not to consider it. It is not evidence in this case."

I sat back down, knowing that I had won the battle but lost the war. The objection as well as Judge Polansky's instruction did the exact opposite of what was intended. By telling the jury that they were to disregard Officer Butler's statement that the police force knew Cecil Bates "and his problems," the likelihood of them remembering it doubled.

Curtis was pleased. She turned to me and smirked, then continued. "Did you approach Mr. Bates?"

Officer Butler nodded. "I did." He was having fun now. "I was concerned I might need to call an ambulance, so I went up to Mr. Bates and sort of nudged his shoulder to see if he was OK."

"And then what happened?"

"He woke up and was very disoriented and agitated. He wanted to fight me."

"Did you believe he was under the influence?"

Officer Butler nodded. "Most definitely." I wanted to object, but I was too slow. The answer came out and I decided to let it go. No need to highlight another bad fact.

"And then what happened?"

"I called for backup and placed Mr. Bates under arrest."

"And the bottle?"

"The bottle fell and broke." The officer shrugged. "Once Mr. Bates was taken to detox, I took a picture of the broken bottle on the ground."

Curtis stood, then walked over to the court reporter holding three large color photographs. "I'm asking these photographs be marked as State's exhibits one through three."

◆ ◆ ◆

The cross-examination of Officer Butler didn't go badly, but it didn't go particularly well, either. He stuck to his story and didn't get flustered or lose his temper. Officer Butler didn't remember most of the details, but that wasn't too surprising. It had been just another night of work. Cecil Bates was one of hundreds of arrests he made in a month.

By the end of his testimony, even I had a hard time believing that Officer Butler was making the whole incident up.

Judge Polansky looked at the clock. He then looked at me and, out of mercy, decided to end the day a little early.

The judge turned to the jurors. "This court is going to stand in recess until tomorrow morning at nine o'clock. In the meantime, you are not to discuss this matter among yourselves or with anyone else. Although the prosecution rests, the trial is not over. You should avoid all media, television, or Internet. And again, do not discuss this matter with anyone or begin any deliberations."

Judge Polansky looked back at the prosecutor and then at me. "Anything you all need to put on the record before we recess?"

Both of us stood. "No, Your Honor."

"Good." Judge Polansky nodded, and then he stood. "Court is in recess. Please rise and wait as the jurors exit the courtroom."

We did as we were told. As I turned to watch the jurors leave, I noticed that Emma and Nikolas were in the back of the courtroom.

Over lunch, Emma had told me that she was going to be coming down to the courthouse to deliver some files for review and "see me in action." But I was surprised to see Nikolas. Except for the night he was robbed in the alley, I don't think I'd ever seen him outside his little office in the back of the coffee shop.

I turned back to the bench. Judge Polansky and his clerk were gathering up their things. As they left, I walked over to Cynthia Curtis. Quietly, so that Cecil couldn't hear, I asked, "Any chance that plea offer is still on the table?"

Curtis pursed her lips into a cruel smile. "Not a chance, Glass." She put her file into her briefcase and slung it over her shoulder. "It's done. Can't wait to see what the judge does to you." She started to walk away, then stopped and looked back. "My guess is that we have a guilty verdict in twenty minutes. How about you?"

She didn't wait for my answer.

"Not a nice lady." Cecil watched her go.

"I agree." I patted Cecil on the back. "Unfortunately, she's not the worst." Then we walked toward Emma and Nikolas.

We were now the only people left in the courtroom.

"What'd you think?" I asked Emma.

She hesitated, considering my performance. "You didn't drool." She paused. "That's good." Another pause, and then a broad smile, and we all began to laugh.

"Cecil," I said, "let me introduce you to Nikolas. He's Emma's cousin."

"I know." Cecil nodded and held out his hand and the two shook like old friends. "How's our project, Nick-o?"

Nikolas was about to answer, but Emma cut him off, nodding toward me. "That's something Mr. Glass doesn't need to know about."

CHAPTER FORTY-TWO

I missed the tour at Parker Catholic. Although court ended early, I still had to return all the phone calls and e-mails that I couldn't respond to while we were in trial. But I was only ten minutes late for the next one at the South County Day School, SoCo for short. I fought through traffic, got off the highway in Clayton, drove down a frontage road, and then pulled into a long drive leading to the main building.

From the looks of it, SoCo appeared to be twice as expensive as the others that I had seen and probably just as expensive as the many other schools that Sammy and the Judge had toured without me. Its campus, once a farm in the late 1800s, unfolded in a series of a dozen classic buildings nestled among a patchwork of gardens and manicured lawns. Despite the late burst of fall heat, the grass was a perfect hue of vibrant green. Through the copious use of magic chemicals, it was unlikely a dandelion had ever sullied the grounds of SoCo.

I parked the car and started walking up to the main campus building. It was solid brick with a large portico. Four white columns rose up three stories, supporting a base that was crowned with an ornate tower, clock, and bell.

It took a few minutes, but I eventually found the admissions office.

I knocked on the door, was told to come in, and stepped inside. Sammy and the Judge were already meeting with the admissions officer. She smiled at Sammy and then at me. "You must be Justin Glass." She stood and held out her hand. As we shook, she said, "Your daughter is delightful." Then she winked at Sammy, and Sammy looked away, embarrassed and proud at the same time.

The admissions officer sat back down behind her desk. "As I was saying, we hire local artists and grad students from Washington University to come after school and help our students pursue their own individual passions." Then to me, "Our curriculum is structured enough to ensure that each child gets a classic education, but flexible enough to provide the appropriate resources for each child to achieve whatever they've set as their goals. In short, we want a place where it is cool to be smart."

. . . and it'll only cost you $50,000 per year to transform your nerdy kid into a cool one.

◆　◆　◆

For dinner, we all went to Carl's Drive-In off Manchester Road. The commonfolk of Saint Louis swear by Steak 'n Shake, but the enlightened find their way to the little white building with a seating capacity of about sixteen off a divided road creeping toward suburbia.

Carl's was a throwback, a restaurant frozen in 1952.

Usually people have to take their order to go in a white sack and eat in their car. We got lucky and nabbed three barstools at the counter. The Judge sat on one side of Sammy and I sat on the other. We were all smiles, watching the people come and go and watching the cooks smash burgers, fry one basket after another of onion rings, and pour frosty mugs of homemade root beer crafted from the original IBC recipe.

After we ordered, Sammy laughed. "Grandma's gonna be mad she missed this."

I put my arm around her. "Maybe we shouldn't tell."

The Judge joined in, playfully scolding. "Now now, secrets are never good."

"I guess not." I pulled some napkins out of the black and chrome dispenser, and then I asked Sammy what had been on my mind since leaving SoCo. "What'd you think of the schools you saw today?"

She kept her eyes on the griddle of burgers. "They're good." She shrugged.

"Seemed like you thought they were more than good during the tour."

Sammy hesitated and then nodded. "Yeah." She took a deep breath. "But I don't want to get too excited."

"Why's that?"

"Because even if I wanted to go"—Sammy looked at me—"I'm not so sure I can. You know?"

I closed my eyes and nodded. Of course Sammy understood what it would take to go to a school like Baxter or Parker Catholic or SoCo. She wasn't a naive little girl. She understood money and our circumstances. Then I opened my eyes. I pointed my finger and touched the tip of her nose. "You're a good kid, Sammy, but you don't have to worry about that. Let's find the right school, and then I'm the one who's going to make sure you get to go."

Then our food arrived.

◆ ◆ ◆

We felt satisfied walking out of Carl's Drive-In. The sun had set. Although the night was still warm, the temperature had dropped fifteen degrees, and there was a cool breeze that hinted of fall.

I was about to ask Sammy whether she wanted to ride back with me to the house in Compton Heights when my phone rang. The screen indicated that it was Emma.

I pressed the button. "You still working?"

Emma didn't take the bait. She was all business. "You need to come back to the office tonight," she said.

I looked at my watch. "It's late. I'm with my daughter, and I want to go home."

"It's not that late." Emma was annoyed. It's always difficult when the employee is working harder than the boss. "We've got something you need to see. Nikolas and Cecil are here, and we're waiting."

"You need me back right now?"

There was a moment of silence, and then she said, "Why do you think I called you?"

CHAPTER FORTY-THREE

All the lights were on. The little storefront was the only sign of life on the entire street. I couldn't help being curious, despite being tired and wanting to be home. It wouldn't be that long before I'd have to be back in court for the second day of trial.

Emma, however, was not a dramatic woman. Although she liked tight clothes and big jewelry, she was a professional. She wouldn't have ordered me back to the office for no reason.

Then I heard the music coming from inside, and suddenly I had my doubts. It was heavy funk—unless I missed my guess, an early Bootsy Collins cut.

I walked to the office, the music getting louder with every step, and when I opened the door, I saw a little party. Cecil and Emma were dancing. Hermes sat in one of the chairs in the waiting area mixing a drink, and Nikolas sat in the chair behind the front desk rolling a joint.

I stood there, unnoticed, for a few seconds, until Cecil saw me as he spun Emma around and into a dip. "There he is," he shouted over the music. He lifted Emma back up and then pointed at me. "Lawyerman himself."

Emma, Hermes, and Nikolas cheered.

"I thought this was an emergency."

Emma laughed. "More like a miracle." Emma walked toward me, took both of my hands in hers, and looked me in the eyes. "If you don't do something stupid tomorrow, you might actually win a case."

◆ ◆ ◆

Emma sat me down at my desk in front of my computer. Nikolas clicked "Play" and the picture began to move. A weird feeling came over me. The last time I'd watched security footage like this, I'd seen my daughter get beaten up in a school hallway.

Emma assured me it was going to be great. Then she clicked a box, and the picture expanded to full screen. "This is perfect."

It took me a second, but then I realized that I was watching Cecil sitting in the park. The time and date stamp in the upper right corner indicated that it was going to be a video of his arrest. I looked at Emma. "Where'd you get this?"

She didn't answer the question. Emma pointed at the screen. "Just watch."

A minute passed, and then I saw a police car drive slowly past the park where Cecil was sitting and stop. Officer Butler got out of the car, and then he approached Cecil Bates. There was no sound, but already there were contradictions between what I was seeing and the testimony that I had heard at trial.

Cecil was not passed out or sleeping. He was sitting up. He looked alert and seemed to be minding his own business.

At first there was what appeared to be a casual conversation, and then Officer Butler pointed. It was clear that he wanted Cecil to leave.

The mood changed, and Cecil got agitated. He folded his arms across his chest. He wasn't going to leave.

Officer Butler started to walk away, and then he stopped.

"That's when I called him an asshole." Cecil laughed. "Not the smartest thing I ever done."

Officer Butler came back, took out his handcuffs, and told Cecil to stand up. When Cecil didn't move, the officer grabbed Cecil and pushed him to the ground. There was no bottle. There was no alcohol.

"And that's it," Cecil said. "That's what I been sayin' happened."

"OK." I ran my hands down my face and closed my eyes, trying to think about how this video was going to get into evidence. "Let's watch this one more time." I opened my eyes and looked over at Emma and then at Nikolas. "When it's over maybe our resident computer expert can clarify how you happened to come by this little miracle."

Cecil piped in. "Came in the mail from the city, responding to my request."

I couldn't believe that a city department would respond to anything promptly, much less a data practices request for a security video. "I hear what you're saying, Cecil," I said, but I was still looking at Emma and Nikolas. "I just want to talk about it."

CHAPTER FORTY-FOUR

The next morning, I held the envelope out to the prosecutor, but Cynthia Curtis wouldn't look at it. She shook her head, telling me no.

"What do you mean you're not going to watch it?" I kept my demeanor calm. I didn't need to get mad. I had all the leverage. "This is the video footage that I had requested. Remember? It's the video that you told the judge didn't exist. I want to give you an opportunity to see it before I show it to the jury this morning."

"You're not going to show it to the jury." Curtis continued to shake her head. "You can't lay foundation for it. You need a witness to authenticate it, and you don't have one."

"The subpoenas went out this morning," I said. "Whether the city staff show up, I don't know, but I do know that I'm going to get them here one way or another. I'll ask the judge to issue a warrant if I have to."

Curtis turned and stepped away from me. "I don't think so." She wasn't going down without a fight. Prosecutors are like that. They hate to lose, even if the case is over nothing.

"Fine." I began walking down the hallway. "Just going to go talk to the judge." I pointed at the hallway that led toward Judge Polansky's chambers. "You coming?"

"I'm not going to talk to the judge." Curtis didn't move and refused to look at me. She was in full-tantrum mode, reminding me of a younger Sammy.

◆ ◆ ◆

I rang Judge Polansky's chambers. The intercom beeped, and his clerk said, "Chambers."

"Yes." I bent over, getting closer to the old wall speaker. It had all been state of the art about fifty years ago; now it was quaint. "This is Justin Glass. We've had a development in the *Cecil Bates* case. I need to talk to the judge before we call the jury in."

"Fine." The door buzzed. The lock retracted, and I was able to enter a long, narrow hallway. At the end, there was another hallway with two judicial chambers and direct entrances to the courtrooms.

I followed the signs, and eventually found Judge Polansky's chambers. His law clerk looked up from her desk, then got up and led me back to the judge. "He's waiting."

"Thanks." I walked into the formal chambers. Then to Judge Polansky, I said, "Good morning, Judge."

"Good morning." His back was turned to me. The judge was hacking away at his computer. "One second. Got all these e-mails, like Whac-A-Mole. I get one out and two more come in."

Judge Polansky pressed "Enter," and then turned. "What's going on?" he asked, but before I could answer, he held up his hand. "Where's Ms. Curtis?"

I wanted to tell him that Ms. Curtis was pouting in the hallway, but thought better of it. "She didn't want to come in, Your Honor. I wanted her here, but I wasn't going to force her."

Judge Polansky grew suspicious. "Why doesn't she want to come back?" Judges are always concerned about having conversations with attorneys without the opposing party being present. It's against the rules, although some judges follow the rules better than others.

"Well"—I paused, thinking about the best way to phrase it—"we have an evidentiary issue. It's a big deal. I don't want the jury to hear the arguments and cause a mistrial. I'd like your advice as to how to proceed."

"Seems fair." Judge Polansky nodded. "I'll send my clerk to get her." He pointed back to his outer chamber. "Have a seat out there until she comes."

◆ ◆ ◆

If I thought that the prosecutor's mood would improve upon further time and reflection, I was wrong. Cynthia Curtis shot me a look that I wouldn't soon forget as she entered the judge's chambers. I was going to pay for this.

Upon seeing her, Judge Polansky smiled. "Good, I'm glad you could make it, Ms. Curtis." His sarcasm was clear. The judge pointed at the chairs in front of his desk. "Now please have a seat."

We both sat down across from him.

Once settled, Judge Polansky took control. "We have a jury waiting, and Mr. Glass has something that he'd like to discuss." He checked his watch. "I hope we can get this resolved quickly, because we've already wasted a lot of time."

"Yes, thank you." I sat up a little straighter and moved to the edge of my seat. "As stated prior to trial, we have been seeking out a security camera video from the City of Saint Louis. It was part of my formal discovery request, and also my client, without my knowledge, sent an open records request to the city on his own prior to trial."

Judge Polansky nodded. "I remember."

"Ms. Curtis insisted that no recording existed, and I believe that she sincerely thought that what she was telling the court was true." I reached into my briefcase and pulled out the large envelope. "But my client received this in the mail yesterday." Instead of handing it to Judge Polansky, I handed it to Cynthia Curtis. I wanted to force her to touch it and acknowledge that everything about it was authentic. "As you can see, it was sent in an official envelope from the city and postmarked last week, but just arrived. Inside, there is a letter from a city clerk acknowledging receipt of my client's information request, as well as a digital recording of the evening in question."

The judge's eyes narrowed and he leaned back in his chair. "And I suppose you've watched this video?"

"I have, Your Honor, and it's exactly what my client has been saying all along. In short, it directly contradicts the officer's sworn testimony. There was no bottle. There was no drinking."

Judge Polansky nodded, absorbing everything that I had said. He wasn't simply thinking about Cecil Bates. I could tell that his mind had started to contemplate other repercussions. A police officer had lied under oath. How many other cases had he testified in? There was potential civil liability for the city and more bad headlines.

The judge turned to the prosecutor. "Ms. Curtis, thoughts?"

"It's a completely unfair surprise, Your Honor. We are in the midst of trial, and I have already rested. This is prejudicial and not timely, not to mention that this so-called video hasn't been authenticated. It may be altered."

"Altered?" Judge Polansky had become irritated. "You are digging a deeper hole for yourself, Ms. Curtis. So I suggest you take a different approach. Humbleness is a virtue, and so is admitting when you're wrong."

Ms. Curtis ignored Judge Polansky's advice. "We don't know what's on this recording. We don't know anything."

"You don't know, because you don't want to know. Mr. Glass offered to show it to you this morning." Judge Polansky's voice was rising. "Unless you're honestly arguing that a homeless man stole an envelope from the City of Saint Louis, forged a cover letter from a city clerk, and digitally altered security footage. Is that your position?"

"I'm saying we don't know." That was the best Curtis could do, and Judge Polansky wasn't going to push her any further. He didn't need to. He was the judge.

"Well then, why don't we all watch the tape together and go from there."

CHAPTER FORTY-FIVE

We stood as the jury came back into the courtroom. Their shoulders were slumped. Some were tired. Some were annoyed. Some were curious. Others were all three. If I had been trapped in a small jury room all morning with no explanation, I think I'd have been in the annoyed category, bordering on anger.

As the jury got to their seats, Judge Polansky instructed us all to sit down. "Thank you." He looked down at his docket. "We are back on the record in the file 23-MD-15-2258, *State of Missouri versus Cecil Bates.* May I have the attorneys note their appearances for the record?"

The prosecutor stood. "Cynthia Curtis on behalf of the State." Then she sat down. Her thunder and confidence were gone.

Then I stood. "Your honor, I am Justin Glass on behalf of my client, Cecil Bates, who is present and seated to my left."

As I sat down, Judge Polansky turned to the jury. "You are probably wondering what is going on." He smiled, hoping to soften them a little before they got the news. "We've had an evidentiary issue come up this morning, and that was the reason for the delay. I truly apologize for the inconvenience." He paused, weighing his words. "While you were all waiting patiently, the attorneys and I were hard at work. The attorneys also had time to discuss this matter in greater detail among themselves, and they have reached a resolution. Therefore, your service on this jury is no longer necessary, and you are excused."

The jurors looked confused. Although many may not have wanted to serve on a jury, once they were sworn and the trial began, they had become invested in the process. Their sudden dismissal didn't feel right.

"Again," Judge Polansky said, "I do appreciate your time and consideration, but your service is no longer necessary. I ask that we rise for the jury as they exit the courtroom. You may all gather your things from the jury deliberation room and go back home or to work, however you wish to spend the rest of the day."

Judge Polansky then stood, and we followed his lead.

The jurors also stood and exited the courtroom. Once they'd gone and his law clerk indicated that it was appropriate for the court to proceed, Judge Polansky sat back down. "Ms. Curtis, you have something to put on the record."

"Yes, Your Honor." Cynthia Curtis looked at Cecil Bates for a moment, then back at the judge. "In light of the disclosure this morning, the State is withdrawing its criminal complaint against Mr. Bates."

"And you understand that"—Judge Polansky leaned in—"since we have picked a jury and started trial, that double jeopardy has attached and that the State may no longer pursue any charges against Mr. Bates for the alleged crimes on this date?"

"Yes, Your Honor, although I don't expect that we've seen the last of Mr. Bates."

The judge let the comment slide. He turned to me. "And, Mr. Glass, any other thoughts?"

"No, Your Honor. I'm glad to see that Ms. Curtis changed her mind, and I appreciate the court's guidance as we worked through the various issues prior to court this morning."

"Justice is done." Judge Polansky smiled.

Sometimes, I thought. *Sometimes.*

CHAPTER FORTY-SIX

The Children's Defense League fund-raiser started at five thirty with a silent auction, followed by dinner at six thirty and the speech at seven o'clock. I ran late, as usual. My mother, Sammy, and the Judge had been thoroughly enjoying my recap of all that had transpired with Cecil Bates after our visit to Carl's Drive-In, and I didn't want the good times to end. Sammy had particularly enjoyed my impression of the prosecutor's refusal to even look at the evidence.

I was following it up with my rendition of the prosecutor's final tortured decision to pull the plug on her dying case when I glanced at my watch. I realized that the fund-raiser had already started, and, to make matters worse, it wasn't until I was halfway to the downtown Crowne Plaza that I figured out the ticket was still in my office.

I signaled and looped back on Thirteenth to North Florissant, then I found a spot to park and hustled inside my office. Emma had left the ticket in an envelope right in the middle of my desk. I swept it up and left in a matter of seconds, but as I was locking the front door, I noticed that lights in the Northside Roastery were still on. Usually they didn't stay open past five. There wasn't the business to justify staying open late.

My curiosity piqued, I walked down the block to make sure everything was OK.

Looking in the window, I saw Hermes on his knees. He had a wrench in one hand and a sheet of instructions in the other. Around him was a collection of metal parts, screws, and pieces of some type of equipment.

I tapped on the window to get his attention.

Hermes turned, saw me, and smiled. He got up, came to the door, and welcomed me inside.

"What are you working on?"

"Oh . . ." He looked at the instructions in his hand and then at the pile of parts on the floor. "New refrigeration unit, hopefully."

"Gonna stay late?"

Hermes nodded. "Need to get this done. Nikolas also here, too, so I not want to leave him alone."

"In the back?" I looked past Hermes to the opening leading to the storage area and the little office where Nikolas had a desk and multiple computer screens surrounded by a mess of wires and hard drives. "Mind if I go back there and say hello?"

Hermes shrugged. "No problems to me. Emma say you had a big day in court."

"Absolutely." I wished Hermes luck in assembling his refrigerator and then walked through the curtain to the back of the shop. At this point, I knew I was going to be late to the fund-raising dinner, regardless. A few more minutes wasn't going to change that, and something had been nagging at me since I first heard about the security video footage and Emma's insistence that it was fine.

I knew the video wasn't fake. It was time-stamped and everything. The letter that had accompanied the disc and the envelope that held them were real, too, but something about the process was off. Maybe Nikolas would tell me, now that the trial was over.

He had his back to me, whacking away on a keyboard. I knocked on the door frame. "I know I've already asked, but now do you want to tell me how you did it?"

He turned around. "Excuse me?"

I stepped farther into his little office. "How you did it?" I asked again. "I'm not going to be mad. It's done. I'm just curious about how you made it happen."

Nikolas grunted and shook his head. "Emma warned me about you." He waved me away. "She says you're smarter than you let on. Pretending to be a regular guy, but not regular guy."

There wasn't an empty chair, so I crouched down to put us at the same level. "I know you did something, but I want to know how. Why not tell me?"

"Don't know what you are talking about." Nikolas held his hands out wide, feigning innocence. "I'm but a humble computer salesman. Give you good deal on eBay."

"I don't believe that for a second, and I'm not leaving until you tell me." I stood, leaned against the wall, and crossed my arms.

Nikolas tried to go back to work but couldn't concentrate. "You gonna be there all night?"

"Better than a chicken dinner in a hotel ballroom."

Again Nikolas tried to work, and again he gave it up. "OK, OK." He shrugged. "But don't tell Emma I said anything. You do not want that woman mad at you, believe me." Another shrug. "I do nothing illegal." He hesitated and then revised his last statement. "Perhaps I do nothing really, truly illegal."

"That's a start."

Nikolas sighed. "OK, like I said, it's no big deal . . . So Emma comes over here. She tells me about this case and your client who won't shut up about the video. He drive her nuts. Every day, he call her about the video. Not shutting up. So she says to me, can you help? And I says, for you and Mr. Justin, OK."

"And then . . ."

"I figure out who handles the requests at the city, and I see that the requests are logged and kept in an electronic queue."

I left alone for the moment the question of how Nikolas happened to unearth this list, which I couldn't imagine was posted on the city's public website. "But this electronic queue," I said, "it's no good?"

"Correct." Nikolas nodded. "The list has Cecil Bates like . . . at the end. Be a year before they get to him. So I bumped him to the top of the list."

So he'd not only accessed this queue, he'd manipulated it. The arrival of the miracle video was losing some of its miraculous patina. "And that's it?"

Nikolas seemed confused by my question. "You want that to be it? If you want—it can be all I do. It be it. Finished."

"No." I shook my head. "I want to know whether you did anything else."

"Sure?"

"I'm sure," I said, although I really wasn't.

"Well last week, Emma says the trial is coming, and we're running out of time."

"And . . ."

"So help the city along a little more." Nikolas considered his words. "I make them more efficient. Here. I show you."

◆ ◆ ◆

It was unclear how Nikolas entered the city's computer system. A blur of keystrokes, and the screens in front of him started to flash. Text and binary numbers scrolled as Nikolas toggled between them. "Takes a few minutes." He typed something when a cursor began to flash, then did the same when another screen changed color.

"What is all this?"

Nikolas didn't hesitate or stop working as he responded to my question. "The network."

"The city's network?"

"In a sense, yes." Nikolas continued to type on his keyboard and move his cursor from one screen to the next, explaining. "You see, all the pretty graphics and buttons on your regular computer . . . it's an illusion. Skin on the body." He stopped, looked at me, and pointed back at the various screens. "These are the guts. This is everything happening behind what you see."

He looked at a yellow Post-it Note on his desk, then typed in a username and password. Text scrolled down the screen, and then he reviewed a list of subfolders. "The security videos are here." Nikolas pointed at a folder named ZZ, and then he pointed at a file about halfway down the list, identified as VID10283740283-ZZ-7-BB-2015. "That's the one. Each traffic or park camera on the street has a letter identification. This is camera ZZ, and then each day has its own file. So I open it like this." He pressed a button. "You see how I now find the video, here, and then I send it via e-mail to the clerk who is responsible for the data requests."

A flash of dread. I wondered whether there was any kind of trail that could lead back to me. "You sent it to her?"

"Yes and no." Nikolas shrugged. "Figured out who does this at the city, and I use his e-mail account to send it to her. Once she got it, she sends it to Cecil."

"You helped them along." *By illegally accessing a public employee's e-mail account and using it to forward a file you plucked from the city's servers.* "Very efficient."

Nikolas smiled. "Exactly. I helped. I make them very efficient for you. Very American."

CHAPTER FORTY-SEVEN

The ballroom at the Crowne Plaza was filled to capacity; probably five hundred people were in attendance. In the back, there was a cash bar and tables for the silent auction. The tables were filled with sports tickets, restaurant gift certificates, celebrity autographs, gift baskets, and bottles of wine.

On the other end, there was a stage, two giant screens, and Judge Danny Bryce at the podium. He was a thin man with an athletic build.

His keynote address had already started, and nearly everybody else, except me, was seated politely at their assigned tables.

Rather than make a scene trying to find my table, I instead went to the bar. "Gin and tonic."

The bartender nodded and went to work. I put my money down, and he handed me the drink. When he made change, I told him to keep it, then turned and listened to Judge Bryce.

He was a charismatic speaker. I'd looked into him a little. Appointed young, he had fifteen years on the juvenile bench well before his fiftieth birthday. He was passionate about kids and had been the presiding judge over the juvenile division for years.

He took the microphone off its little stand and walked away from the podium with it, pacing the stage like a preacher. His image projected even larger on the screens. "Every day," he said, "I see kids with nobody. Thirteen-, fourteen-, fifteen-year-old kids charged with serious crimes." He shook his head. "I look down from the bench, and I see lawyers and probation officers, but I often don't see a parent with these kids. I don't see a grandma or an aunt or a cousin. I don't see anybody. This kid is there, all alone in the courtroom—and the system is supposed to fix that."

Judge Bryce ran his hand through his hair. "Let's be honest with one another: the system can't fix that." He took a moment, taking a deep breath and letting it out. "But you all can. The people in this room. You're the educated. You're the powerful. You're the elite, and you can make a difference in the lives of the at-risk kids in our community."

Here his voice intensified. He gripped the mic with both hands. "But I'm telling you—however hard this is to hear—I'm telling you it has to happen *before* those kids ever set foot in a courtroom or are placed in the back of a squad car. Once they get involved in the criminal justice system, our likelihood of success—our likelihood of any kind of meaningful intervention—plummets.

"Back in the 1990s I was very young—a baby judge. I created a new model. We brought together folks from all different disciplines—social workers, psychiatrists, doctors, teachers, community mentors, cops—and we wrapped ourselves around the kids entering the system. And we had tremendous success. People called it a miracle. But that was well over twenty years ago. Times have changed. The types of kids we're dealing with have changed. They're harder. The wraparound works, but it's not as effective as it once was. There are certain kids that are too far gone for the system to reach—ever. Once they're in, they'll continue to be in and out of correctional institutions for the rest of their lives—a life sentence, on the installment plan—and they'll leave a trail of victims along the way.

"I'll keep doing what I can on my end, but let's not wait for miracles. Let's act. Support the Children's Defense League and help these kids before they come to me. We need to focus on the younger ones, ten and under. That's where we'll be successful. We have to *act* to save the kids who can be saved."

The man really is a firebrand, I was thinking, when I felt a tap on my shoulder.

It was Annie. She smiled.

I smiled back. "Madame Mayor."

"Mr. Glass." She turned and ordered a glass of wine from the bar. "Heard you might be coming to this."

"And how's that possible?"

"Power has its privileges." She took the glass of red wine from the bartender and paid. "I have spies everywhere, you know?"

"Should've known that."

"Feeling better about your brother?"

I didn't respond right away, because I wasn't sure how to answer. With the trial and Sammy and the Lost Boys, I'd been too busy to think much about it. "I guess."

"Well"—she took a sip of wine—"I think you made the right decision."

"Figured you'd say that." I quietly laughed and shook my head. "Because you didn't want to share me with anybody else. Keep me on the down-low."

Annie nodded. "Perhaps." We listened to Judge Bryce a little longer, and then Annie leaned in closer. "Got plans for later?"

"Don't know."

She paused, thinking over my response. Then she reached into her clutch purse and removed a small envelope from the hotel. A room number was written on the outside. A key was inside. "If you're available, maybe we could meet." Annie slid the envelope with the key into the front pocket of my suit jacket.

She touched my shoulder. Then Annie walked away.

◆ ◆ ◆

As most of the crowd gathered their things and filed out the door, I worked my way up to the stage. There were a half dozen people gathered around Judge Bryce. I waited along the wall for the various well-wishers to say their words of thanks and praise.

Eventually Judge Bryce was alone, and I walked up to him. He was in his midfifties but looked younger. He had a full shock of hair, and his face was lean, like a runner's.

"I know you want to get out of here," I said, "but my paralegal and your law clerk have been exchanging e-mails, trying to find a time for us to meet, so I decided that I'd do it the old-fashioned way and just introduce myself to you in person." I held out my hand and we shook. "I'm Justin Glass. My dad is Congressman Glass, and my grandpa is Judge Calhoun."

Judge Bryce nodded. "Of course. I should've known. Seen you in the newspaper." He smiled. "And I also read in the paper that Congressman Glass announced that he's calling it quits." He took a step back and raised his eyebrows. "Lucky man."

"He'd be the first one to call himself lucky, I'm sure, but I don't think he's actually retiring."

"Politicians never do." Judge Bryce subtly looked at his watch and then back at me. "What can I do for you?"

"Well you may have heard that I'm representing some of the families of those boys that have gone missing. It's been in the newspaper."

Judge Bryce nodded. "Oh I've seen it. I even recognized some of those kids from court."

"My grandpa thought you'd be a good person to talk to about it. Nothing specific, just about the juvenile court and anything else you might know."

"I'm always happy to talk to people about what I do . . . or don't do . . . or, more likely, what I try to do with somewhat mixed results."

"You're being modest."

"No"—Judge Bryce smiled and laughed—"I'm being honest." Then he put his hand on my shoulder. "When I first got sworn in and put on that black dress, I was pretty naive. Then you start seeing the kids of the kids that you tried to save coming into the system. That's when reality hits."

Judge Bryce took a business card out of his pocket. He wrote his cell phone number on the back and handed it to me. "Pretty tired right now after all this. Call me and I'll give you a grand tour of the juvenile courthouse, and we can maybe find someplace more private to talk."

"I'd love to hear your thoughts."

"I'm sure you'd love to hear some gossip, too."

◆ ◆ ◆

Like all middle-aged men who were about to have a romantic liaison in a fancy hotel, I called my mother first to ask for permission.

She told me that Sammy was reading a book in the library with the Judge. She'd tell her that I was working late and that she should sleep in the guest bedroom at the main house. We talked a little about when I might be home, keeping it vague. Then the conversation wound down, and my mother's last words were, "Everything will be fine here."

I can't imagine that she approved, but at the same time, she also knew better than anyone where I'd been and what I'd gone through since Monica died. Perhaps any relationship was better than no relationship at all.

As weird as our exchange was, it set me at ease. I didn't want Sammy waking up in the middle of the night only to find out that she was alone.

On the elevator to the eleventh floor, I thought about Annie and her marriage that wasn't really a marriage, and about our relationship that wasn't really a relationship. After a month of absence and avoidance, we were finally coming together, but I didn't know why.

The doors slid open, and I walked down the hallway, figuring out how the rooms were numbered.

Our room was at the end.

I slid the key out of the envelope, stuck the card in the slot, and waited for the click of the lock as a small green light turned on.

I opened the door.

Light from the hallway cut into the room, but the rest was dark.

I stepped inside, the door closing behind me, and then I saw Annie on the bed. There was a single candle on the nightstand, burning behind her. It cast Annie in a silhouette. A sheet covered her, but I knew that she was naked underneath.

I took off my shoes and then my jacket. My tie was undone, and then I took off my dress shirt. Annie reached out to unbuckle my belt, and I bent forward to kiss her forehead and then her lips.

She didn't say a word. It was silent, and everything seemed staged. Her movements were slower than normal, more deliberate and thoughtful. Nothing was rushed. Annie's constantly buzzing phone was nowhere to be seen.

That's when I understood what we were doing. I figured out why Annie had slid the hotel room key into my pocket, and why Annie offered an invitation after so much time and distance.

She was saying good-bye, once and for all.

CHAPTER FORTY-EIGHT

I think I should've been more upset about the end. I wasn't happy, but I wouldn't exactly say that I felt sad, either. Part of me wondered whether Annie and I even had a relationship. Two lonely people who had found someone to lie next to at night, maybe that's all we were. Perhaps I wasn't upset that it ended because it had never started.

In any event, it was resolved.

Most men my age were either single by choice or divorced. I wondered whether a widowed man who still loved his deceased wife could ever really find love again, whether there were parts that would never be available because of the loss.

Those thoughts kicked around my head as I drove to the office the next morning after going home to shower and put on a fresh set of clothes.

When I walked in the door, Emma was already there. "Have a good night?" She smiled like she knew that I didn't sleep in my own bed.

"It was OK." I walked to the back but stopped in the doorway. "You happen to talk to the mayor yesterday about where I was going to be?"

She hesitated. "Maybe."

"Well it wasn't such a terrible breach of confidentiality, if you did." I continued on into my office. "Quite enjoyed it, in fact."

I sat down at my desk and turned on my computer. Then I pulled up my e-mails and calendar for the day.

Emma had scheduled me to attend the funeral for Devon Walker. She hadn't previously mentioned it to me, and if she had, I would have come up with some excuse. But my mood had shifted.

Taking control of Sammy's schooling, winning the *Cecil Bates* trial, and saying good-bye to Annie on good terms gave me a sense that I might be stepping out of the darkness. Fragmented pieces of my life had fallen away. I felt focused rather than overwhelmed.

There was also something else that was new: a little bit of confidence, threatening to grow.

◆ ◆ ◆

After the church service, I was glad that the interment was going to be at Bellefontaine Cemetery, and it wasn't just because of its proximity to the office. Devon Walker was a kid who probably never knew nature. He never had peace. He was never confronted by the larger picture or surrounded by beauty, but in this place, there would be no escaping it.

As the line of twenty-five cars drove through the main gate and onto the 314-acre property, the procession drove past the manicured gardens, mausoleums, fountains, small lakes, and brooks. Century-old trees provided shade and lined paths that wound through the tombs of the city's famous and infamous.

We stopped at the far edge.

There was an elaborate gate that was no longer in use. In the past it had served those arriving at the cemetery by streetcar.

I turned off the engine, removed the key, and stepped out into the heat.

I waited a moment and watched the pallbearers remove the casket from the back of the hearse, then I followed them to the gravesite along with family members and friends. I hung back from the group, but I was still able to see and hear.

The pastor stepped forward.

I recognized his face from the billboards. Each advertisement had a picture of him and his wife with a website address for the Church of Everlasting Love, as well as a promise for a hot meal after every service.

"My name is Reverend Harold Battle, and I bless each and every one of you. I want to thank y'all for being here today." He paused. "I ain't gonna pretend that I knew Devon Walker. Truth is, I ain't never met him. I also hadn't ever met his mama or the rest of the family until they called me this week to help lead this service." Reverend Battle held up his hand. "But that's OK. Never too late to call. Never too late to put a little God in your life."

Reverend Battle took a moment to look at the family members that were gathered to his right. He smiled at the mother and nodded. His grace filled the space. All was forgiven.

I looked at Tanisha, dressed in her Sunday best. She had been crying but was now trying hard to be strong. Her siblings and cousins were also standing in the line, some fidgeting more than others. The toddler, Dice, had already wandered off to play by himself under a tree. That's what he liked to do.

My initial instinct was to dismiss Reverend Battle as a huckster, but the more he talked, the more I liked him. It'd been a long time since I'd attended church or listened to a preacher. Maybe I needed to go again. Maybe Sammy needed to learn that there might be something more out there, even if she later went her own way, like most do.

I had become one of the growing number of people who claimed to be spiritual, not religious—whatever that meant. Whether I believed in God or not was an open question. It's hard to maintain faith when life gives you such pain and organized religion seems to have been co-opted by the cruel and self-righteous.

But on this day, Reverend Battle's words about redemption rang true.

"This is one of the biggest cemeteries in the country," the pastor continued. "Eighty-seven thousand people are buried here. All races. All classes. All religions. Rich. Poor." He paused. "It is truly sad that this is the most diverse neighborhood in Saint Louis. Truly sad that the most diverse neighborhood in our city is one for the dead and not the living.

"We have much work to do." Reverend Battle looked at me. "You have work to do."

CHAPTER FORTY-NINE

I found a quiet table in the back of the Beale Street BBQ after the funeral service. Beale's always had a steady stream of customers, but there was never a long line like there was at Pappy's Smokehouse. The food was just as good, but Beale's was harder to find and located in a tougher part of town.

It was small, probably six tables, and served mostly take-out meals to the hardhats. They worked at the chemical plants between I-70 and the Mississippi River.

I opened my white Styrofoam container and the smell of sweet, acidic sauce burst up from a pile of pulled pork. I dumped the coleslaw that came with it on top of the pork, Memphis style, then took a long drink of sweet tea and got to work.

There were a dozen boys that were gone and a dozen families that deserved answers. I hadn't sought the job, but it was mine. If the police weren't going to follow all the leads, then I'd have to do it for them. I'd need to learn their files and their backgrounds for myself, not just rely on Emma and her spreadsheets. Their mothers needed to trust me, and I needed to trust myself with them.

I took a big bite of my sandwich, wiped my fingers clean, and pulled a notepad and pen from my briefcase. I took another drink of sweet tea, allowed the sugar to jolt up my brain, and made a list.

The first thing that I needed to do was personally interview all the family members of every identified Lost Boy, thoroughly. What we had wasn't going to be enough. Second, I needed a copy of each boy's file. I knew that we had some, but Schmitty needed to get me a copy of everything ever connected to the boys. Third, I needed to follow up with Judge Bryce. If I should be looking even closer at Jimmy Poles, he'd be the one to tell me where to look.

CHAPTER FIFTY

I had wanted Emma to shut down my law practice so that I could focus solely on the missing boys, but I knew that wasn't going to happen. I wasn't just a street lawyer anymore, and my obligations went far beyond finding a paying client to fix a broken air conditioner.

Lawyers needed to bill. Emma needed to get paid, and I needed to take care of my daughter's education. So I made a compromise with myself.

Each morning would be spent on the care and feeding of existing clients as well as nurturing more. When there weren't any court appearances, the afternoons would be spent sifting through the boxes of documents, police reports, and court histories that Schmitty had sent over related to each victim. Then there was the second round of family interviews. In the evening, after Sammy went to bed, I'd have to evaluate whether to work on paying clients or the Lost Boys, but having a beer and watching television wasn't going to be an option.

I knew the system was unsustainable in the long run. It'd eventually kill me if it went on too long, but in the meantime, it worked.

Over the next few weeks our spreadsheet of data grew. I got to know them all personally, but in truth, I was still no closer to finding the actual proof that Jimmy Poles was responsible or a link to anyone else. I felt myself losing some steam, so I decided to get out from behind my desk.

◆ ◆ ◆

I grabbed my briefcase and walked into the main reception area. "I'm getting out of here."

Emma said good-bye to whoever she was talking to and hung up the phone. "Where you going?"

"I need to talk to the Turner family." Emma had scheduled them to come back for an interview with me four times. Two interviews were cancelled at the last minute by the mother, due to sick kids or transportation. The other two times they didn't show up. "They're the only ones who have something concrete, and I haven't even heard the information myself. All secondhand. Should've talked to them right away, a month ago. You got the address for me?"

Emma pressed a few keys on her keyboard, pulled up a document, and wrote down the address on a Post-it Note. "Here you go." She handed the little yellow square piece of paper to me. "Good luck."

"Thanks." I read the address and nodded. "If they're not going to come to me, I'll go to them."

"Fair." She turned her attention back to her computer screen. "Just don't forget you've got court tomorrow morning and a meeting with Judge Bryce tomorrow afternoon."

"I won't forget."

"Good," she said. "Because you still have to pay my salary."

CHAPTER FIFTY-ONE

The boy kept looking at his mother. There were stutters and stops as he kept his head and eyes down. "Go on," she encouraged him as I waited.

It took some time, but eventually Isaac Turner started to talk. It was circular, in the way that kids talk, but once it started it came in a flow that seemed beyond Isaac's age.

"Was hanging out. Bored 'n' all that. Gone down to Popeyes, see what's going on—who there—and then TeeTee wanted to talk to these girls at the bus stop and these other kids were throwing, talking about staining somebody for some ganja."

"TeeTee is your brother, Thomas Turner?"

"Yeah, and then these other kids were throwing and TeeTee wants to talk to the girls, you know, and I was getting tired and I wanted to go into Popeyes to get something to eat, you know? But we didn't have no money, and so TeeTee just went ahead and talked to thems girls, and the other nig—"

"Don't say that word," I said. "We don't say that word."

"What?" He looked at me, and then he looked at his mother.

She told Isaac to continue, and Isaac's eyes went back down to the floor as his flow of words started again. "So we gots to be hassled by them guys and one of them flashes his nine, you know?" Isaac made a quick movement with his hand, imitating someone pulling a gun. "So he flashes his gat, and I tell him we gotta go, because it's getting real, and we walks away, and then TeeTee says he needs to chill and needs to hit some chronic for his glow, man, and so . . ." He looked over at his mother, and she nodded at Isaac to keep going, despite his repeated references to guns and marijuana. "So we decide to head back home to see if we can find somebody who's gotta stash, 'cuz we ain't got no money, and so we get on our street and we walking, and I say I gotta take a piss, and that's when I duck by this building and TeeTee keeps walkin' a bit. He's not waitin' 'cuz he's wantin' the chax, you know? So I come out and that's when I sees it."

I leaned closer, and Isaac said, "Po-Po van, clear as day."

"A police van?"

Isaac shook his head. "Naw, like the probation. They drives them blue vans. I see TeeTee talking to somebody through the window, and then he gets in the van and they drive off."

"There are lots of blue vans."

Isaac looked up, staring at me. "I know what I seen, man, and that's what I seen. Blue van. Probation. They got him, man, and they the ones who killed him."

"You're sure."

"Yeah."

Then I looked at Isaac's mother. "And you're sure about the date?"

"Positive." She looked at her son. "He be coming home and telling me TeeTee got arrested. That's when I start calling the detention center, find out his court dates and all that, but they say he ain't there." The mother opened her purse, took out her cell phone, pressed a button, and handed the cell phone to me.

I looked down at it.

The mother, Naomi Turner, had pulled up the cell phone's call history. "Thems numbers there." She pointed.

When I checked the number, there were twelve calls to the Saint Louis Juvenile Justice Center. I wrote down the dates and times of the phone calls in my notebook, and then I looked at both of them.

"Ever hear of a probation officer named Jimmy Poles?"

Isaac Turner and his mother shook their heads. "Never heard of him."

◆ ◆ ◆

I called Schmitty on my drive back to the office. Adrenaline pumped. I was getting closer, and I had to work to keep my voice steady, staying professional.

"Hey, this is Glass." I told him Isaac Turner's story, trying to include every detail. "One of the few cases that we actually have with a solid date of disappearance. The other ones are a total guess. Might give you something to work on with Poles, see if you can figure out where he was on the date Isaac's brother disappeared. See if he's got an alibi."

"Might be a break," Schmitty said, then sighed. "Wish it wasn't an inside job."

"Well," I said, "that ain't exactly my problem."

CHAPTER FIFTY-TWO

After a moderately successful morning as a lawyer, I ate lunch at the Northside Roastery and then drove down North Grand and over to the Juvenile Justice Center. The JJC was tucked behind Saint Louis University's ever-expanding sprawl. On one side, pristine athletic fields. On the other, vacant lots and barbed wire.

From the outside it looked like a worn-down 1970s school, featuring light-tan brick and futuristic curves. The arches were likely intended to mirror the famous Gateway Arch, but these arches weren't dramatic. They were squat, resulting in a building that looked like it was frowning at you.

Inside, it wasn't much better. The lighting was dim. The linoleum tiles were chipped at the edges, and everything smelled like cleaning antiseptic.

I went through the metal detectors. As I walked through the security gauntlet, the machine beeped loudly. A beefy private security guard pulled me aside and wanded me. The scanner didn't like my belt or my shoes, but the security guard didn't seem to mind.

He patted me on my back. "Good to go."

The security was lax, but I was wearing a suit and tie, after all.

Judge Danny Bryce's chambers were on the third floor. I found the elevator with a young mom and kid. She got off on the second floor, and then after another jerk upward, I got off at my stop.

To my left were two courtrooms and four small conference rooms. The hallway expanded into a waiting area, which held a smattering of parents and their delinquent kids.

A sign pointed me in the other direction, and I followed it to a thick wooden door with a series of buttons on the side.

I pressed the button labeled "Hon. Bryce" and waited.

A voice came through the speaker, clouded by static. "Chambers."

I leaned over. "This is Justin Glass. Here to see Judge Bryce."

"Yes. Come back." There was a loud buzz, and then the magnetic locks released the door.

◆　◆　◆

Judge Bryce's chambers didn't look like any judicial chambers that I'd ever seen before. There was no ego wall filled with awards, degrees, and certificates. There also weren't any law books that I could see. Instead, the shelves were filled with children's toys. Some of them were old, probably played with by the judge himself when he was a kid. Others were new.

By the door, there was a bulletin board filled with the pictures of kids and notes from grateful parents. The rest of the walls were covered with children's artwork from floor to ceiling. None of it was in a frame. It was hung on the wall with Scotch tape. There was no order. Wherever there was an empty space, a picture covered it.

Judge Bryce smiled. "Like it?"

"I do." I walked over to the empty chair in front of his desk. "Ever rotate them?"

Bryce nodded. "In the summer, the humidity causes the tape to lose its stickiness." Judge Bryce looked over at one of the pictures that was crooked and partially folded over. "Like that one." He pointed. "When it falls, I'll throw it away and then put a new one up in its place."

"Ever keep any?"

"I used to keep the ones if they got sent to prison. Thought that somebody had to remember these kids, and it might as well be me." Judge Bryce's voice trailed off, and then his face tightened. "But then the stack got too big. Better just to throw them away."

◆ ◆ ◆

We worked our way through the juvenile courthouse, starting at the top. Each floor had the same plan. There were two courtrooms per floor, conference rooms, and a secure area for the judges and their chambers. In the far corner of each floor somebody had built bookshelves and filled them with used books in various stages of neglect.

On the main level, Judge Bryce took me toward the back of the building. There was a woman behind a window made of bulletproof glass. He smiled and waved at her. She smiled back.

Then Judge Bryce leaned closer and spoke to her through a small opening. "My friend needs to sign in."

I signed the clipboard, and a light above a steel door turned on. Judge Bryce opened the door. We walked into a small entryway, and then he let the steel door close behind us. Once it was closed, another light came on above another door, and we were allowed to enter the secure area where juveniles were held while waiting for an initial appearance, trial, or placement out of the home.

"I want to welcome you all to one of 'America's Top Ten Places to Work.'" A large, grinning correctional officer approached us with his hands held out wide. "Who's the Honorable Danny Bryce brought to us today?"

Judge Bryce shook the man's hand. "This here is Justin Glass. He's an attorney, and you've probably heard of his dad."

"Of course." The correctional officer held out his hand, and we greeted each other. Then he gestured to the hallway behind him. "Let me show you around."

He turned, and we started walking down a hallway with a half dozen doors. "This is our administrative area. We don't ever have any kids on this floor. All staff. Sometimes a visitor will come through here or a parent visiting their kid. We greet them out here and take them where they're supposed to go."

He then walked us to the elevator, continuing to explain the mechanics of housing juvenile delinquents. "One floor down, we got a visiting area for attorneys or family that want to talk with the kids. Above us, we got a floor that has a place for medical, cafeteria, as well as a school and gym. The top two floors contain the pods. Our capacity is about one hundred twenty, but since JDAI, the numbers are way down."

"JDAI?"

"Juvenile Detention Alternatives Initiative." Judge Bryce laughed. "One of those wonky programs that we do."

"But this one actually works, as Judge Bryce is quick to tell anybody who will listen." The correctional officer put his hands on his hips, goading Judge Bryce to elaborate. "Correct, Your Honor?"

"Correct." Then Judge Bryce turned to me. "In the past, we were convinced that the Scared Straight approach worked. So we were locking kids up for all sorts of stuff, even a truancy or a petty theft. Then it turned out that Scared Straight was causing serious problems, and the outcomes for kids who spent just one night in jail were horrible. Criminality is like a contagious disease. After JDAI, we don't do the shock incarcerations any more. Now instead of one hundred twenty kids we have about forty-five on any given day."

I thought about the two floors of pods. "So most of this place is empty?"

"Yes. And we haven't seen any real uptick in crime. The media doesn't report that or make it seem that way, but that's what the actual data tells us," said Judge Bryce. "And it's the same thing at all the JDAI sites throughout the country."

◆ ◆ ◆

After the tour was done, Judge Bryce led me out of the detention facility. I was once again given the clipboard, this time to sign out, and once again I slid it back through the slot.

Judge Bryce checked his watch. "Well that's kind of the end of the tour."

I nodded. "Thank you." Then I thought about Isaac Turner and what he'd seen the night that his brother disappeared. "How do they transport the kids here or send them out to placement?"

Judge Bryce thought for a minute. "Oh . . ." He walked to a window at the end of the hallway. He pointed down at a little parking lot behind the JDC. "We got these vans. They're down there. Want to see them?"

I nodded. "A closer look would be great."

Judge Bryce hesitated. "It's getting late."

"Please." I smiled, keeping it light.

"OK." Judge Bryce caved pretty easily. He was a social guy, and I could tell that sitting alone in his chambers was killing him. He liked talking to people.

Judge Bryce led me back toward the main entrance, then back to the administrative offices, where he held his identification card up to the magnetic reader. The door clicked open, and we entered an area where clerks pushed and sorted the massive amount of paperwork that flowed through the juvenile and family court system. Unlike the adult criminal cases that had been converted to electronic files, juvenile and family courts still conducted business the old-fashioned way.

Judge Bryce greeted all the staff by name as he led me to another elevator. "This is the secret one," he said. "It allows us to go from our cars up to our chambers without ever going in the public common area." He pressed a button. A few seconds later, a bell dinged and the doors slid open.

We got in the elevator, and Judge Bryce pressed the button labeled with a capital *B* for *basement*. The elevator brought us down a level.

"Not the nicest place in the world, but the parking is free, and it's convenient." Judge Bryce led me out into the little parking garage. It was the basement of the Juvenile Justice Center. There were no windows. It was all concrete with large columns that supported the building above us.

Judge Bryce kept walking, and I followed as he made conversation. "Not too many people get to park under here—there's the judges, and then the managers of the juvenile courts and the probation supervisors." We walked a little farther toward a large metal garage door. "Of course the probation officers are always trying to park down here during the off hours, but they really shouldn't."

As we got closer to the garage door, Judge Bryce pointed to a rack of keys. "So here are the keys. Then when a PO—I mean, probation officer—wants to pick up a kid for court, he grabs a key and takes a van. Same goes for anyone who has to transport a kid to a placement somewhere. They grab a key and take a van."

"No sign-out or anything."

"There's supposed to be, but we don't have one. You know Saint Louis. A little weird like that—a big city that acts like a small town sometimes." Judge Bryce pushed a button, and the garage door rolled open with a clatter. The noise echoed off the garage's concrete walls. "Why're you interested in all this?"

As we walked out into the parking lot behind the detention center, I said, "We had a kid who says he saw his brother being taken. The brother—he's one of the Lost Boys I represent." I pointed at the row of blue vans. "Says the guy who took him was driving one of these."

Judge Bryce took in the information. Then he nodded. "That explains the whispers I've heard about Jimmy Poles."

◆ ◆ ◆

When we got back to the elevator, Judge Bryce and I took a ride back up to the main level. I could tell that he wanted to say something more, but not in the building. We walked out the front door together, and then I pointed at my rusted Honda in the corner of the lot. "That's me."

He nodded, and then, when we got to my car, Judge Bryce said, "Thank you for coming to see me today."

"I should be thanking you."

"No." Judge Bryce shook his head. "What you're doing for these missing kids is important. If this was helpful at all, I'm glad I could do it."

"No problem." I turned and unlocked my car. I was about to get inside when I felt a hand on my shoulder. I stopped. "Something the matter, Judge?"

"Maybe."

I turned back around so that I could face him. "What is it?"

"I was thinking," he said. "You should go public with this."

"With what?"

"With what you know," Judge Bryce said. "The van, the probation officer, maybe even identify Jimmy Poles . . . I don't know. Just letting these families tell their stories from their perspective." He shook his head darkly. "Good God. You go public, you'll get people

to come forward. There'd be outrage. It's the only way that the investigation is going to move forward. They may say that they won't treat
Poles differently—because he isn't a real cop, just probation—but he's
part of the system, and the system protects its own. It's called the blue
line, and nobody wants to cross it."

"I'm pretty sure they're working on it."

Judge Bryce shook his head and rolled his eyes. "Suppose Sergeant
Schmidt told you that."

CHAPTER FIFTY-THREE

I had hoped that the momentum would continue, but it didn't. Judge Bryce was right. The investigation had stalled.

There wasn't enough. The fact that Jimmy Poles was the probation officer for most of the Lost Boys and that Isaac Turner had seen his brother getting into a probation van on the night he disappeared hadn't resulted in any arrest. If the JJC had kept a record of who took the vans out and when they were returned, then there'd be something, but there were no records.

When I talked with Schmitty and told him what Judge Bryce had said about going public with Jimmy Poles, he told me that he'd think about it, but I knew that he didn't like the idea. Maybe Schmitty was protecting the system, maybe he wasn't.

The second interviews were over. The files had been read and reread. The spreadsheet was done, and I couldn't think of anything more to do. I wondered whether anything would happen, and then I remembered what the police chief had warned me about when we had met at Castlewood State Park. He had told me that it was a "tense time."

Anything could happen, he said, and it turned out the police chief was right.

◆ ◆ ◆

I was getting ready for bed when Lincoln called with the news. It was a little after ten. Sammy had already gone to bed.

Lincoln was constantly on Twitter. When he saw it, Lincoln knew it was going to be big. "You gotta get in front of this, bro." Then he turned conspiratorial. "People are starting to line up for my state Senate seat. I been trying to respect your space and hold them off from announcing, but this could be a real opportunity. Me run for Congress. You run for my spot. Perfection."

My stomach turned at my brother's political calculations as I scrolled through a series of Twitter posts on my cell phone. "Now's not the time," I said, squinting at the tiny screen. "I'm serious about running, more serious than I've ever been, but I'm not quite there. I got a real job to do, and I still have to find Sammy a new school and get her settled there."

Lincoln sighed. Even over the telephone, I could tell that he was rolling his eyes at me. "That's where you're wrong," he said. "This is the perfect time."

"Whatever." I tapped through a series of links and eventually found the original source. "Thanks for letting me know about this." I hung up the phone and stared at the string of Twitter posts, trying to make sense of who had posted them and why.

As I read each one, an uneasiness rolled over me.

This isn't good.

It started with a picture posted of Jimmy Poles holding a gun and a Confederate flag. I remembered the photo from the file that Emma and Nikolas had compiled. Below the photo was the statement: *Why is this man suspended? #LostBoysRemembered #STLtruth.*

The post was made by a person called @STLtruth. It was a relatively new Twitter account, but there were enough followers to plant the seeds.

An hour later, another photo with the same hashtags, this one a picture of Jimmy Poles wearing a black T-shirt with a pair of large, cartoonish white eyes printed on the front. Below the eyes were the words OUR PRESIDENT. This one had the descriptor: *Saint Louis Probation Officer Jimmy Poles #LostBoysRemembered #STLtruth.*

An hour after that, another photo of Jimmy Poles was posted. He wore an orange prison jumpsuit, blackface, and an afro wig. Below the photo was the statement: *Two things all Lost Boys have in common: Jimmy Poles and they are black #LostBoysRemembered #STLtruth.* It was an exaggeration, but few people would know.

Black Twitter picked it up first, and the story built to a boil; then the traditional media couldn't ignore it anymore. Questions were asked. Accusations went back and forth, and then the Jimmy Poles story got bigger.

The speed at which information and the pictures spread was stunning. The Lost Boys were no longer merely a tragedy in flyover country. Each minute that passed, the intensity grew and, with that, a movement.

@STLtruth began posting pictures of the Lost Boys, including pictures of the crime scene. Photos of bones and shallow graves. Then came the boys' juvenile system files.

The posts and information established credibility. Although the true identity of @STLtruth was unknown, it didn't matter. What he or she was posting was clearly authentic.

Monthly probation officer reports that Jimmy Poles filed for each of the identified Lost Boys were posted. One every ten minutes. Most of the information was blacked out, but the reports themselves weren't important. @STLtruth wanted to prove that Jimmy Poles was the common thread that ran through the murders, the person who connected all the Lost Boys together.

The furor grew.

The anonymous person had put Jimmy Poles on trial and convicted him through the Internet. It was inflammatory. It wasn't fair, but it was effective. No mainstream reporter could have done what he or she was doing. This was the new world. The fact that Missouri law made juvenile files confidential didn't matter.

◆ ◆ ◆

The next morning, I sat in my office and watched it unfold, going from the anonymous fringe of the Internet to the mainstream by midmorning. "You seeing all this?" I scrolled through the Twitter feed again, on my computer.

Emma stood over my shoulder, taking it all in.

I looked up at her. "I have to call Schmitty."

She nodded and then stared out at her desk in the other room. The phone had been ringing nonstop all morning as the story grew. "What do you want me to do about all the calls?"

I shrugged. "Don't know. Guess we have to answer. Can't just shut down."

"Fine." She patted me on the back, then returned to the reception desk.

As she was closing the door, I shouted at her. "Hey, Emma."

"Yes." She poked her head back inside my office.

"Any chance Nikolas is doing this? Maybe he thinks it's helping me."

She paused, considering the possibility. Then she shook her head. "Don't think so. Not really his style, but I will ask."

"OK." I nodded. "Thanks." I picked up the phone, looked at the Post-it Note on my desk that had Schmitty's phone number, and dialed as Emma shut the door to my office.

Schmitty picked up after one ring. "Glass. What the hell?"

"I was going to ask you the same thing."

"So you're not doing this?"

"Of course not," I said, perhaps too defensively. "Thought maybe you were doing it, trying to smoke him out."

"Are you kidding?" I could hear the panic in Schmitty's voice. "This ain't gonna end well, my friend. Gotta go. The damn governor is on our ass, worried about another Ferguson. Call me if you figure out who's posting this stuff."

◆ ◆ ◆

By sunset, there were a thousand people gathered outside Jimmy Poles's house, shouting and chanting. Somebody on a megaphone instructed the crowd to disperse, but the command was ignored. Two helicopters circled overhead, one a police tactical unit, the other a news crew. There were moments where it looked like the two would collide. Plus there were at least five knuckleheads flying remote-controlled drones with cameras mounted on them.

In a McDonald's parking lot six blocks away, four armored Missouri National Guard vehicles reviewed maps of the area. A small army of police officers suited up in full riot gear. A similar contingent prepared at a pharmacy on the other side of Jimmy Poles's house.

The plan was to simultaneously approach the protesters from each side, press them together, pinch them at one end, and push the crowd toward the highway and out of the residential area.

It was the best strategy that they could come up with. Nobody expected it to go smoothly, but somebody should've known that it was going to be a complete failure.

◆ ◆ ◆

A call was made, and the two units started their slow march. Squad cars and police officers eventually formed a corridor leading from Jimmy Poles's house toward the highway. The squads and police officers were intended to limit the choices that the protestors could make by keeping them together and cutting off alternative routes.

Contain and control.

The crowd received another warning, ordering them to start dispersing or face arrest. The bright lights shone down on the crowd, growing bigger as armored vehicles crept closer. Riot police with masks and shields flanked the edges.

Chants grew louder as the units pressed.

As the protesters were pushed together, some started moving down the street and toward the highway as expected, but the police were too slow to pinch them from behind.

That was how the plan fell apart.

Rather than go toward the highway, hundreds of protesters moved in the wrong direction. They went off the street and onto Jimmy Poles's front lawn. Then somebody threw a bottle through the front window.

More glass shattered. Cops got spooked. A half dozen canisters of tear gas shot into the crowd. Protesters panicked as their eyes watered. They got disoriented and didn't know where to run. Some fell to the ground, coughing and seeking clean air. Others tripped or were pushed. Everybody was screaming as the vehicles and the line of police continued to push forward.

Then Jimmy Poles's house was lit on fire.

CHAPTER FIFTY-FOUR

The governor called a state of emergency. A curfew was imposed across the entire city, but the protests continued night after night. Every day, television and newspapers were filled with images of the conflict. Reporters from around the world descended on the city. Gun sales were at a record high, and permit-to-carry classes filled as the frightened prepared for the worst. The community splintered into protests and counter-protests, with others stuck in the middle.

Saint Louis had always had an identity crisis. It was the intersection of North and South, East and West. The tension had always been below the surface, but now it was out in the open. Past police shootings and riots were prologue. This was different. It wasn't going to end with a task force and a march to Jefferson City.

"Your father wants me to go to Washington, DC, for a few weeks." My mother poured herself some more wine and then took a bite of her dinner salad. "Let things calm down. Sammy could come."

I looked across the table at Sammy, but she didn't say anything. "I'd rather Sammy stick with me." I smiled at her and winked. "We're getting the schools narrowed down to the top three. I want to get that started."

"Now?" My mother's look turned skeptical. "With everything going on?"

"Can't stop living." It sounded odd coming from me, a man who had been frozen for years and who—even now—was only partially thawed at best.

An awkward silence hung over the dinner table, and it stayed there until I broke it. "OK, OK. Y'all are given permission to laugh at me. I'm Mr. Corn-Dog. I get it. I got no business giving people life lessons." I gave Sammy a goofy grin. "'Can't stop living.' Hear that? 'Keep on living.' Go ahead. You can laugh now."

And laugh they did.

It was a release, and it felt good. When it tapered down, the Judge knocked on the dining room table, suppressing his smile. He declared to the world, "I'm staying put." Then he poured himself another glass of wine. "Down with the ship, I say. Not going to be driven from my home by a bunch of idiots. A lot of them aren't even from here. Traveling to our fine city to cause trouble. Anarchists and professional protesters. Ridiculous."

Then a small voice said, "I want to go to the lake."

We all turned to Sammy.

"The lake?"

"It'd be nice." Sammy smiled and looked at me. "And you promised we'd go last summer, but we never did." She continued to justify her recommendation. "Peaceful. No Internet. No television. Doesn't that sound good?"

"Yes." I nodded. "Sounds about perfect, except I got work and we got to get you back in school, remember?"

CHAPTER FIFTY-FIVE

The next morning, I met my brother for breakfast at a box tucked between Broadway and the historic Route 66. Lincoln had wanted to get together since the press conference, but I had been able to put him off until now.

There were a few pleasantries, but it didn't take long for Lincoln to get to the point.

"You know I still want you to take my spot." Lincoln put his arm around me. He was ready to forget about the threats made to Annie and the other hard feelings, if I was. "What I told you was the truth. You'd be great. Wasn't a bunch of BS, brother."

"Sometimes I think I've got too much going on already." I looked back at the cook working in the Eat-Rite's cramped kitchen. "I've been leaning toward it, really I have, but then I'll snap back to thinking maybe politics isn't for me."

"You talking about Sammy? Worried about whether she could handle it?"

I thought about what I should say before responding, trying to figure out how much to reveal and how much was already known. I didn't like being guarded with my brother, but I was. "Yeah," I said. "That's a big part of it."

"But this would be good for her and you." He leaned in. "A state senator will have clients coming out of nowhere. And I'm not talking shady clients or criminals. I'm talking about legit companies who will hire you for five hundred dollars an hour, maybe more, for some legal advice. You'll be taken care of."

"Like bribes."

My brother recoiled. "Ain't bribes, man. That's what you're worth. That's what real lawyers charge nowadays." He paused and looked me straight in the eye. "Listen to me." Lincoln pointed at my chest, then spoke every word with deliberation. "That's what you are worth."

"Maybe." I watched as the cook plated our eggs and pancakes and then, as he brought them over to us at the end of the counter, our conversation paused. Lincoln started eating, but I'd lost my appetite.

He raised an eyebrow. "So now you're not going to eat?"

I picked up a small piece of scrambled eggs with my fork and put it into my mouth. "I'm eating," I said. "See?"

"You're disgusted by how crass I can be," Lincoln said. "I get it." He sliced off a piece of pancake. "But somebody's got to be real, man. If not, why'd you invite me here?"

"I thought you called me?"

"Technicalities," Lincoln said, dismissing the chronology. "You want to hear the crass stuff. Admit it."

"No," I said. "I want to get your ideas and thoughts." I sighed. "This is a big decision for me. I'm trying to work it through and just get it done and . . . you're better at this stuff than me."

Lincoln smiled wide. "A compliment," he said, raising his voice. "My big brother complimented me." He leaned over and patted me on the back. "I talk like that sometimes 'cuz I know it gets you fired up. I'm just playing with you."

Lincoln took a breath. "I know you want to do the right thing. You're pretending like there's a downside, because you're afraid of putting yourself out there. Afraid of disappointing people." He paused, winding up his pitch. "But there is no downside. There's some crazy stuff going on out there right now, and you can help in ways that I can't. That's why Dad did what he did, even though it hurt me. I get it, too." Lincoln was actually sincere. "Remember, though, you don't have to be like Dad. You can do your thing while you're there and then move on, if you want. You don't have to do it forever. Just try it out. It's up to you."

Our waiter came over. "One check or two?"

"Two," I said, but Lincoln overruled me.

"One check, and it's on me." He pulled out his wallet and put his credit card down on the table. "Glad you called me." He was serious, although he was, again, factually incorrect. "We gotta do this more."

"You mean scheme?" I kidded him.

"I mean *think*," Lincoln said. "Think big thoughts. Look out for each other. Like it or not, we could be good partners again, like when we were kids."

"Dangerous partners."

"JFK and Bobby." Lincoln laughed. "And dangerous and good ain't mutually exclusive."

CHAPTER FIFTY-SIX

The march was my idea. I had to *do* something. For over a week, the city had burned. Every night at dusk, a militarized police force confronted young black men who had been reduced by the media to statistics: half as likely to graduate college, four times as likely to be unemployed, three times as likely to be in jail, twice as likely to be convicted of a felony, 20 percent less likely to ever marry, and so on.

I was tired of watching it happen. The news reports were caricatures—information and images manipulated to support the political priorities of either the Left or the Right. I felt the humanity fade in the numbers and the conflict. The reality was that the missing boys were sons who were thrown away, disconnected from the institutions that were supposed to care—schools, churches, the government, and even, sometimes, their own families. Where was the collective responsibility to never allow these boys to fall so far away?

Nobody talked about that, but I could.

My last name gave me a platform that I had been afraid, until now, to use. I didn't want to be seen as a fraud, and I thought it'd be easy to dismiss me. I didn't grow up in poverty. Half my relatives were white. I had the schooling. My family had the money, and my father had the power. When I examined my own life, it wasn't hard to surrender to the voices in my head that sounded a lot like the bullies at Sammy's school, questioning whether I was black enough.

It was time to silence those voices and lead.

I stood on a bench outside my law office with a bullhorn. Over a thousand people showed up. I didn't know how they had found out about the march, but that was the Glass machine.

"Good morning." I looked out over the crowd. "My name is Justin Glass. Like you, I wish we didn't need to be here, but we don't have a choice. We need to stand up. We need to march, and we need to demand answers for what has happened. We need to know what is going to happen. And we need to hold the person or people who did this responsible."

Directly in front of me were the families of the Lost Boys, my clients. I'd gotten to know every one of them. I'd sat in their apartments. I'd shared in their grief, surprising myself and letting them get closer to me than a lawyer should probably allow.

I had made sure that each family held a sign with their son's name. Each family also had a black coffin hoisted on their shoulders. They floated along on the sea of people. "We can't burn our own community. We need to organize. Put pressure on the police to stop harassing us and start investigating in earnest for these families right here in front of me."

There was more that I wanted to say, but I couldn't put the ideas together as a coherent whole. I didn't know the right words, and perhaps that was the problem. Everyone standing in front of me knew that something far bigger was wrong. They knew that the system was broken, but we all lacked the language to express it, and so we were here to grieve these lost boys.

But the issue wasn't just about troubled black boys who disappeared. That was only on the surface. The real reasons lay beneath. We were people who had been wronged. We were protesting bad schools, run-down housing, high unemployment, no credit, regressive taxation, exorbitant fees for government services, unnecessary fines, and the list could go on.

Rigged.

That was the only word I could come up with to express the situation.

I put the bullhorn down, and then I looked at Lincoln, who cued the Dirty Thirty Brass Band. The drummers struck a slow beat. Then the trumpets came in, followed by the trombones, tubas, and a couple of guys on sax.

Our protest was a New Orleans–style second line—a funeral parade from my law office to the Juvenile Justice Center. At first the music was solemn, playing the classic hymns, and then, per tradition, it picked up. By the time we crossed Page Boulevard, it was an expression of life.

Schmitty hadn't returned my phone calls. He hadn't updated me on any information. This would, hopefully, get his attention. I was done waiting. And, looking at the crowd, I could tell that they were done waiting, too.

CHAPTER FIFTY-SEVEN

The vast majority of the marchers were gone after a few hours. They had dispersed easily; some walked to the light rail station on Grand, and others had rides waiting. Lincoln had also arranged for buses to take people back to the start of the march.

About a hundred or so appeared to have set up camp on the corner of the Juvenile Justice Center's parking lot. The police weren't going to like the idea of a permanent protest, especially in front of the court, but I didn't know what I was going to be able to do about it.

Emma honked her horn to get my attention. I waved at her, said a quick good-bye and thanks to a group of pastors who had spoken at the rally, and got into her car. "Thanks for the ride back." I buckled my seatbelt as Emma pulled away from the curb. I asked, "Any coverage?"

"Every channel," she said. "Most carried it live. I think they were hoping to see some violence, but had to settle for speeches."

I smiled. "You'd think they'd be tired of the violence by now."

She pulled into the left lane to go north on Grand toward the office. "Oh, Mr. Glass, they never get tired of violence." Then she looked out the window at the sky, maybe thinking about all the violence that she'd seen in Bosnia, thinking that most Americans didn't know how fragile things really were.

She snapped back to the present and looked back over to me. "Plus all the other stuff happened at night. This time they had good light for all their pretty photographs."

◆ ◆ ◆

I decided I'd check my messages and then go home. I figured that it wouldn't take too long, and that I could still get home for a late dinner with Sammy, my mother, and the Judge.

I was, ultimately, wrong about the length of time I'd spend at the office, but I was right about Schmitty finally returning my phone calls.

"Want to tell me what the hell that was all about?" Schmitty was not happy at all. He started talking the moment I answered the phone. "Thought we were on the same team, had an understanding."

I didn't match his intensity, although I was tempted to come back at him by pointing out his failure to update me on the investigation. "I didn't do anything wrong, Schmitty."

"Great," he said. "I'm so glad *you* don't think you did anything wrong. Within seconds of that little speech you gave, Chief Wilson was up my ass, calling you a traitor. Said you were inciting violence."

"There was no violence."

"Not right then. Not right now," he said. "Wait till tonight."

"Tonight's going to be no different than every night for the past two weeks," I said. "You guys need transparency. You need to communicate."

"Transparency?" Schmitty was still agitated. "You're smarter than that. It's a damn investigation. You don't tell the public how and when you are investigating a dozen murders."

"Well maybe you need to communicate with me. That would be a start." There, I'd laid it on the table.

Schmitty grunted. "Surprised by you, man," he said. "Thought you were different than your brother, playing games."

"I don't have to take that, Schmitty," I said. "Been working hard, asking nothing in return. You asked me to do this, remember? I know these families. I talk with these families all the time now, and they deserve better." I collected my thoughts. "And don't criticize my brother to me. He is what he is, and I am what I am."

There was silence, and neither one of us wanted to fill it. If I waited long enough, I knew that Schmitty would break. Whether he felt betrayed or not, the police needed me on their side.

At last, Schmitty cleared his throat. "You just gotta give me a heads-up when you do stuff like that, that's all," he said. "I'd been meaning to call you, but there's been a lot going on."

"Good," I said. "Glad you agree. If there's stuff happening, you need to tell me that. Give me direction. We can get the feedback loop going again."

"Fine." He was cooling off. "But the chief is going to have my ass if there are any more surprises. I'll give you some more information, but you leave the real investigating to us."

I wasn't going to promise that, so I deflected. "Seems like I'm the only one doing the real investigating."

"Glass." Schmitty sounded offended. "Give me a break, man. You know that's not true. Easy to believe, but you know that's not true. I can give you what I can, but more important, I want to prevent you from embarrassing yourself, like today."

"Embarrass?" I shook my head. "You think I embarrassed myself?"

"I do," Schmitty said. "Because Jimmy Poles ain't the guy. All that shit in front of the JJC, calling for his arrest, calling for an indictment, it ain't going to happen."

"I didn't call for an indictment."

"But your people did," he said.

My people, I thought.

Schmitty continued. "We aren't going down that road, because Poles didn't do it."

The news took a moment to register, and, when it did, it hit hard. I wasn't going to accept it. "Everything points at him."

"No," Schmitty said. "The little bit we knew used to point toward him, past tense. Now it doesn't."

I folded my arms across my chest and leaned back in my chair, the phone still pressed to my ear. "Elaborate."

"We followed up on the interview that you did with Turner," he said. "We looked at the JJC records for the night that the kid saw his brother get in that blue van. There were calls made by the mother to the JJC, we got records of that, just like you said we would. The mama called, but Jimmy Poles was on a float trip in the Ozarks that weekend."

"Are there witnesses for this alibi?"

"A half dozen rednecks," Schmitty said. "They all say he was with them."

"A half dozen rednecks *would* say—"

"There's also credit card receipts for food and the property damage agreement for the cabin where they stayed. Poles signed it."

"He could be working with other people." I was grasping at straws and knew it. Jimmy Poles was far from a criminal mastermind. I doubted that any of his buddies were, either. Weakly, I kept reaching for an alternative. "Couldn't that all be faked?"

"The receipts and the thing from the cabin are legit." Schmitty remained patient. "We did a warrant for his phone records, got all the cell tower information, too."

I knew from defending clients that cell phone records and cell tower information had been a major boost to law enforcement in recent years. Every cell phone has a GPS tracker in it, which allows the mapping apps to work and the phone to locate the nearest cell phone tower to relay calls. "And?"

"Poles, or at least his phone, was in the Ozarks, like he said. It was pinging off the cell towers along the Missouri–Arkansas border the entire time."

"That doesn't mean he didn't kill the others."

"Except we got *all* his records." Schmitty sighed. "Guy has had the same cell phone company for five years, and he has never been anywhere near Castlewood State Park. If he goes anywhere, it's either fishing in Troy or down south to the Ozarks. That's it."

"Well maybe he just knows better than to take his phone with him." But I was running on fumes, I knew. The news had gone from bad to worse. The high I had felt after the march was gone, and now I was just confused. I sunk a little lower in my seat. "What now?"

"We're looking at rival gangs, but that seems like a stretch," Schmitty said. "After today, you seem to be the expert. You tell me."

"Whatever." I hung up the phone and ran my hand hard across the back of my neck, trying to work out the knots that had formed. I closed my eyes, trying to think of my next move, but nothing came. I decided to give it a little more time. Maybe something would come after a good night's sleep.

I'd just stood up when the brick flew through my window, showering the floor with broken glass.

Expecting more, I ducked down. But nothing happened.

I got up, ran around my desk, and yanked open the front door. I expected to hear the squealing tires of a pickup truck or see a mob of skinheads who had seen me on television, but there was none of that. The street was empty and dead quiet.

CHAPTER FIFTY-EIGHT

I was anxious to leave. I was tired and discouraged after my phone call with Schmitty, and now I felt exposed. I waited two hours for the handyman to arrive, stewing over who threw the brick and why. The truth was that I had no idea whether it was a random kid, an Internet crazy, or the beginning of a riot.

After the boards were screwed into the window frame—both on the outside and the inside—I paid the handyman cash, and then we were both on our way.

I checked the time. It was now too late for dinner, and I decided that I'd drive back over to the Juvenile Justice Center. My confidence had been shaken. If Jimmy Poles wasn't responsible, who was? I needed to find the other thread that connected all the Lost Boys together, and I felt myself being pulled back to that building. Maybe if I stood there long enough and stared at those blue vans, a name would come.

I pulled into the JJC parking lot, stopped the car, and noticed that I had two new texts from Annie. The first said, **Nice speech**. I smiled. Even though we had our final night at the hotel, it felt good to know that she still thought of me, confirming that we had left on mutual terms. The second text said, **Be careful**. I stared at the screen. The two words could be read different ways. A warning, or only concern? Maybe she'd been talking with Chief Wilson and knew about Poles.

I put the phone in my pocket and got out of the car. The protesters had made a small bonfire on the edge of the parking lot. They had lawn chairs, a small barbecue, a few coolers, and some tents.

The remaining crowd was now down to about thirty.

Tanisha Walker and her mother were among them. I walked over, and we talked for a few minutes; then I noticed Isaac Turner, with his mother and aunt, by the fire.

I waved, then beckoned to Isaac. "Come on over here," I said. "Let me introduce you to somebody."

Isaac looked at his mother, who gave him a nod of approval, and then he got up from his lawn chair and came to me.

"Isaac," I said. "This is Tanisha Walker. I think you two are about the same age. Tanisha was the first person to hire me. Wouldn't be involved in any of this, if it wasn't for her."

Tanisha smiled and made brief eye contact with Isaac, then looked away.

"Tanisha," I continued the introductions, "this is Isaac Turner. He's been very helpful to me." That earned him another quick, shy look from her, but I was thinking about my conversations with Isaac now. Just because Poles was no longer a suspect, nothing that Isaac had told me about the night that his brother had disappeared was necessarily wrong. There were no logs or formal check-out system. Anybody who worked at the JJC could have taken one of the blue probation vans.

To Isaac I said, "You mind taking a walk with me?"

Isaac glanced back at his mother and then shrugged. "I suppose."

I looked at Tanisha. "You can come, too, if you want." I pointed up the street. "Going to take a look at something."

We walked a half block down Enright Avenue, along the side of the JJC building.

It didn't take long before we were in front of a tall chain-link fence. On the other side of the fence were a half dozen blue vans. "See those?" I pointed. "On the night that TeeTee disappeared, is that what you saw?"

Isaac nodded. "That's them." He looked up at me. "Been tellin' you that. Seen TeeTee talking to somebody and then he done get into one of them vans. Ain't never seen him no more after that."

I glanced at Tanisha and then back at Isaac. "You're sure?"

"Positive."

CHAPTER FIFTY-NINE

Sammy was in her bed reading, waiting for me to get home. I knocked on her door frame. "Sorry I'm late." *How many times have I said that to her?* I walked over to her bed and sat down. "New book?"

Sammy smiled. "*Redwall.*" She held it up so that I could see the book's cover featuring a monastic mouse lifting the legendary sword of Martin the Warrior.

"Looks like a good one."

"I think so." She looked at the cover once more, then set it aside. "Seems like you had a busy day." Sammy sounded like my mother. "Saw it all on television. Grandma thought it was great. The Judge, not so much."

"He's more about the settlement than the protest," I said. "But there's a need in this world for both."

"Going to arrest that probation officer now?"

I considered how to answer Sammy's question, then told the truth. "I don't think so."

"But he did it, right?" Sammy furrowed her brow. "They said that he did."

"That's certainly what we thought." I touched her knee. "But now I'm not so sure."

She nodded, considering this new piece of information. Then she shrugged. "Well I know you'll get him."

"Thanks." I leaned over and kissed the top of her head.

We sat in silence for a bit longer, and I felt myself starting to cycle down from all that had happened during the day and refocus. "Are you ready for us to make a decision?"

Sammy nodded. "Time's up, isn't it?"

I smiled at her, trying to add a little levity. "Wish it wasn't. Kinda like you hanging around, not getting any smarter than your old man."

"Already smarter," she shot back.

"Oh you think so, do you?" I started to tickle her, like when she was a little girl, and Sammy squealed in delight. I kept at it until she recanted.

"OK, OK," she said. "Maybe you're smarter."

With that I let her go, and we moved comfortably apart. She emitted a final laugh and smiled at me, then leaned over and took my hand, serious again.

"So where are you thinking?" I asked.

"Well I liked all the schools we visited." Sammy picked up her book and put it on her nightstand. "But some were a little too fancy, you know? Like, not any fun. Like . . . I don't know . . . too clean or something."

I nodded. "Agreed."

"But I liked that one that was pretty close to us, over by the arboretum."

"You did?" I thought about all the schools that we had toured, or that Sammy had toured with the Judge. "Clement City?"

"That's the one." She nodded. "Clement City Day School. All the kids learn Latin, and I saw one of the teachers had a poster of the Greek gods. That's pretty cool."

"It is cool."

"And maybe I could ride my bike there." She offered the suggestion on the sly, trying to catch me at a weak moment.

"Maybe," I said. "Have to think about that."

"You could ride with me." Sammy didn't give up easily. "To keep me safe, you know? And make sure I make it on time. Like hold me accountable and stuff."

"Have to think about that bike thing." I smiled and nodded. "But Clement City is a great choice. I'll call tomorrow, and we'll make it work. I want to get you started right away."

Sammy looked at me, beaming. "Thank you, Daddy."

I leaned over and kissed the top of her head. "You don't need to thank me."

◆ ◆ ◆

After Sammy had fallen asleep, I heard a car drive through the alley a little too fast. I peeked out the window, watching it go, and I felt an unease return. I waited and watched, looking for something more, but nothing happened.

I hadn't called the police about the brick, because I knew there wasn't anything they could do about a broken window. Now, in the quiet of my house with Sammy, I wished that I had.

I took my cell phone out of my pocket and texted Schmitty. After our phone call, I didn't know where exactly we stood, but I thought he might be able to do something. I sent a quick text message about the brick. Then I asked him to send a squad past my office, as a precaution, and also past my house.

On my way to the toy room, I stopped for a bottle of beer and a glass. It was a Belgian-style beer from a microbrewery over on Michigan Avenue.

The Saison de Lis was created by the owner of Perennial Artisan Ales in honor of his daughter, and so I thought it'd be appropriate.

I stepped into the room and closed the door behind me. I took a Preservation Hall Jazz Band record off the shelf, removed it from the sleeve, and placed it on the record player.

Music popped to life as I sat down at my worktable and poured the beer into the glass. Then I removed the framed photo of Monica from the drawer and got to work.

My hero's little antagonists were carved and ready. The clay figurine with the top hat and his henchmen—the giant and the troll dressed as the aristocrat's butlers—had hardened. All I needed to do was paint.

I put some butcher paper down on the desk, set the figurines on top, and removed my paints and brushes from the drawer.

As I worked, I told Monica about the books Sammy was reading and about Clement City Day School. I had made a promise to Sammy, and I intended to keep it. Clement City wasn't the most expensive private school in Saint Louis, but it wasn't cheap, either. The school was filled with kids whose liberal parents loved the city but hated the city's school system. We'd fit right in.

Then I told her about Schmitty and Jimmy Poles and what Isaac Turner had seen the night that his brother had disappeared. As I finished painting the final figure and put it on the shelf to dry, I knew that I wasn't going to be able to sleep. My mind was still going.

I was missing something. I felt it. There was a small piece of information in each of the files connecting all the Lost Boys.

I went into the corner and grabbed one of the boxes off the stack. Each box was filled with copies of police records and criminal histories, the backgrounds of the kids that nobody had been looking for.

I took the top binder out and started reading.

CHAPTER SIXTY

It took another three days to go through all the files again. When it was over, I wasn't any closer to finding the link that I was looking for. I was still sure that there was a piece of information in each file that would link the boys together, but I couldn't find it.

I looked at my watch, then put a lid on the last remaining box. I left the toy room and went out into the kitchen. It was still early in the morning, and Sammy was finishing up her cereal, dressed and ready to go to school for the first time in over a month.

I couldn't contain my smile. "All set." I clapped my hands together.

"One more bite." Sammy shoved a final spoonful of cereal in her mouth and then swallowed. "Done." Then she picked up her bowl and spoon, took them over to the sink, and set them down. "I'm ready."

"Then let's go." I checked my watch again. "Don't want to be late on your first day."

We hustled out at a quarter to eight, got in my car, and drove over to the Clement City Day School. It didn't take long. The school was located just on the other side of the Tower Grove Park.

"That would've been easy to bike," Sammy said as we pulled into an empty parking spot on the street.

I looked over at a huge bike rack filled with bicycles. "Maybe next time."

The school was located in a large, redbrick building that used to be the Saint Thomas More Catholic School, but after years of dwindling enrollment, the archdiocese sold it to a real estate developer in the early 1980s.

The master plan was to convert the old school into condos, but then the condo market crashed. This seemed to surprise the investors, even though condo markets crash about every six years. Financing fell through, and the property got foreclosed. A decade later, a group of professors and artists bought the building from the city for a dollar and started Clement City Day School.

As we neared the front steps, we were greeted by my mother and the Judge. I had tried to convince them to stay home, but they insisted. I was worried that Sammy would be embarrassed by all the fuss, but she didn't seem to mind.

Sammy walked over to them and gave each a big hug, then she turned back to me.

"You ready?" I asked.

Sammy nodded and took my hand, and then we all walked into the school together.

◆　◆　◆

After dropping Sammy off at school, I met with Schmitty at the Sunshine Café on Morganford, just south of Tower Grove Park. The pastry and sandwich shop was in the middle of a rejuvenated block between a soccer bar and a Vietnamese restaurant.

I felt like I needed to make sure we were OK, and I also wanted to thank him for increasing the patrol around my office and the carriage house.

"Lots of hipsters." Schmitty glared at the bearded man with the MacBook sitting at a table near the window and then at two young women wearing vintage clothes and sporting large, elaborate arm tattoos. Even after the morning rush, the place was pretty crowded.

"Well I like it." I took a bite of my croissant. "Just wish there were a few more of these little strips on the north side."

"A few more?" Schmitty snorted. "How about *one* of these places on the north side?"

I shook my head. "You're just not looking hard enough." I set my croissant down and leaned back, ready to get down to business. "I read all the criminal files again," I said. "And I'm still not seeing anything that connects them except Jimmy Poles."

"But Poles *doesn't* connect them. Not all of them. Some of them had different probation officers." Schmitty sat up in his chair and leaned in. "I'm telling you, Jimmy Poles isn't the one. You have to get off it." Then Schmitty leaned in even closer. "The chief is serious. Back off it."

"I'm not on it, OK? I hear you loud and clear. It's not Poles." I took a sip of coffee, letting Schmitty absorb what I had just said and hoping he understood we were on the same page. "But if not Poles, what about the others? Have you looked at them?"

"We've looked at the other probation officers, security guards, even some of the lawyers, and we got nothing."

"But we got the blue van."

Schmitty shook his head. "Pretty weak."

"Well you got something better for me?"

He looked away, then turned back to me, looking at me straight with a little bit of panic in his eyes. "I told you we got nothing. We've got nothing on anybody."

And I believed him.

CHAPTER SIXTY-ONE

Emma's list for the afternoon was long. I had spent multiple days working exclusively on the Lost Boys files, and she needed me to make some money. After being presented with the first bill for Sammy's new school, I also felt the pressure to bring in some revenue. My goal was to pay a quarter of Sammy's tuition for the first two months and then slowly increase that portion. The Judge had said from the beginning that he didn't care, and I believed him; but in my mind it was my promise to Sammy and my obligation.

With no leads or clear direction about what was next for the Lost Boys, I put it all on the back burner and met with a new civil client out in Clayton. I spent over an hour returning phone calls and setting up new appointments, and then I walked over to the nearby courthouse for two court appearances before heading back to the office.

Traffic on Forty wasn't too bad. I took the Jefferson exit off the highway and wound up the off-ramp into the city proper. The ramp dumped me at an intersection that only a traffic engineer could love. It was a tangle of old city streets, highway, service roads, alleys, and some sidewalks that were never used.

I pulled up to a white line and waited while cars and semitrucks zipped past me in all directions. When the light turned green, I was going to take a left, cross back over the highway, and cut across downtown.

The light, however, did not turn green.

It held steady on red as the other traffic lights and arrows cycled, theoretically giving everybody an opportunity for safe passage.

My mind wandered. Then a knock on my car window brought me back. I turned and saw Cecil Bates smiling at me. He held a cardboard sign, obviously panhandling.

I rolled down my window. "How's it going, Cecil?"

"Not too shabby, Counselor." His head bobbled, and as Cecil exhaled, the car filled with the odor of cheap whiskey. "Making a little something something, here and there."

I got my wallet and took out a ten-dollar bill. I held it up but out of reach. "I'm giving this to you, but you gotta promise me first."

"Promise what?"

"To stay out of trouble," I said.

Cecil gave me an exaggerated look of great offense. "Absolutely," he said. "Not breaking any laws."

"You sure?"

"Cross my heart." Then Cecil laughed. "Plus I got me my backup plan now."

"Backup plan?"

"The cameras, man." Cecil pointed at a pole above us. It had four cameras mounted on the top in each direction. "Don't do nothing where there ain't cameras. Videos don't lie." Then he winked at me. "Keepin' it legal."

"Got it." I laughed, then looked back up at the cameras. Somebody behind me honked their horn. I looked over at the traffic light, which had turned green—and, at that moment, I had an idea.

"Take this." I handed Cecil Bates the ten-dollar bill. "You earned it." Then I pulled away, deciding that I wasn't going to go straight back to the office.

CHAPTER SIXTY-TWO

It took about eight minutes to get over to the Juvenile Justice Center. I slowed as I drove in front of the building. The protesters camped at the corner of the parking lot had dwindled from a hundred to two dozen, and now to about ten.

I didn't see anything at first. Then I turned on Bell Avenue and circled it again. Still nothing.

The angles weren't right, and even driving slowly, I was going too fast. Too excited.

I pulled into the parking lot in front of the Juvenile Justice Center. After grabbing my cell phone, I got out and gave a quick acknowledgment to the remaining protesters. Although Tanisha Walker and Isaac Turner were gone, the people that remained looked familiar. "Talk to you in a minute." I waved again, then started walking down the sidewalk that ran along the south side of the building.

I knew they had to be there, but I was worried that they wouldn't be in the right spots.

I walked a little farther, toward the back parking lot. Then I saw it: a little silver box attached to the side of the building.

A camera.

I took a picture of it, and then I stared at it, trying to figure out exactly where it was pointed.

I walked up to the chain-link fence that surrounded the blue vans that were used by probation. There were no cameras on poles here, and no cameras atop the high fence posts, but I found one attached to the back side of the building.

I took a picture of it, getting even more excited. The camera was pointed directly at the vans. If it didn't capture a face, it would have certainly captured the general physical characteristics and body type of the person who took the van on the night that Isaac Turner's brother, TeeTee, had disappeared.

I had just taken another picture when a security guard came outside. He was a big guy, probably eighty pounds overweight. The look on his face was one of panic as he ran toward me from the front of the building. Every few yards, he'd stop, wave his hands, and yell at me. "Can't do that! Can't do that!" Then he'd double over, head between his legs, trying to catch his breath.

◆ ◆ ◆

He wanted to confiscate my phone. That much was clear, although it was difficult to understand him. His face was bright red by the time that he'd made it all the way down the block. Sweat ran down his cheeks. Midsentence, he'd stop, take a deep breath, point at my phone, and say, "No."

"You're telling me I can't stand on a public sidewalk and take a picture of a public building?"

"Says you can't do that." He was out of breath. "You need to give me your phone." He pointed at it, bent over, and shook his head.

"Listen." I tried sounding contrite. "I'm not giving you my phone." I looked over his shoulder, hoping that somebody rational would arrive. "Why don't we call Sergeant Schmidt of the Saint Louis Police Department? He can clear things up, tell you who I am."

This stopped him. He looked at me with suspicion. "Telling me you a cop?"

"No, I'm not a police officer, but I'm working with—"

"Then you need to give me that phone."

"Why?"

"You know, terrorists. September eleventh." He wiped more sweat off his forehead. "Against the law to take pictures of a public building."

"It is not against the law to take pictures of a public building." I put the phone in my pocket. "Listen, I'm just going to leave now. OK?"

"Not OK." Now the security guard was pointing at the pocket that held my dangerous cellular device. "You need to leave that with me until I get it cleared."

"I'm not doing that." I turned and started to walk away, and then I felt a firm hand on my shoulder.

"Told you that you cannot leave." The security guard grabbed my wrist. "Going to have to place you under arrest."

I yanked my hand away from him. "You're not even a police officer."

"Sir," he said, shaking his head. "You need to obey me."

"This is ridiculous."

As the security guard started to unclip his handcuffs from his belt, the high chain-link fence to the parking lot began to jerk and squeak to life. We both turned, surprised, as the fence opened and a black Jaguar XJ emerged from the lot behind the Juvenile Justice Center.

The car pulled up alongside us. The passenger side window rolled down. "Jameson." Judge Bryce leaned over, shouting out of the car window. "What are you doing to Mr. Justin Glass?"

The security guard's chest pumped up. "Yes, Judge." He nodded toward me. "This man was taking photographs of our building, sir."

"So what?"

"With all due respect, Judge Bryce"—the man shifted from one foot to another, starting to get nervous—"it's against the law to take photographs of any courthouse."

"That's ridiculous." Judge Bryce pointed at me and then looked back at the security guard. "Leave him alone or I'll have to report this to your supervisor. I happen to know that Regal Security's contract is up for renewal, and they will not like hearing about this at all."

"But sir." The security guard looked at Judge Bryce with a mixture of disappointment and exasperation. "The law says—"

"The law does not say that." Shaking his head, Judge Bryce dismissed the security guard with his hand. "Go on back, now. Don't make me get out of the car."

"But . . ." The security guard put his hands on his hips.

"Now." Judge Bryce turned off his car and stepped outside, slamming the door shut. He then walked around the front of his car and stood toe to toe with the guard. "I'm the presiding judge of this court. I'm in charge of this courthouse, and I'm telling you for the last time to go back inside and leave Mr. Glass alone."

That was it.

The security guard took a final deep breath, staring at Judge Bryce with a mixture of respect and resentment familiar to any enlisted grunt that ever had to deal with a commanding officer, then slightly bowed his head. "Yes, sir."

We watched in silence as he shuffled back toward the front of the courthouse, rounded the corner, and disappeared.

When Judge Bryce was sure that he was gone, he turned to me and shook his head in dismay. "My apologies." He paused, as though thinking about whether he should elaborate. "Been having trouble with Jameson for years. He has applied to be a police officer in every city and county in Missouri, and never made it . . . mostly because he's a moron."

"Well thank you for stopping. Thought I was going to be put in jail."

Judge Bryce laughed. "Maybe handcuffed, but as soon as he got you into the courthouse, somebody with a brain would've intervened."

"Hope so."

Judge Bryce looked at the building and then back at me. "Mind if I ask why you were taking photos of one of the ugliest courthouses in America?"

"A theory." I kept it vague.

"Seem to still be very interested in the blue vans."

"I am." I paused. "But I'd better go and let you be on your way."

Judge Bryce nodded and looked back at the vans on the other side of the fence. "I thought your march was wonderful," he said. "Call me if you have any updates, will you? I feel terribly out of the loop."

"I will."

"Maybe coffee or lunch sometime." Judge Bryce rubbed his chin, thinking. Then he sighed and stepped a little closer to me. "But be careful."

"About what?"

"Well." Judge Bryce looked around. "I know you're working closely with Sergeant Schmidt."

I shrugged. "He's my contact."

Bryce nodded. I wasn't telling him something he didn't already know. "I've been around a long time, you know? Remember, I was a prosecutor before I was ever a judge, and I'd be careful with Sergeant Schmidt. That's all I'm saying."

"Something specific here that I need to know?"

Judge Bryce shook his head, then he talked softly and slowly. "Plays the game very well. Easy to underestimate, and I've seen things and I've heard things . . ." He stepped back. "Shouldn't go into too much detail, but my warning is a fair one. We got a city on edge. Jimmy Poles is nowhere. Supposedly he's fled the state because he fears for his own life. Last night was the first night it was a little better, but I think it's just the calm before the storm. Too much pressure. The city's gonna pop." Judge Bryce stepped back and started walking to his car. "I can feel it."

He opened his car door, and he stuck one foot inside. "Plus the birds tell me he's gonna be the next chief if he plays this right."

CHAPTER SIXTY-THREE

What Judge Bryce told me about Schmitty rattled around in my brain for the rest of the day. It probably troubled me more because I knew that at least part of it was true. It was convenient for me to consider Schmitty a friend, even though he wasn't. We'd never seen each other for non-work-related reasons. Never hung out because we enjoyed each other's company or for no reason at all.

It was convenient for me to consider Schmitty a good guy, because he'd passed along some information or let me see a confidential file. But it was just as plausible that he was playing me, knowing that one day he'd need my family's support when his name was dropped as the next chief. And given all the favors he'd done for me over the years—with little given back in return—I'd gladly offer him my endorsement and tell Annie, my father, my brother, and the rest of the Glass machine that he was a good choice.

Or maybe Judge Bryce's warning went beyond simple politics. He'd heard the whispers about Jimmy Poles. Maybe there were whispers about Schmitty, too. He certainly knew his way around the system, but I couldn't imagine Schmitty being dangerous or hurting anybody.

It nagged at me.

Emma knocked on my open office door. "You doing OK?"

I looked down at the stack of papers for my review and the small notebook filled with phone messages that I needed to return. Then I looked back up at her. "I guess so, just . . ." I wondered whether I should tell her about Judge Bryce's warning. "What do you think about Schmitty?"

The question caught her off guard. "The cop?"

I nodded. "The guy who's been working with us on the Lost Boys."

Emma paused, as if picturing him in her mind. "What about him?"

"Think he's using me? Using my name? Using my connections?"

Emma smiled. "Of course he is." Then she shifted her weight to her other foot and put her hand on her hip. "That's how it goes with cops. Doesn't mean it's bad. That's their job." She started to turn, but stopped. "Anything else?"

"Well." I pointed at the chair next to my desk. "Why don't you have a seat?" I thought for a moment, then, as Emma sat down, I warned her. "It's only a theory."

◆　◆　◆

I told Emma about my drive back from Clayton, my intersection epiphany with Cecil Bates, and my confrontation with the security guard at the Juvenile Justice Center. Even though it got later and later, Emma sat patiently and listened.

Then I told her what Judge Bryce said about Schmitty. "Think it's possible?" I shook my head. "It wouldn't surprise me if Schmitty wants to be the next chief, but I don't understand how burying evidence about these kids is going to help him. Why would he get the videos and never act on them?"

Emma shrugged. "You never know about people, but it doesn't seem like him. It doesn't make sense." She thought more about it, trying to reason it out. "The police are tight, like a brotherhood. Maybe he keeps a video tight to protect the integrity of the department, maybe to prevent the violence from escalating, maybe as a favor to get somebody's support for a promotion. Perhaps all three."

"Maybe." I stood up. "I should give him a call and tell him about the cameras." I paced behind my desk, feeling like I had become a conspiracy theorist. It was a rush of paranoia, and it made me suspicious of everybody. "I mean, we don't even know whether the videos exist. Maybe they delete them all after a week or something."

Then I had an idea. "What about Nikolas?"

"To sneak a peek?"

"Something like that, like an insurance policy." I talked up the idea, trying to convince myself. "If we peek, find nothing, no harm done. Or maybe I find something, and Nikolas makes a backup copy, just in case Judge Bryce is right."

"Maybe." Emma remained noncommittal. It was one thing to play a little loose with Cecil Bates and drinking in the park. It was another thing to start hacking the courts' security system on one of the highest profile criminal investigations in the country.

"That's it." I nodded, folding my arms across my chest. "We're doing it."

"Correction," Emma said. "You're doing it."

◆ ◆ ◆

The Northside Roastery was closed, but Emma had a key. We went in through the back door. Emma called out, letting them know they had visitors. She looked over her shoulder at me. "Don't want to get shot."

Hermes was cleaning the front of the shop, and Nikolas was in his little room.

I went to Nikolas, and Emma turned back, leaving. "You're on your own, Mr. Glass."

"Thanks for reminding me." I took a step into room where Nikolas was working.

He was concentrating on the information displayed on one of his three computer screens. He typed another line of code and then turned. "Can I help you?" Nikolas had dark circles under his eyes, and his beard had grown bushy. It looked like he'd been working nonstop for a few days. The place smelled like a locker room.

"I think you might be able to help," I said. "It's the Lost Boys case. The one in the news."

Nikolas nodded. "Yes?"

"I think I might know a way to find out who's responsible, but I'm not sure the police are going to help."

"Don't trust the police?" Nikolas smiled. "Me neither. What you need?"

I handed him my phone and we looked at the pictures that I had taken of the cameras outside the Juvenile Justice Center, as well as a picture that I took of one of the blue probation vans. "I'm looking to see if there's any footage of who took the van on this date and about this time." I took out a piece of paper from my notebook that had the information written on it and handed it to him. "And if there's other videos from inside showing the person walking through the hallways, or maybe even a video of the van driving on the street near the place where Isaac's brother was taken, that would be amazing."

"That's a lot." Nikolas turned and looked at his computer. "Got something in the hopper right now." He held up his hands. "All this you're talking about, probably different systems. Street cameras, probably public works or department of transportation, maybe Homeland Security or cops. The courthouse, maybe city or cops or bailiffs, or even a private security company. I have to figure out the main system where it's stored."

"But you did it for Cecil."

Nikolas nodded. "True, but that was one little traffic camera that nobody cares about. This is a courthouse, more complicated."

"So you're not going to do it?"

Nikolas laughed. "No, I do it for you, Mr. Glass. Just might take a little time. Give me time."

"Like a week?"

Nikolas shrugged. "Don't really know. Some, I get quick. Others, more difficult."

CHAPTER SIXTY-FOUR

The next few days passed without incident. Maybe it was the novelty, but every morning Sammy got up, got dressed, and headed off to school without complaint. By the end of the week, a pattern had already developed. It felt like she had been going to Clement City her whole life. Sammy seemed more at ease and more confident.

Then, on Friday evening before dinner, the phone rang. This time, however, Sammy wasn't in trouble.

It was a girl from school. I handed Sammy the phone, and they talked for a few minutes. Then Sammy said into the receiver, "I'll check and call you back."

They were assigned to be partners for a history project, and the girl wanted to know whether Sammy was willing to come to her house to work on it and then go to a movie on Saturday.

It was the first time that Sammy had been invited to a playdate in years, although I didn't say it was a playdate out loud. I knew that I'd be scolded for using such a babyish term, and that Sammy would give me the heavy eye roll.

I normally found the teasing to be quite enjoyable, but not this time. I didn't want to do anything or say anything that was going to ruin it.

"I'll make sure we get you over there." I played it straight. "You can call her back and get the address after dinner."

"Will do." Sammy smiled. Her personality was lit up, and it was quite possible that she might float away.

"You ready to go?" I asked.

"I am," she said, and then we walked over to the main house for dinner.

◆　◆　◆

The weekend went by in a blink and the next thing I knew, I was in my office on Monday morning prioritizing phone messages and gaming out the week. Emma updated me on new hearings that had been scheduled, and then it was almost time to go.

Although the arraignment calendar wouldn't start until ten o'clock at the earliest, I wanted to stop into the Northside Roastery before heading downtown.

Nikolas and I needed to talk.

I grabbed my battered briefcase, hustled out the door, and walked down to the coffee shop. Hermes came out from the back. I ordered a dark roast and then asked whether I could go back and see his brother.

Hermes shrugged as he put the money I paid in the drawer. "Human interaction might be good for him."

"Supposedly it's good for everybody." I picked the cup of coffee off the counter, thanked Hermes, and walked around the counter to the backroom.

Nikolas was sitting in front of his three screens. A cold, half-eaten box of Chinese food was on one side. Three bottles of Mountain Dew were on the other.

I knocked on the door frame. "Got a minute?"

"A minute or two." Nikolas fired off another barrage on the keyboard and turned around. "What's happening, my friend?"

"Nothing much," I said. "Just wondering how you're doing."

Nikolas nodded. "An update on the security camera project?"

"That'd be nice."

"Short answer is that it's tough job." Nikolas considered his words. "Like I thought, it's not on the same system as the traffic cameras. Those are city cameras, and the system protection is weak. These cameras are state court system, separate from the city and more sophisticated. More protections because court data is more sensitive than cars driving down the road or your friend getting drunk in a park."

"Hey now," I said. "Cecil wasn't drunk."

"Well," said Nikolas. "He wasn't drinking in a park. May have been drunk."

I conceded this, and we moved on.

Nikolas explained, "The state court system, they're used to being attacked by hackers from China and people who do it for fun."

"But you can get in?"

"Maybe," he said, "but it'll take a long time to figure out a path."

"Are we talking weeks?"

"Months," said Nikolas. "If at all."

"I don't have months."

"You can go to your cop friend, see if he do it."

After Judge Bryce's warning about Schmitty, I wasn't sure I wanted to play on that team. "Are you sure there isn't a quicker way?" I asked. "I don't know what, something more direct?"

Nikolas sat for a moment, thinking. Then he turned away from me and located a half-empty Mountain Dew bottle. He unscrewed the cap, took a drink, and set it back on his workstation. "I got an idea," he said. "But it's risky."

CHAPTER SIXTY-FIVE

The plan we devised in the half hour before I was due in court was destined for failure. In hindsight, it's quite clear. One should never commit a major felony or violate multiple federal laws in haste. Variables should be limited. Opportunities for discovery and identification should be minimal, if not nonexistent. And, with things going pretty well professionally and personally, I was just plain pushing my luck.

Getting the lunch appointment with Judge Bryce was a fluke. It should've been another sign that this was too easy and that I needed to stop and think. Judges are notoriously busy with meetings and court during the day, but when I'd called, he'd told me that he was available. My guess was that Bryce had rearranged his schedule to meet with me. I thought that the judge was merely anxious to hear the latest gossip about Jimmy Poles.

I arrived at the Juvenile Justice Center a little after noon. The overweight security guard that had almost confiscated my phone and placed me under arrest was working the metal detector. As I placed my briefcase onto the conveyer belt for the X-ray machine and passed through the metal detector without a beep, he gave me the skunk eye and didn't say a word.

I retrieved my briefcase, walked down the corridor to the elevators, and rode up to Judge Bryce's floor. His law clerk ushered me back to his chambers, and then I sat down across from him. We made small talk about the weather and where we should go to eat.

"There's a little Indian place about a block from here through campus." Judge Bryce considered his own recommendation. "Not a bad buffet, the price is right, and it's quick."

"Sounds good." I nodded and then stood.

The cell phone was in my hand. The text had already been typed. I just needed to press "Send" when the time was right.

As I walked out the door, Judge Bryce grabbed his coat and followed behind. He said a few words to his law clerk, and then we walked into the hallway.

We got about halfway, and then I turned to Judge Bryce. I've never claimed to be a good actor, and my guess is that this is where the plan started to fall apart.

"Oh," I said. "I forgot my briefcase in your chambers."

Judge Bryce shrugged and kept walking. "You can come back up here when we're done."

"No." I turned. "I better get it." I started back, not wanting to give Judge Bryce an opportunity to argue. "Afternoon appointments." I took another few steps, and then I looked down at my cell phone.

The text message to Nikolas was one word: Ready.

I pressed "Send" as I walked past Judge Bryce's law clerk, then entered the judge's chambers without pausing. I went past the chairs, past my briefcase, and around to the other side of the Judge Bryce's desk.

His computer had gone to sleep. I pressed a key on the keyboard, and the screen came back to life. Then I clicked on the icon for Microsoft Outlook.

As the program opened, there was a gigantic rock in my throat.

My hand shaking, I moved the cursor and scrolled up to the most recent e-mails. It was there, waiting for me. I opened the e-mail that Nikolas had sent to the judge. The message appeared to have been sent from the judicial district's IT department. There was a link, and above the link, the words:

YOUR PASSWORD WILL EXPIRE IN TWO DAYS.
PLEASE RESET YOUR PASSWORD.

Neither Nikolas nor I knew how savvy Judge Bryce was with computers. Nikolas figured that we should set it up like a typical phishing scheme. If I had the opportunity to click the link, then he'd be able to install the malware onto Judge Bryce's computer. If not, we hoped Judge Bryce would read the message and do it himself.

I clicked the link, and the screen flashed. Nikolas was in. Then I deleted the e-mail message, took a deep breath, and stepped back from the computer.

I checked my watch. Less than a minute had passed. And then I looked up.

Judge Bryce was standing in the doorway, looking at me, puzzled.

I glanced at the computer and then back at the judge. I forced a smile. "Better get some food. I'm hungry."

"Don't you want your briefcase?" Judge Bryce looked down at the floor by the chair that I had been sitting in. The briefcase was still there. "Or was that not what you were really looking for?" Judge Bryce took a few steps farther into his chambers and closed the door.

"Sorry." I slowly walked out from behind Judge Bryce's desk. "Must be going blind or something." I reached down and picked my briefcase up off the floor. "It was there the whole time." I nodded. "Ready to go?"

Judge Bryce held out his hand. "No." He shook his head. "I'm not ready to go." He stared at me. His eyes cold. "I think you need to explain why you snuck back into my office and were doing something with my computer."

I held out my hands. "I don't know." My mind was blank. I couldn't think of any plausible explanation.

Judge Bryce didn't flinch. His demeanor remained stiff. "I think you do know, and I think you better start talking to me."

I swallowed, unsure of exactly how much trouble I was in. "I can't really . . . I think maybe I should just go. Have lunch another time."

I started toward the door, but Judge Bryce didn't move. He knew that I wasn't going to push him aside. "You're not leaving here until you tell me what you're doing."

I looked at him. We stared at each other in silence, and then I bowed. "Fine." I took a few steps back, gathering my words. "I think you may have been right about Schmitty," I said. "He's stalling on the investigation. They all are. We've only talked and met once over the past few weeks. He's not returning my calls again, so I thought I'd try and get it myself."

Judge Bryce's eyes narrowed. "Get what?"

"The security videos," I said. "We know the date and approximate time that the Turner boy disappeared. So I want to see the security footage of who took the probation vans that night."

Judge Bryce studied me, and then he looked over at his computer. "You think I have the security videos on my computer?" His voice dripped with skepticism and disappointment.

I shook my head. "No, but the videos are stored in the judicial district's system. It's pretty well protected, I'm told. But if we get past the first security gate, it's easier."

"*We?*"

"A friend," I said.

"Does your friend have a name?"

"Of course."

"And?"

I hesitated. "It doesn't matter."

"I think it matters."

"Just a guy at a coffee shop near me. He sent you an e-mail. I just needed to click the link, and he'd be able to get inside, break through a few more firewalls, and find out if there's video of who's been taking these kids."

"A guy at a coffee shop." Judge Bryce shook his head and took a step toward me. "And you didn't trust the police to do this?"

I shook my head, thinking of Schmitty. "Not really."

"And nobody else knows you did this?"

"No."

Judge Bryce didn't respond. He stood in silence, thinking about my response. I could see him silently processing everything that I had revealed, working it through. Eventually he stopped staring at me and looked down at the ground.

The silence seemed like an eternity.

Then Judge Bryce took a deep breath, put his hands on his hips, and looked up at me. He had a huge smile on his face. "Well that was a ballsy plan, Glass." Judge Bryce started to laugh. "Incredibly stupid, too." He walked over to me, still smiling, and put his hand on my shoulder.

"You should've just asked me to do it." He patted me on the back. "I can't wait to nail the asshole who's responsible for all this shit."

CHAPTER SIXTY-SIX

The cell phone's ringtone distantly rattled some part of my brain, but the vibration on my nightstand really did it. A mini-jackhammer pounding on the wood top.

I reached for the phone. "Hello?"

It was Nikolas.

I rubbed my eyes. "Can this wait, man?" I was trying to figure out whether this was a dream. "Connect in the morning or something?"

Nikolas told me I had to come down to the shop.

"Seriously?" I tried to sit up, but my body refused to follow any commands.

"Just come down to the shop," Nikolas said. "Need you to come down to the shop, right now."

"Why?" I asked, but Nikolas had already hung up.

I turned on a light, looked at the clock—3:19 a.m.—and considered calling Nikolas back to tell him I wasn't coming. It would have been the right decision, but as I sat there and actually processed what was going on, I started to get excited. Maybe he'd actually found something.

◆ ◆ ◆

I left a note for Sammy, just in case she got up in the middle of the night and wondered where I was.

In the dead of night with no traffic, it took me about ten minutes to get to the office.

The street was dark. No lights were on, except at the Northside Roastery. I pulled around back and parked behind the coffee shop.

I was now wide awake, positive that I was about to watch a video of Jimmy Poles driving out of the Juvenile Justice Center's parking lot on the night that Isaac's brother went missing. Maybe, if I was lucky, there'd be some video picked up by a random camera near where the kidnapping actually occurred. It was a long shot, but it was possible. Cameras were everywhere.

I got out of my car and went to the back door. I knocked once. Nobody came. I knocked again, louder this time, and waited. "Nikolas, it's me." I tried the door, and it was unlocked.

Opening it a little wider, I took a step inside. "Hey, Nik, it's Justin." I peeked around the door. There was a light shining from the room where Nikolas worked.

Everything else was dark.

I took one step farther inside. Then an odd feeling rushed through me. Something wasn't right. As I took a step back, I heard a click; then I felt a sting as two small fishhooks attached to my chest. Fifty thousand volts of electricity pulsed through my body and pushed me hard to the floor as I blacked out.

◆　◆　◆

When I woke up, my mind was in a fog. Each breath took effort. My fingertips felt numb. I wasn't sure where I was or how long I had been unconscious, but I knew the hard tile floor wasn't my bed. I wasn't at home.

There was talking. An angry voice barked orders. It was a familiar voice, but I couldn't place it. I was too confused.

Lifting my head, I finally opened my eyes.

We were in the back office at the coffee shop. Recent events started to come back to me, and I realized that I was in trouble.

Nikolas was in his chair in front of his three computer monitors. Standing over Nikolas was a man. It wasn't a local thug. It wasn't Jimmy Poles. It wasn't Sergeant Schmidt.

My mind was scattered and it was difficult to put the pieces together. I rubbed my face and tried to prop myself up.

He must have seen me out of the corner of his eye, noticing the movement.

Judge Bryce turned and smiled, pointing his gun at my head. "Nice of you to join us."

CHAPTER SIXTY-SEVEN

Judge Bryce wasn't happy with how long it was taking. He became agitated whenever Nikolas scrolled through pages and pages of code. Judge Bryce thought Nikolas was stalling, which maybe he was. Nobody knew for sure.

"Judge," I said, "what are you doing? Why?"

He looked back at me, annoyed, and then returned his attention to Nikolas without responding.

I figured he was going to kill me no matter what, so I didn't have much to lose by being annoying. Even though my body ached, I pushed myself farther upright and tried again to engage. "You're being stupid, Judge. Think this through."

Judge Bryce looked back at me, pointing the gun. "Shut up." I thought I saw a flicker of doubt in his eyes. There was nervousness.

"Schmitty already knows," I lied. "I thought about your warning. I also thought about your enthusiasm for my investigation today. It didn't feel right."

"Don't believe you." Judge Bryce turned back to Nikolas. "I've been watching you for a long time. Even knew about him"—he nodded down toward Nikolas—"figured he'd be the one that was getting the stuff on Poles."

"I'm telling you that Schmitty knows about you," I lied again. "In addition to those videos, there's other stuff out there connecting you to these murders. The cops are building the case, getting the warrants."

Judge Bryce scoffed at me, arrogant. "You're bluffing."

I tried to think of something that would make him stop. We needed to buy some time. "Schmitty gave me all those files," I said. "Your name is in every single one of them."

Judge Bryce looked at Nikolas and then turned to me. "My name's in a lot of files." His eyes shifted, another moment of doubt.

"But *every* single file?" I asked, even though I had no idea what I was talking about. "Improbable. What are there, five judges working down there, maybe six?"

"You know nothing."

I was starting to get under his skin, so I pressed him some more. "Thought you loved those kids. You certainly enjoyed getting your awards and giving your little speeches."

Judge Bryce stared at me, hard. "Mercy. I showed mercy on those boys. We both know where they were headed. I stopped the cycle."

"You sound like Jimmy Poles."

"Somebody has to make the tough calls."

"And your legacy?" I thought about the Missouri Miracle. "These kids probably aren't too good for your statistics."

"They're not worth the resources."

"And you get to make that choice?" I forced a laugh. "You're that smart?"

"If not me, then who?" Judge Bryce's face turned up into a satisfied smirk, then he added, "And yes . . . I am that smart." He turned his attention back to Nikolas.

"The investigation isn't going to stop, you know?" I paused, waiting for a response that never came. "Killing us isn't going to solve the problem. Others know about the videos." I thought about the files, still trying to think of a connection that I could never find. Then I remembered when my grandfather recommended that I talk to Judge Bryce, early in the case. His name triggered something, but I couldn't place where I had heard it and where I had seen it. At the time, I wondered whether it was because I had seen Judge Bryce on a panel or read about his work in the newspaper, but that wasn't right.

I thought about Devon Walker. His pictures. His progression from a little chubby kid in elementary school to the young tattooed man running the streets.

Then it came together.

"You signed all the warrants," I said.

Judge Bryce turned back, looking at me.

I continued the thought. "Even though the cases were spread out among all the different judges and probation officers, you were the one who had signed the arrest warrants. As the presiding judge, you were responsible for signing the warrants. You read their histories. You saw they had been given multiple chances. And then you decided to kill them."

Judge Bryce took a step forward toward me. "You don't know anything about me."

"I think I do," I said as I looked past him. Nikolas turned and nodded. It was a sign, and I got ready. "So we're supposed to thank you for killing these little kids."

"They're not little kids anymore." Judge Bryce laughed at me. "I'm preventing hundreds—maybe thousands—of people from being harassed and hurt by these thugs. I'm saving the taxpayers a lot of money, too, millions wasted on treatments that are years too late." Judge Bryce came closer. His eyes were filled with belief, righteousness. "It's for their own good, to be put out of their misery. I weep for them, but I know that we are all—"

Nikolas spun his chair around and awkwardly threw his body into Judge Bryce's backside.

The gun went off, exploding just over my head as I rolled to the side. On all fours, I crawled out the door and then tried to run toward the front of the shop. My legs were heavy. Still feeling the effects of the Taser, I tripped and fell.

Behind me, I heard Nikolas and Judge Bryce fighting in the office. Computer equipment crashed to the ground; glass shattered.

I kept going in the darkness.

Stumbling, I came through the curtain and into the front of the coffee shop. I sprinted to the counter and reached under the cash register where Hermes kept the gun.

Groping, I felt in the back. I grabbed it, and then the entire coffee shop flooded with blinding light.

My eyes adjusted enough to allow me to see Judge Bryce no more than six feet away from me, frozen. All color was gone. In the blaring white light, he was a ghost. An outline holding a gun.

His own eyes adjusting enough to find me, Judge Bryce pulled the trigger, and I shot back as we both fell to the ground.

I don't know how many shots I fired. I just kept pulling the trigger.

CHAPTER SIXTY-EIGHT

Schmitty stood over the body. Judge Bryce's chest was painted red. Thick blood seeped from underneath him, expanding into an irregular pool on the hardwood floor.

Schmitty didn't say anything. There was no need to state the obvious.

He shook his head, took a final look, and turned to me. "Let's get your friend and go have a chat someplace private."

We walked to the back. There were a half dozen cops standing around. Schmitty told them to get outside and help make sure there was a decent perimeter.

Nikolas stood near a pile of burlap sacks containing green coffee beans from around the world. I walked over to him and reached out, patted him on the shoulder. "You OK?"

Nikolas shrugged. "Beat up, but still standing."

"You got nine lives, my friend." I smiled, then gestured to the door.

Nikolas understood, and he followed me outside. Schmitty trailed behind.

Once we were in the back parking lot, I stopped. There were cops everywhere and a helicopter overhead. "I think we're even now," I said to Nikolas. "I saved you, and you saved me. All debts are paid."

Nikolas nodded. "Fair enough."

Then we walked around to the front to my law office. "This should work." I took out the key and unlocked the door, and all three of us went inside. Then I locked the door behind us to make sure we weren't disturbed.

◆ ◆ ◆

Schmitty wanted to hear the whole story from our perspective. He didn't let me ramble. He interrupted, when necessary, pressing me for more and more details. Why did I go to Judge Bryce in the first place?

I told him about the fund-raising dinner, the keynote address, and the tour of the Juvenile Justice Center. I told him about Cecil Bates and the security footage that captured his arrest, and then I told him about the traffic cameras I'd seen coming back from the court in Clayton, my decision to go back to the Juvenile Justice Center and take pictures, and, ultimately, being caught by Judge Bryce after tampering with his e-mail.

"That was what set him off," Schmitty said. "We've been monitoring Judge Bryce for a few weeks, since we traced the leaks about Jimmy Poles back to him. The Twitter account, the images, some of that stuff was done with his court-issued laptop. He took precautions, deleting browser history and creating fake e-mail accounts, but not enough. You'd think he'd know it all leaves a record, but guess not."

"You knew he was at the coffee shop the whole time?" I was angry. "We could've been killed."

Schmitty held out his hands, defensive. "We didn't know what was going on inside. We didn't think he actually killed those kids, for God's sake." Schmitty looked at Nikolas for support, got none, and decided to explain. "You're the one who told me that Judge Bryce wanted us to go public with it. Then when we found out he was the guy posting all that stuff, fanning the flames; some people thought you might be in on it. You know, telling the public about Poles."

"Really? So you were actually monitoring me?"

"I told them that they were wrong," Schmitty said, unconvincingly. "But it looked bad. Then there was that damn protest march, and it looked even worse when we watched Judge Bryce go into the coffee shop after hours."

I was still angry. "So you had cops sitting there while I got tased and shot at?"

Schmitty shrugged. "Sort of." He looked at Nikolas. "We had two cops staking it out, but we didn't know what was going on until Nikolas sent me an e-mail. That's when we mobilized. About to bust in when the shots rang out."

◆　◆　◆

After downloading encryption software, Nikolas used my work computer to access the part of the Internet without any pretty images and colors. It was all numbers and text.

Schmitty and I stood over his shoulder as he pulled up the video of Judge Bryce walking down from his chambers late at night. He was wearing the khaki pants and blue polo shirt usually worn by the juvenile probation officers. He also had a backpack slung over his shoulder, likely containing the plastic zip ties, his Taser, and other tools he'd need later in the evening.

We watched him walk through the parking garage, take one of the van keys off the rack, and drive the van out of the lot. He didn't need permission to exit; the gate automatically opened.

Nikolas paused the video. "You see the card reader?" He pointed at a post outside the gate near the street. "I check and he didn't use his own pass card to get back in." Nikolas looked up at Schmitty. "Something to check. Maybe setting up Poles or somebody else."

Nikolas turned his attention back to the computer screen, and we watched him work. Then Nikolas said, "When he came inside the shop, his plan was to get you to come. I'm not sure he knew what I was doing, but he saw the screens and put it together." Nikolas kept typing, scrolling through lines of code and working through different programs. "Glad he did, because that's what kept me alive. He was telling me to delete, so I faked that."

Nikolas stopped and looked up at Schmitty. "See this? You cops are familiar with this." He turned his attention back to the computer. "This is his cell phone record. You get the cell tower data and it'll show when he went to that park to dispose of the bodies. It's all here."

Schmitty looked at me and nodded. "Don't send it to me," he said. "We have to play this carefully. I want warrants. I want it official, just like the warrants we got on Poles."

◆ ◆ ◆

The plan was straightforward. Everything told to the public would be true, except some facts and events would be omitted.

Schmitty would state that they had traced the leaks about Jimmy Poles to Judge Bryce and had him under surveillance. He'd establish that he'd been in contact with me throughout the investigation, and that they became concerned when Judge Bryce went to the Northside Roastery late in the evening. When officers heard a gunshot, they entered the coffee shop, but Judge Bryce was already dead.

Judge Bryce would be named the prime suspect in the Lost Boys investigation, warrants would be obtained, and Schmitty would express confidence that further evidence linking Judge Bryce to the disappearance of a dozen Northside juveniles would be unearthed.

Discussion of Nikolas would be kept to a minimum. He'd be referred to as a private contractor that the police department had hired to help me with the Lost Boys investigation as well as the leak of confidential documents. Schmitty would state that Judge Bryce had learned that Nikolas was the contractor hired for the investigation and had gone there to stop him. If any reporter pressed for more information, Schmitty would politely decline to answer because there was an ongoing internal investigation.

My job was simply to go home and not say a word. It was a job that I fully embraced.

CHAPTER SIXTY-NINE

We are, whether by nature or nurture, episodic. We find a problem and then we fix it. We want there to be a beginning and an end. Everyone wanted the death of Judge Bryce to be the end, but life isn't that simple.

We are in a constant relationship with one another, a series of communications sent and received through word and action. An unrelenting feedback loop that either gets louder or softer, but never goes away.

The death of Judge Bryce was not the end. It was a disruption of the cycle.

The fires may have stopped. The tension that had erupted with the protest in front of Jimmy Poles's house may have sunk back beneath the surface, allowing the systems to lurch forward. But the tension wasn't gone. The relationship wasn't over. Post-racial America did not emerge. The long history of violence and control continues to be unresolved. It only waits for another moment in the future to remind us of our sins, even as we all do our best to just live our lives.

Jimmy Poles quietly resigned and moved out of state. A severance package in an undisclosed amount was approved by the Saint Louis Board of Aldermen in a closed session. It wasn't reported in any newspaper or on television.

Sammy continued classes at the Clement City Day School, and she seemed genuinely happy. The bullies were gone, and she was no longer considered a rich kid. There were plenty of others at her new school competing for that title.

I settled back into my law practice, hustling clients and making court appearances. Emma made it all routine. She managed the office with ease, and I talked to her about the possibility of her going back to law school to get licensed in the United States.

I just had one more loose end to take care of.

◆ ◆ ◆

Lincoln picked Sammy and me up sharply at eight o'clock. We sat in the backseat while Buster drove us downtown. It was a beautiful morning. The humidity had blown through. The temperature had dropped, and seemingly overnight the tips of trees had started to change from green to bright-yellow, orange, and red. Fall had arrived. It was late, but it had finally arrived.

We cut over to Broadway, and Buster drove us to the Fox Recreation Center. The Glass machine had done its advance work. By the time we arrived, the stage was built; the microphones and speakers had been tested; red, white, and blue balloons decorated the stage; and **GLASS FOR STATE SENATE** signs were everywhere.

"Lincoln," I said, "can you give us a second?"

He looked back at me and Sammy and smiled; then he opened the door and got out of the car. Buster did the same, leaving us alone.

I watched my daughter staring out the window at the crowd and the signs. She looked a lot like I did at her age, watching my dad at his meetings and rallies, fascinated by the process.

"What do you think?"

Sammy nodded. "It's cool."

I laughed.

Then she asked, "What do you think Mom would have thought?"

I pictured Monica, beautiful Monica, standing in the kitchen of our old house as I told her that I'm finally going to run for office. I could see a gorgeous smile spread across her face. "She'd be proud," I said. "She'd tell me that she loved me. She'd support me, but she'd make sure that I wouldn't go and get a big ego or nothing, keep me grounded."

Sammy nodded. "That can be my job now. Keep you humble."

"Well," I said, "you've already got a lot of experience at that."

Sammy rolled her eyes. Then she turned away from the car window and looked at me. "I *am* proud of you, though, just like Mom would've been."

"Thanks," I said. "So you're ready to do this?"

"Totally."

"Then let's do it."

I opened the door, and as we emerged from the car, hundreds of people erupted in applause. They cheered and shook my hand and gave Sammy hugs as we pushed forward down the middle of the assembled crowd.

When we finally made it to the front, I was escorted up the steps, onto the stage, and toward the podium. Sammy was led to the side next to my mother and my father. All three of them smiled at me. The cheers swelled as I approached the microphone. Sammy cheered the loudest.

At the podium, I looked down at all the cameras and out at the crowd. My grandfather, Judge Michael M. Calhoun, stood off to the side. He felt his status as a retired federal judge barred him from endorsing candidates or attending political functions, but he couldn't stay away. I also saw the mayor, Annie Montgomery, and Schmitty among the friendly faces in the crowd.

I pulled a sheet of paper out of my front jacket pocket. I looked down at the words that I had spent hours writing, and then my vision blurred.

I had a knot in my stomach, and I started to tear up.

I closed my eyes. Then I opened them, deciding to forego my prepared remarks.

"My first decision as a candidate is to not give a long speech." I folded my paper up and put it back in my pocket as a few people in the crowd clapped and others laughed. "My second decision is to try not to be like my brother or my dad." I looked over at my father and then at Lincoln, who had now joined us on the stage. "I can't be them. They're each one of a kind. But I can be me. And I care very deeply about our community. I've been through tough times. When my wife—Sammy's mom—died, I wasn't sure I was gonna make it. Sometimes I still don't know. I'm just like all those people out there right now who aren't so sure they're gonna make it. Whether they're gonna make the rent, whether they're gonna be able to buy the groceries, whether they're gonna be able to keep their head up above the water.

"We have problems." I took a deep breath, and let it out slowly, letting my voice grow and my confidence build. "But there is hope. As bleak as things seem today, they're certainly better than fifty years ago or a hundred. We can't lose our sense of community. We can't give up; we just have to think smaller and make incremental changes. We can work to make things a little better here in our neighborhood—and they can get better. One piece at a time. We start with our neighbors, and we work out from there. Ignoring the kids who are too easy to forget is not the answer. Ignoring the city is not the answer. Bashing the suburbs is not the answer. We're in this together, you and me. All we have to do is try, and keep on trying."

ACKNOWLEDGMENTS

Many thanks to Thomas & Mercer and Jacquelyn Ben-Zekry for making the development of this book a great experience; not too many writers get to say that. I also want to thank the readers who contact me with encouragement, advice, and enthusiasm. Don't stop! You can visit my website at www.JDTrafford.com and send me a note.

ABOUT THE AUTHOR

Photo © 2016 Gwen Kosiak

Award-winning author J.D. Trafford, described as a "writer of merit" by *Mystery Scene* magazine, has topped numerous Amazon bestseller lists, including reaching #1 on the Legal Thrillers list. IndieReader selected his debut novel, *No Time to Run*, as a bestselling pick. Trafford graduated with honors from a top-twenty law school and has worked as a civil and criminal prosecutor, as an associate at a large national law firm, and as a nonprofit attorney. He's handled issues of housing, education, and poverty in communities of color. Prior to law school, he worked in Washington, DC, and lived in Saint Louis, Missouri. He now lives with his wife and children in the Midwest, and bikes whenever possible.

TRAFF　　　　　　　　　　　　　　**FLT**
Trafford, J. D,
Little boy lost /

11/17